Nappily Married

TRISHA R. THOMAS

 O9-BUD-703

St. Martin's Paperbacks

This is a work of fiction. All of the characters, organizations, and events portrayed in this novel are either products of the author's imagination or are used fictitiously.

NAPPILY MARRIED

Copyright © 2007 by Trisha R. Thomas.
Excerpt from *Un-Nappily in Love* copyright © 2010 by Trisha R. Thomas.

For information address St. Martin's Press, 175 Fifth Avenue, New York, NY 10010.

Library of Congress Catalog Card Number: 2007061722

ISBN: 978-0-312-53139-3

Printed in the United States of America

St. Martin's Griffin trade paperback edition / August 2007
St. Martin's Paperbacks edition / June 2010

St. Martin's Paperbacks are published by St. Martin's Press, 175 Fifth Avenue, New York, NY 10010.

10 9 8 7 6 5 4 3 2 1

Nappily Married

Make a list, I told myself.

Things I swore not ever to do again:

1. *Go out drinking with my best friend, Wendy, which somehow always got me into trouble.*
2. *Return to the relaxer chair, where I now sit.*
3. *And most important, never ever fall in the path of Clint Fairchild again. Dr. Clint Fairchild to you, the man who broke my heart, stomped all over it, then gave it back, telling me we would always be friends. Nothing good ever comes out of dealing with the past.*

"All right, Miss Thing, you know there ain't no going back. Once I lay this product on, it's *O-V-A,* over." Shane stirred the white mixture until it looked like a perfect Betty Crocker icing. I stared at myself in the mirror. I'd stopped counting how many people confused me with Melanie B, the chocolate spice of the Spice Girls. I had the same coral-toned skin, wild spirals coming out of my head in some spots, and a serious Pam Grier–Foxy Brown style in others. Count-less times I'd been asked who did my weave. No add-ons, no glue or thread, just me, 100 percent, the real deal.

The woman in the next chair spoke with her chin pushed down to her chest, with long straight extensions attached to a winding circle of cornrows on her head. "I can't believe she's about to put a chemical on all that natural hair."

"You putting a chemical on her, Shane?" Josie, the salon owner, was so engrossed by what she was about to witness, she could barely lead her closed-eyed customer to the washbowl, bumping her into the chair. "Oops, I'm sorry," she told her customer, then turned her attention back to Shane. "You thought about just pressing it out, see if she likes it straight?"

"I'm just giving her what she asked for." Shane took notice of all the eyes upon him. "I'm not selling crack, here, ladies. Back up off me." He waved a plump hand to his peers.

My mother had made sure I got my monthly dose. It was all coming back to me, from the age of five years old when my mother stood on one side of me and pulled my hair out of the barrettes and bands. "Do something with this. I can't work this hard anymore."

"Yeah, it's thick. Pauletta, how have you gone on as long as you did, girl? You were right for bringing her in. We'll start out with a mild."

"Mild?" someone questioned. "You ain't gone do nothing but tease that child's hair with mild. Put some super on there." The first perm was thirty years ago, and nothing had changed. It still took a congressional meeting over my head to decide what to do.

"Everybody in here would pay for that hair, solid cash, and you about to put the heat to it," Stella chimed in from two stations away.

"What a waste," Tikki said in between the smoke

rising from the flat iron going through her customer's hair.

Women lined the dryer seats, the waiting chairs, and the hot seats where they'd been ordered not to move or they'd be burned, but no one could resist spying on the frantic young woman with the healthy natural mane who'd demanded chemical assistance. Pronto.

Few black women even knew what their natural hair looked like and probably hadn't seen it since the baby pictures their mamas still held in a chest at home. It was the curse of the Dark & Lovely boxes and Ultra Sheen ads from fifty years ago. Nothing had changed. But when one soldier was bold enough to rough it, discover her true natural beauty, everyone else cheered for her freedom. Offered support and praise. *Run like the wind, child, be free!*

Shane combed through the parted center of my hair. He took two handfuls and twisted them in a clip. "Now, Miss Thing, I know I just met you. You coming in here flashing hundreds, offering anybody with an available chair five big ones to straighten you out, but I am a sympathetic black man. If you want to talk about it, we can. No charge."

"I don't need a therapist. I need my hair straightened." I pushed back the heavy mass of hair nearly covering my eyes. "Do you think you can give me some blond highlights while you're at it?"

The room went into a dizzying hush. Blow dryers clicked off. Gossiping voices turned down to silence.

"Miss Thing, you will lose every strand of hair on your head if I do a color lift on top of a relaxer. I don't care how much money you got in that, Gucci via Rucci, or whatever bag of yours. I am not going to let you ruin my good name."

"Okay. Fine. Just straighten it then."

The salon door flew open as if a gust of wind had carried the woman who stood panicked with a weave so tight, her eyes bulged. "Where's Cee Cee? Where she at? Look at this." She spun around, "Cee Cee! You gone fix this, you hear me? I paid two hundred cash, and I can't sleep 'cause my damn eyes won't shut."

A few snickers came from behind the partitioned wall where fingernails and toes were being tended to. The woman was tall and lean and used her height to peer over the top half of the wall. "Who the hell thinks this is funny?" She was a fright with her eyebrows in permanent flex. "I said, who the hell thinks this is funny?"

"Cee Cee is not here," Josie said with a hand on her blow dryer like she was ready for a duel at the O.K. Corral. "Now, you've called here ten times, and I've told you the same thing. She doesn't work here no more. And you and a few more unhappy customers are precisely the reason why. Now I'm sorry about your hair, but nobody in here is responsible."

The woman's eyes bulged even more. "Well, if this is your shop, you are responsible."

"No. I'm not. I wasn't the one to do your hair, 'cause if I did, it would've cost five hundred instead of two. This is a simple case of you got what you paid for."

"You hired that heffa. This is your shop, so I'm suing you."

"I didn't hire anybody. She rented a space from me. Everybody in here is a free agent. Now if you'd like someone in here to remedy your situation for a modest fee, you're going to have to act with a little more civility."

"You think I'ma let somebody in here steal some more of my money? I already paid once. I'm not paying again. This place ain't nothing but a fake. Just 'cause you in the nice part of town, got your fancy shiny floors and your painted walls, I should have known better. High rent

don't make you better than anybody else. You ain't nothing but a chop shop, messing up people's heads. I
could've gone to any hole in the wall and got better."

Josie was a stocky woman who looked like she
preferred giving a good beatdown to a monotonous
treadmill workout any day. She took a step toward the
lean brown-skinned woman, prepared to do whatever
was necessary to protect Josie's House of Style's good
name. "That's it, you're out of here. I've tried to be
reasonable, but you've got to go."

Shane leaped between the two women. "Okay, now,
this is a place of business. Now look, we all sympathize
with your problem, but the party responsible is only
two blocks up at Weaves R' Us. . . . Oops, did I say
that?" He put his fingers to his lips.

The lean woman started crying in a painful whimper. Her tight scalp prevented her face from falling into
the full grieving frown. "My wedding is Saturday, and
I'm out of money. Not a cent left. I can't show up at my
wedding looking like this."

Shane wrapped one of his burly arms around her,
then waved Josie away. "You're going to be a beautiful
bride."

A few snickers could still be heard scattered about.

"I'm not. I'm not going to be beautiful, not like this."

I would have to agree she looked like Medusa's spawn.
The hair attached to her head stood up in bountiful spirals shooting in every direction. A reasonable-minded
person would have gotten right out of her seat and
headed to another salon with less drama. That reasonable-
minded person was not me. I felt sorry for the woman, I
suppose, as sorry for her as I did for myself.

"It's supposed to be the happiest day of your life," I said
out loud before I could contain myself. "The day when
you marry the man of your dreams, isn't it supposed to

be the happiest day of your life?" I wiped the tear that trickled down my face. "Is he the man of your dreams?" I asked the woman who'd begun crying in the midst of everyone else's amusement.

She nodded silently. "I've loved this man since I could tie my own shoes."

"I'll pay for her hair." I twirled my chair around to face the woman instead of staring at her through the mirror. I went into my purse and pulled out more ones— one hundreds, that is. I'd married well for all that didn't know. My husband, Jake Parson, owned JP Wear, an urban clothing line based on his reputation as a rapper. My Jake was a successful businessman, just as safe and sound as any doctor. Dr. Clint Fairchild wasn't special. So what he was in the business of saving lives. Rap and urban clothing had its special place in society as well, did it not?

Shane rushed over and pulled out a tissue for each hand. "Oh, this is bad. Worse than I thought," he announced. "We got a full stock of sanitary napkins in the bathroom for the rest of you crazy bammas."

Josie looked around, miffed by the contagious blubbering. "I'll do your hair for free, just stop crying. Everybody, stop that," she ordered. From the hair dryer to washbowls and back to the stationed chairs, not a dry eye in the salon. No one knew what she was crying about. A universal tear of sadness for every trust betrayed and every hope dashed by a cheating lying man or in my case, a woman.

As I said, if I'd made a list and stuck to it, I wouldn't have traveled down this road again. Women did that from time to time, traveled the same path knowing what waited at the end, yet unable to stop and turn around.

"It's always a man, isn't it?" Shane said, spinning my chair back around to face the mirror.

"Sometimes it's two," I said, sniffing and wiping with the beaten tissue in my hand.

"Whew, I know that's the truth. Sometimes three or four, but we're not counting today." He paused long enough to hand me another tissue. "You poor thing."

I couldn't help myself. The *chair* is a vulnerable place to be.

I'd fought long and hard to stay out of the chair. Rehab had been a son of a gun. Breaking a lifelong cycle of chemical dependency was something to be proud of. Black women yearned for that freedom and celebrated others' success when the spell had been broken. Feeling themselves helpless, always citing excuses of why they couldn't do it: not strong enough, pretty enough, secure enough, or just plain crazy enough to go natural. Besides, there were no African-American super-natural beauties for role models, none recognized in the host of magazines or on the entertainment circuit. When a black celebrity donned natural hair, it was store bought, a prop for a photo shoot, an added wig, or extensions. The word *natural* meant cut from the head of another woman somewhere in Asia or Africa then sewn or twisted in. And here I was, the exemplary model of what we were trying to achieve, backsliding. All the way back, all because of a man, which only made matters worse.

When I first cut off all my long straightened hair, it was about the freedom. Not Angela Davis–type freedom. It wasn't a black power movement; it was one woman's quest for sanity and clarity. Get control of your hair and you get control of your life. Little else in one's world could be controlled: Weight, ha! Shoe or dress size, double ha. A man, ha ha ha, with two more on the end. Hair, yes, fast and easy. An instant charge in spirit and attitude could easily be found in a new hairdo.

I'd made a terrible mistake somewhere along the way.

Being in control was a lot of work, a daily siege of contact with every side of the big picture frame. A frame I'd created, by the way. Control meant staying in between the lines. Functioning within the space I'd defined. I was tired. I'm not going to lie, being a Black American Princess required daily affirmations and continued renewal of the vows.

Be strong.

Be diligent.

Be right.

Shane interrupted my thoughts. "So, I've already sent two of my best customers to the waiting chair. They're not going to stay over there long, at least not peacefully. Tell me what you want me to do." Shane picked up the long-handled comb.

I swallowed hard, but the lump wouldn't remove itself from my throat. I tried to speak again, but it stayed, tight and resolute. He placed his large hands on my shoulders. The weight felt good. A grounding swell moved through my body. "Do you love him? My bad, do you love 'em both?"

I nodded my head. "Different love."

"Now see, I don't believe you can ever love two people at the same time. Not in the same space and time. I think sometimes our lines get crossed and we're living in multiple spaces, you know like *Star Trek* in the episodes with parallel universes. Something's happening over here but at the same time it's happening over there. But eventually you have to decide which universe is real. Which one is just a visit to the past and which one is your future."

"Ooh, listen to Shane-man over there getting deep. Tell it, Shane. Preach, my brotha." Josie had the unruly customer controlled and sedated with a plastic cape around her chest and shoulders. I'd long associated the plastic beauty cape with the straitjacket in mental hospitals. Once placed around a woman's body, she went into a mind-numbing state, losing all track of time. I looked around the salon and noticed there were no clocks, at least not any visible to the paying customers.

"Hush over there and mind your business." Shane bent down and whispered near my ear. "You want to hear a joke?" He asked, not giving me a chance to answer. "Okay here it goes. This guy worked construction, every day he'd sit up on the scaffold with his buddy and open his lunch box and be like, 'peanut butter sandwich again. I hate peanut butter, damnit, if I have to see one more peanut butter sandwich, I'm going to jump.' His friend got tired of hearing the same complaint every day so he asked, 'why don't you tell your wife to stop making peanut butter sandwiches if you hate 'em so much?' The guy stares into his lunch box. 'It's not her, it's me. I make the gah-damn peanut butter sandwiches.'"

Several women sputtered with laughter, even the woman with the scary fixed eyebrows.

Shane was right. I'd fixed my own peanut butter sandwich way too many times. I put my hand over my mouth and nose to try to contain the mixture of tears and laughter. Shane reached over and sat the entire box of tissue in my lap. "Oh hell, we're not going to do this today. You have way too much to think about. Whatever needs fixing can't be done in this chair."

Little Red Corvettes

It's difficult to explain what spurred my little break-down. I could start at the beginning, but time, as you can tell, is of the essence. I could start from the middle, but then it would never be clear why I wasn't content with my life, the perfect life I'd made for myself. After all, I had everything a girl—a woman—could ask for. A girl because when she's five years old, she only knows the basics of the game. Make him love you. When she becomes a woman, say around thirty, she learns the real rules. Make him stay in love with you. I'd succeeded. Jake Parson had fallen in love with me and would have stayed that way had I not made a terrible mistake.

Jake was completely justified in straying into the arms of another woman. I see it clearly and without bias. His side of the story will make mine look tame in comparison. But if I was watching from across the street, peering into someone else's yard, I'd say, She got what she deserved. Letting a man that fine run around un-attended—well, what'd you expect? Right on all counts. I was guilty.

So I'll start, not in the middle, but somewhere closer to the end. I was out drinking with Wendy, I admit, breaking my first rule.

It was the first week of the first month of a brand-new year. Wendy had finally received her divorce papers and felt a celebration was in order. I'd offered something more reasonable, like a trip to the spa where they fed you strawberries dipped in chocolate and champagne in real crystal glasses, but, "No," she'd said, "I want to dance."

So there we were, in a nightclub, for goodness' sake. Gotham Hall in Santa Monica, a full-fledged "get down and shake your booty on the dance floor, neon lighting, and waitresses with their booties flinging around when they walked demanding you fill a two-drink minimum or sit somewhere else" kind of club. I was far too sophisticated to be there. I had principles. *I was a married woman of eighteen months, seven days, and a solid twelve hours.*

I wasn't supposed to be there while strange men breathed down my face, sniffing for levels of female desperation. The whole scene was far beneath me. Wendy, too, but where else could we dance if we didn't want to dance with each other? (Which by the way was a white thing. Black women, no matter what the alcohol content read on the Breathalyzer, did not turn to each other and say, "Let's dance." In college, I tried to explain this to my white and other roommates. It wasn't that I was a bump on the log; I wanted to party as much as the next guy, but with a *guy*.)

"Venus, you in here, where you at?" Wendy's voice bounced off the bathroom walls.

"In here! I'll be out in a minute." After five mojitos, getting too-tight jeans off was aerobic exercise. Relief washed over me when I finally won the struggle and squatted in praying yoga position over the commode.

"No hurry. The party will continue. Did you see that guy with the fake tattoo? Oh my gawd, what has the world come to? He must've been forty, easily, looking like a broke Coolio." She snickered to herself. Wendy was only one year away from the big four-oh herself, even though her lean figure and flawless dark skin radiated good health from five days a week at the gym. "I'm going back to the table. Take your time, less competition." She let the door teeter back and forth.

I took my time. I had little choice, struggling to get the too-tight jeans back over my hips and thighs. Let's face it, all my jeans were too tight, not just the ones I was wearing. Being in my late thirties added thirty pounds. Distributed evenly, I thought, until taking a peek down my low-slung halter top. After giving birth to Mya, I'd had voluptuous breasts for an entire month. Once the overstock of hormones cleared, I was left smaller than I'd started, a mouthful or a handful, depending on whose hand or whose mouth. If it was Mya's, yes; if it was Jake's, I fell slightly short.

"Someone in here?" My bathroom door shook. The woman's slurred voice echoed against the tiled walls. "This one's open," she said to the other pair of heels clicking across the floor. "I can't stand this anymore," the slurred voice continued from the stall next to mine.

"Stop worrying about him. The world is full of married men. He's just one more."

"How many times have I told you, he's not just a married man?" The other voice echoed. "I care about him. He's my friend."

"Why do you keep hashing this up? You're either in or you're out. Married men don't need friends. They need extra punanny. They also don't leave their wives for the extra punanny, and the two percent of them that do, end up leaving you, too."

"It's already over. I just want him to stop lying to himself. He's miserable. It breaks my heart to see him so unhappy. I knew it. I knew exactly where his marriage was headed. Failure. He felt sorry for her. That's the only reason he married her in the first place, because her baby's daddy dumped her. Pitiful. He came to her rescue. He was played for a fool."

With a valiant deep breath, I got the button on my jeans to close. I was secure and safe to breathe. I peered past the stall down to the woman's excellent painted red toes. Glossy like shiny new red Corvettes on a lot. Ten of them. And the strappy sandals to match. I owned the same pair, though I hadn't worn them in a while.

"The worst part is that the heffa was running around on him. Seeing her ex behind his back. Dr. Ex-Lova." Slurred laughter matched her slurred words. "I could see if he was like a plastic surgeon or something, but he's just a charity doctor, broke like the rest of us."

I tried to stop the ringing in my ears. Dr. Ex-Lova? Charity doctor? Chills ran up my bare arms. I was hallucinating for sure, hearing things. Had someone dropped something in my drink? *C'mon, breathe,* I told myself.

Her toilet flushed. "Anyway"—the strappy stilettos moved and the stall door banged open—"things are coming to a head, you mark my words. Jay is not going to stay with her, not when she's messing around on him. She hung herself."

Breathe, damn it! Stay calm. I stood up and touched the latch, then stopped myself. I didn't want the two women to see me, but I needed to see them.

I attempted to step on the toilet seat to peer over the top. The nonflexible fabric of my jeans permitted only an awkward knee prop, then another. I came down and pressed my face in the crack above the hinge. A red dress. A rounded shoulder. Skin, lots of cinnamon brown skin. A flip of streaked blond hair.

"I mean she spends half her time in D.C., the other in Los Angeles, spending up his money like she's Ivana and he's Donald."

"Ivana and Donald aren't married." The voice out of eyeball's reach said.

"Ivana's still spending his money."

"How do you know everything going on in his world anyway?"

"He tells me," she snapped. "That's what I mean, if he loved her so much, why is he telling me all their business?"

"Don't get hostile on me, girl. All right. You know him better than I do."

"I do. I know him. Jay is one of the good ones, and we're destined to be together."

By the time I struggled with the latch and freed myself, they were gone. The music lunged at me as I burst into the nightclub. Neon lights coming up from the dance floor bounced with the rhythm. Swaying bodies crowded the dance floor.

"Hey, shorty, want to dance?" A slim white guy with his shirt unbuttoned nearly to his navel blocked my way. I stared into his hairy midsection before making a beeline around him looking for what . . . the shoes. Nice ankles and nice calves. Red dress. Blond-streaked hair.

"Venus, over here." Wendy was waving from the dance floor, both her long arms over her head while another pair of arms looped around her waist from behind. She turned around and did a freaknik, going down on her dance partner. I grabbed her by the wrist and pulled.

"Okay, wait, damn. How fine is he?"

"Wendy, I am not trying to show you a man!" I said, unable to keep my focus. There were so many women.

Never before had it dawned on me this way: so many women for Jake to choose from.

But I was looking for just one. Red strappy shoes, red dress, long straight hair. The predator planning to steal my husband was getting away.

"What, girl? What's wrong?" Wendy's honey-colored eyes peered deeper into mine.

How could I put it into words? I knew I deserved whatever was coming my way. The way I'd treated Jake, the way I'd totally disrespected him by lying about Clint—now it was my turn.

"I'm sick." I grabbed my stomach to emphasize.

"Oookay," she said suspiciously. "You need some water or something?"

"Wait! Stop," I called out, taking off in the opposite direction. Wendy was right behind me. The mystery woman disappeared into a crowd. I pushed through the various women, unable to see anything but silicone-enhanced cleavage and long legs attached. "Let me through."

"Venus, who are we chasing?"

I reached out and took Wendy by the wrist. "Come on." I pushed and wrangled until reaching a clearing on the other side. We were outside nearly in the street with no hopes of getting back inside. Then I heard the toilet stall voice coming from a short distance in the darkness of the night. Promises to call. Slight laughter.

"This way." I pulled Wendy, knowing I'd need backup.

"What . . . is . . . going . . . on?" Wendy uttered through jiggling jaws while I dragged her to keep up.

The sound of an engine came, then headlights. It was a convertible, but the top was up. When the car came toward us, I was busy staring into the dark reflection of the windshield.

"That's it . . . Venus, what is wrong with you? I want

an answer right now." Wendy used her long arms to snatch me out of the way. I struggled to get back into view. The car's license plate was out of sight.

"Somebody's . . ."

"Somebody's . . . what?" She stuck her neck out and dropped her chin. "Spit it out!"

"Somebody's trying to steal my husband."

"Oh gawd, what else is new?"

Good question. It's not like I didn't have this problem often. But this was different. I still had hopes the entire scene was a bad hallucination. Maybe that guy with the fake tattoo did drop something in my drink?

"The woman in the bathroom, she called him Jay." I was nearly hyperventilating. "Dr. Ex-Lova, she was talking about Clint."

To Wendy, I was speaking Spanish with a twist of Greek. It didn't make sense, but I couldn't shut myself up.

"The girl in the bathroom said, 'The heffa is running around on him seeing her Ex behind his back.' Get it? Dr. Ex!" I screamed, "Get it? Clint! How would she know about me and Clint unless Jake was crying on her shoulder?"

"Who is *her*? And since when are you and Clint something to talk about?"

I blinked twice for guilty.

"This is crazy." Wendy shook her head. "I can't believe you've been seeing Clint . . . behind *my* back." She started toward the car. "If anything, that's what you ought to be ashamed of."

Disney Tunes

Six months earlier, I had a good life. I'd basically become the stay-at-home mom I'd always dreamt of being. In some circles, *housewife* was the proper term. Being able to stay home with your child and take care of your loving husband was like winning the California lotto. The odds were like a million to one.

I'd won. The battle was over. Jake made it clear he wanted me to be his wifey and put all my energy into taking care of him. A man's greatest honor, he'd said, was knowing you could afford to take care of your family. My greatest honor, in turn, would be to take care of him.

At eighteen months old, Mya was starting to wield her power as the new princess of the house. So on this day, a miraculously clear afternoon in Los Angeles, it felt good to get out of the house. Blue skies in late August just didn't happen. This hot time of the year was considered heavy smog season, when the wind didn't blow hard enough, the rain was nonexistent, and commuters sat in traffic sending out extra exhaust from the exertion of their air conditioners.

I drove along humming to the Disney radio station, the

only child-safe listening in the entire Southern California area. Then again, they played a lot of Britney Spears. Little Britney's Mouseketeering days were long over, as she showed off cleavage and thongs. But if Madonna could write children's books for little girls, exalting the virtue of being true to yourself, why not have Britney singing "My Prerogative" as the main play on a children's radio station?

The crystal blue sky and the moderate temperature of the day were fine enough, but that's not why Mya and I were so happy. The excitement came with the new teeth finally breaking through her tired achy gums, offering us both a shimmer of relief. A free get-out-of-jail card from her anguish and mine, too. I'd virtually closed myself up in the house during the difficult teething period, knowing the minute I set foot in a mall, a restaurant, or out for a stroll on the beach, her wails of misery would end all world peace.

The day was crisp and ripe with possibility. No more use for the cold teething rings. Mya hadn't used them for much except to bang me over the head. Worse was the gum-numbing gel that made her face squish, giving a clear impression of, *"Mama, that's just nasty."*

The only true relief came from my fragile nipples, which despite their lack of stature provided Mya with a full belly and mind-numbing comfort. I knew she was getting too old, but we'd struck a deal that I found hard to break. The second I pried my drained bosom from her suction, her lips arched down, her eyes watered shut, and she sobbed uncontrollably until her lungs bordered on collapse. I secretly feared someone from social services was watching, taking notes, ready to arrest me. I feared a punishment of being chained down while Mya had her way at my tender nipples all day and into the night if she desired.

Those two new pearly nuggets in my baby's mouth became my ticket to freedom. We were out minding our own business, on our way to browse for the little red clearance tags at Target. The thrill of the hunt, finding a good bargain, brought as much joy as coming across a twenty-dollar bill lying on the edge of a sidewalk. Afterwards, I'd planned to lunch at Bolivia's, a nifty little sidewalk café, without the usual fear of Mya pitching a hissy fit and making the patrons stare.

A beautiful day? No. Instead we were cut short. Clear out of nowhere, a clunker of a car rammed us from the right side at full speed, sending my silver SUV spinning out of control. We landed into a streetlight pole sideways wrapped like a half-eaten bun on a hot dog. Blood dripped down the side of my face. My leg twisted awkwardly in the wrong direction. None of that mattered. My only concern was Mya, strapped in her car seat, tipped over on the side, her mouth bent in panic, but no sound leaving her lips. I couldn't reach her. I couldn't move. She stretched her hands out for me to save her, and all I could do was curse and scream. I should have been able to fly, leap out of my seat, lift her up in my arms, and swoop her to the nearest hospital, but I was only human.

I heard voices all around, frantic 911 calls. A woman trapped, bleeding from her head. That woman was me. After a dizzying mix of images, appropriately called my life flashing before my eyes, I saw Clint Fairchild walk away from me at the altar and marry someone else. I saw my mother lying in the hospital with tubes feeding the chemotherapy into her veins. I saw Jake coming toward me like an angel with open wings.

In the hospital I awoke panicked. "Where is she? Where's my baby?" I tried to get out of the bed, ready to scour the hospital.

A nurse pushed through the door and grabbed me. "Relax, now. C'mon."

"Where's my baby? Her name is Mya. She's eighteen months old."

"She's one floor up, resting. She's fine."

I struggled to get out of bed, not realizing my leg was elevated in a cast.

Another nurse came into the room and took a hold of my flailing arms. "What's she screaming about? I heard her all the way down the hall."

"She wants to see her baby. I think we ought to give her a sedative."

"She's already had a full dose."

"I won't tell if you won't."

"Hey! Hello! I just want to see my daughter. Please." I added a mild whimper. I gave up momentarily and stared into one of the nurse's dark nostrils. "My baby," I purred, hoping to appeal to her feminine side. Her grip tightened as if she'd been bamboozled by my type before.

The older nurse with gray feathered wings for hair was in the process of plunging a needle full of morphine into my saline bag when in walked Jake to save my life, something he'd become quite good at.

"How's it going?" My husband sort of smiled, finding the entire scene amusing, two plus-sized women necessary to hold down his five-foot-two, welterweight wife. Most women stopped short of whatever they were about to do or say when Jake walked into a room. He exuded masculinity, a combination of strength and kindness all at the same time. Topped off with being well dressed and groomed to perfection, he stirred a lot of hearts, young and old.

But not this time. The nurse with hairy nostrils still wouldn't let go of my arms. "Sir, can I help you?"

"This is my wife."

"Sorry for you." The winged nurse smirked. "She's trying to leave her bed even though we've tried to tell her it isn't a good idea."

Jake came closer, gently nudging the nurse aside. "All right, I think everybody needs to calm down." He took my hands one at a time away from their grasp. "How you doing, sweetie? I just left Mya." He talked low and soothing. "The doctor says she has to stay in the brace and shouldn't be moved for a few days. If you go up there, there's a good chance she's going to want to leap into your arms instead of resting and staying put." Jake was one who believed honesty was the best policy. This, of course, would be a problem between us soon enough.

Picturing Mya in a brace sent me over the edge. He held me and whispered over and over, "She's going to be fine."

After a while, I fell asleep. Jake left, expecting me to stay in quiet slumber. In the middle of the night I woke up right where I'd left off, screaming hoarse demands to see my baby. Once the nurses realized they couldn't stop my yelling regardless of how many cc's of happy juice were intravenously delivered, they relented. One of them helped me into a wheelchair and rolled me onto the elevator and up to the third floor.

Inside Mya's room, parked by the side of her bed, I wedged my hand through the steel bed rail and stroked her smooth cheek. Mya slept with her mouth open, her eyelids fluttering. Her round cheeks mimicked sucking every few seconds, no doubt picturing her mommy's weary nipple in her mouth.

"She yours?" The voice cast from behind sent a familiar chill down my spine. I wheeled myself around, leg poking straight ahead in a cast.

That's when I saw him, Dr. Clint Fairchild.

"Venus," he said in quiet shock. Not V, like he used to call me when he'd loved me.

"Clint," I said, the same as I'd always called him when I loved him and when I loved him not as much. I'd look pretty silly calling him Clinton. His mother named him for success, only she didn't stick around to see the results, abandoning him and his older brother and sister when Clint was only ten. I'd stuck around, meeting him in his first year of medical school. We started living together right away. The fact that he was six years my junior hadn't bothered me. I worked and paid the bills while he studied and cut up cadavers. After finally completing his residency at Howard University, he rewarded me with a shiny little cocker spaniel I'd named Sandy, instead of the engagement ring I was expecting for my thirty-fourth birthday. The last time we met, I was telling him through clinched teeth how he deserved every piece of unhappiness life had to offer.

Time had passed and seemingly healed all wounds, but this wasn't how I wanted him to see me, a swollen mouth, a gash in my forehead sewn together with five stitches, mouth dry and eyes wet.

Clint's dark chocolate skin gleamed. His head was a perfect oval shape for the new Mr. Clean look. A small diamond glistened in his earlobe. He maintained his doctor composure, reading the clipboard he'd carried in, "Mother, Venus Parson. Father . . ." He paused, taking a moment to smooth a hand across his razor-clean scalp.

I knew the father section wasn't filled out, left blank. I touched my face, trying to figure out where the sudden throbbing was coming from.

"Eric, right?" He started to write.

"It's with an *A,* Airic, but we didn't work out."

"So you're not married?"

"No . . . yes, I'm married, not to Airic. I married Jake Parson. JP, the rapper." I began to hum the tune then did my best with the main lyrics. ". . . your thick luscious lips and round juicy hips . . . c'mon baby I want a ride." The look on Clint's face made me realize how ridiculous it sounded. I reached out and touched Mya's tiny foot through the blanket and decided to return to the subject at hand.

Clint moved to the side of the bed where Mya slept. "She's going to be fine," he reassured. "She's beautiful, just like you."

Even on morphine, I knew when I was being set up. I blushed in pain. Mya hardly looked like me; her fair skin and mass of silky ringlets were courtesy of Airic, my ex-fiancé.

Clint went back to his clipboard. "There's a slight contusion on her upper spine. It'll heal in about two weeks. She has to wear the brace until it does." He stopped talking and looked down at me as if he wanted to say something important, maybe even profound but changed his mind. "I bet she's a lot of fun." He handed me the clipboard. "Go ahead and fill out where it's highlighted and her birth date." I could see him doing the nine-month math in his head. Trying to figure out if I was already pregnant the last time we saw each other.

I took the clipboard. I filled out the "father" section. *Jake Parson,* because he was the only father Mya would ever know. I signed my name on the consent form and handed the clipboard back to Clint.

"She's been my life from the moment I knew I was pregnant." For whatever reason, I needed Clint to know I was a good mother. I hadn't used the baby's Enfamil to mix a White Russian before noon or added a couple of Benadryl drops to Mya's bottle to get her to fall asleep. I'd avoided many of the offenses I'd heard about from the other mommies in the playgroup, though I admit to giving their suggestions a bit of thought.

"The accident was awful. The guy came out of nowhere," I said, trying to keep my focus on his eyes instead of on the perfect form of his lips.

"She's going to be fine." Clint broke the awkward silence. "So what about you? How're you holding up?"

"My face hurts. My ribs hurt," I said, wiping the stupid tear, then the second one steaming off my cheek. "I can't feel anything in my leg except itchy-scratchy. This robe makes me feel overexposed, and my nurses were trained at the Sumo Wrestler Nursing Academy. Other than that, I'm fine."

"Good, what I like to hear."

I spat bubbles from laughter. The morphine left me a bit loose. I hoped I hadn't given too much information, like *Damn, he looked good*. But hadn't he always? Hadn't he been the one that got away, at least in my mind?

"I'm the head of Pediatrics here. I'm on the advisory board, too," he said, waiting for me to clap like a seal for his accomplishments.

"I guess Kaiser knows a good thing when they see it."

"No, Jackson Memorial," he corrected.

I sucked in all the available air in the room. "I'm at Jackson Memorial?"

Clint nodded his head up and down. "Jack the Ripper" was a well-known epithet in Los Angeles County. The hospital in the hood was known for doing more harm than good. Emergency victims left dying in the aisles. Doctors with good intentions but overworked with only half the pay. I swallowed hard.

He frowned, knowing what I was thinking. "Jackson was the only trauma center open. Trust me, you're in good hands."

"Ah-huh," I said, looking for the nearest exit.

"I know what people say, but it's not true. This hospital is special."

Understatement.

"All it took was one look at the babies in Neonatal, and I couldn't walk away. Kandi was especially concerned. She thought my career was doomed once I signed on to a place like Jackson Memorial."

The mere mention of Kandi's name made my stomach boil. Kandi married Clint on the rebound after I'd kicked him to the curb. The curb was supposed to be temporary, teach him a lesson not to take advantage of the hand that fed him. A hard lesson that turned out to be mine. She wasted no time seducing Clint and carrying him off by his britches. She took him home, fed him a bunch of bullshit until he was stuffed, wiped his mouth, belched him, and said, there, there, you'll not have to be bothered by that nasty Venus again.

I beat myself up about the fact that I let a good man go—a doctor, no less. But once I saw clearly, I knew Clint and I were never meant to be together. Didn't mean I agreed with his choice. Kandi was a gold digger with long legs and big breasts and the determination of a long-distance track runner. She wanted Clint and she got him.

Victorious

"So you're still together?" I asked, petrified that if he said no, I would jump up and cheer, bad leg and all. Not that I cared, really.

Clint looked down at his ring finger that held no band and then looked up, "Yeah, Vee, still together." He sat on the edge of Mya's bed, one leg on the vinyl floor for balance. "She was already mad about me coming to Los Angeles, then furious because I accepted this position. She said my name would be mud after working in a hospital like this. But she softened up after I brought her in, showed her the babies, same way I knew she would. She works here in the hospital in Administration but volunteers in my department. The babies need holding."

I wanted to stand up and put my cast foot up his ass. Kandi was a gold digger. I didn't care how many sick babies she swaddled during the day. Once a gold digger, always a gold digger. Instead, I smiled politely. "Do you guys have any children?" It had been only a couple of years since I'd last seen him, but Kandi could work pretty fast.

"No. Not yet. Soon, though."

Finger in mouth, commence to hurl.

I looked over at Mya, who was sleeping. I held fast to the fact that I'd still won. Regardless of what Clint put me through in the past. I was victorious. I had a beautiful daughter. A wonderful husband. Forget the picket fence—I had an iron gate with the letters *JP* swooped through the center. Four bedrooms and a view of the water. So, ha!

Clint touched my shoulder. "I better get back to my rounds. Hey, you want to roll with me if you're not too tired?"

I blinked. "Uh, no. I better get back downstairs. The nurses need to help me empty my bladder and supply me with more happy juice."

"Please, just for a minute."

I couldn't resist him begging, even if it was for something that had so little to do with me. Clint rolled my wheelchair into the corridor. He pushed me while he talked about the babies in the neonatal ward. "You'll see. Your heart is going to melt when you see them. You'll understand," he said as if he were the one in need of convincing.

The station was painted light pink with a forest mural traveling the length of the hallway. All the magical art couldn't erase the stuffiness of disinfectant and fear. He helped me cover my face with a hospital mask, then opened a slightly upgraded cotton gown for me to stick my arms through.

"They just break your heart, don't they? A lot of them are crack and meth babies, HIV positive, not to mention low birth weight. I never thought it would go on this long, generation after generation being affected by the same craziness that killed my father. You realize no drug has wiped out an entire community the way these man-made amphetamines have?" He didn't wait for my answer to his rhetorical question. He maneuvered me inside.

"How's it going, Frieda?" He spoke to the nurse sitting at the desk.

"You know, same o', same o'." Frieda stood up and rubbed her eyes rimmed with dark circles. She sneered at me and rolled her eyes.

"This is an old friend. I'm just showing her what we do up here."

Frieda's disgust receded to mild annoyance. "Look like you took a fall or something."

"A car accident," I said, still wondering why she'd given me the evil eye only seconds before.

Peaked with exhaustion, she raised her voice when she thought of something positive: "Baby Gaines opened her eyes about an hour ago."

"Serious? That's cool." Clint rolled me near the incubator with the name *Gaines* scribbled on a small white placard. The tiny brown infant lay listless with tubes traveling in and out of her body. I looked around and realized there were at least eight babies exactly like her, slackened bodies, tubes, and tape over their tiny faces.

He put on gloves and reached inside with both hands though the infant was barely the size of one of his palms. "Hey baby girl, you opened your eyes today? I want to see those pretty brown eyes. You going to open them for me?" The tiny little girl lay quiet.

"Clint, I better get back to my room."

He acted like he didn't hear me. "When she gets better, she's going into a foster home. Her mother is doing ten years for grand theft."

I bit my lip, trying to contain the eruption of emotion I was feeling. "Clint, I better go."

He faced me after gently putting the baby back in her sleeping position. "I'll walk you out."

I was in a hurry to get out of there. The thought of Mya being born that way . . . any child for that matter, sent a chill down my spine. I wiped my face and tried to get my composure. I managed to get to the elevator and push the button.

Clint caught up with me. "I shouldn't have scared you off like that." He reached out and touched the tear sliding down my cheek. He stuck his hands in his Dockers pant pockets as if realizing he had no business touching me.

"You didn't scare me."

"Then it was Frieda, right? She thought you were one of the mothers. She's old school. Her philosophy is just say no. Don't do drugs and don't sell your body on the street. Babies wouldn't be born this way if the mothers treated themselves with some respect. Frieda and me debate about it all the time. I tell her it's not that simple. Don't blame the victims."

"I guess you're both right," I said, still angling for an escape.

"So will you come back in?"

"Clint, no, really. I'm tired. Been a rough day, broken bones and all."

"You still think all doctors are the anti-Christ?"

"I never said all doctors. Only you."

"You still feel that way about me?"

"No. You've done good."

"So have you," he said, rocking on his heels. "Besides the battle scar, you look well. I like your hair. You let it grow back. I like it."

During our breakup, it was part of my burgeoning self-discovery: instead of washing that man right out of my hair, I mowed him down entirely, right down to the root. Clint was not impressed, to say the least. So I knew he was just being polite. My current look was matted up in the back from lying down, giving me an "ode to Jimi Hendrix" style.

"So what've you been up to? Still trying to take over the world?" he asked, not even close to saying good-bye.

"I've got the best job in the west: wife and mother. I stay at home taking care of Mya."

"So you're happy?" He questioned my sincerity.

"Absolutely," I said with a straight face, though lately the little voice on my shoulder was screaming for me to get out and start working again. I wasn't the stay-at-home type. I had too much energy. I needed to feel a certain amount of success and accomplishment. Cleaning up spills and picking up toys didn't quite do it for me.

"Well, if you get restless, I know of a position here at the hospital, something right up your alley—public relations. All the attention this place is getting, if someone doesn't step in soon, we're going to get crucified."

"I'll spread the word, see if I know anyone."

"Come on, V. It has your name written all over it. Nobody else has got your skills."

"Thanks for saying that, but no, really, taking care of my family is serious work. I'll see you, Clint." I waved a baby bye-bye and took the first elevator smoking.

Dr. Ex-Love

Even with the happy juice, sleep didn't come easy. I awoke to Jake kissing me on the forehead. He'd replaced the cheap standard-issue carnation with a healthy long-stemmed rose along with a Starbucks coffee and a bagged croissant.

"How was your night? You get some rest?"

I struggled to push myself up on my elbows.

He stroked my unruly hair and pushed it behind my head like a second pillow. "I spoke with Mya's doctor," he said. "She's going to be fine."

"Her doctor?" I pictured Jake unknowingly buddying up to Clint.

"Okay not *her* doctor. The doctor *here,* currently, now, how's that? I know how much you and Mya like Dr. Wang."

"Wong." I corrected.

He handed me a get-well card. I opened the yellow envelope and pulled out a giant-faced sun. Inside was a bouquet of happy-face flowers. *Sunshine and rain make the flowers grow, hope you are well soon.*

I surfed all the signatures. JP Wear employees. Scribbles on top of more scribbles of names I didn't recognize. At one point I knew everyone. I worked for Jake, where we'd first met. I was in charge of marketing, changing the kiddie-wear image of JP Wear. Then I realized Mya was growing so fast without me. I wanted to be a full-time mommy. Jake conveniently agreed. I could still do marketing and reports from home, which eventually phased out to a discussion or two over dinner while Mya pulled on my bottom lip as she nursed.

The door of my hospital room pushed open with a rush.

"How's the crash survivor doing this morning?" Clint entered, looking highly respectable. He didn't see Jake standing off to the side. "Hope you got some rest."

Jake stepped forward and stuck his hand out for a firm shake. "Oh, hey, Dr. Fairchild, she's doing well. This is my wife, Venus. You know, mother of Mya, up-stairs." He pointed up, then gave it some thought. "You're Pediatrics. Covering a lot of ground, aren't you?"

"Right. Yes." Clint and I stared at each other, waiting for who would say something first. "So you're doing okay?" he asked.

"Great!" I spouted like a shaken bottle of soda water. "When can Mya go home?"

"Tomorrow, free and clear, except for the brace."

"Great," I said again with less fizz.

Clint nodded. "Great, then. Okay, then, take care." He made his way to the door for a quick exit. He waved one last time then left the door swinging.

"Okay, then. Bye-bye," my voice cracked.

Jake stood silent, arms crossed over his wide torso. He immediately sensed something not quite right. He turned to me, then back to the swinging door. "Something I need to know?"

When we first got together, Jake used to go straight

into his educated gangsta mode; how you gone play me—wassup—I'm outta here, and then do the magic disappearing act. But here he stood, no threat of disappearing. His hands soft, his nails manicured. A well-dressed, well-liked urban clothing entrepreneur with the patience of a Dalai Lama.

"Something you need to know?" I repeated the question with a question, giving myself a moment to think. "Clint." I figured one name ought to do it, like Cher, Prince, or Brandy. From the look on his face, one word wasn't enough. "I told you about Clint, honey. Dr. Ex, my ex, the puppy instead of the engagement ring. Remember?"

"I see." A brick landing on his chest. "Why didn't you just say so? Why'd you let me make a fool of myself introducing you two like you'd never laid eyes on each other?"

"I didn't know what to say, I'm sorry. I saw him last night for the first time in a couple of years. I had no idea he was here, I had no idea I was here . . . at Jackson Memorial." I sneered. "Why didn't you move me and Mya? Gawd, this place is an accident waiting to happen." I was working hard at shifting the blame. It seemed to be working.

Until.

"I'm sure having your ex-live-in-doctor-lover-boyfriend at your bedside made it all better."

"Please don't be like that. I'm sorry." I held my arms up for the group hug that would include Clint, though he'd left the room minutes ago. I dropped my tired arms to my side and covered my face. "I'm sorry. I should have said something right away."

"Yeah, you should have. Don't disrespect me like that, Venus."

"I'm sorry," I said, leaning forward, arms stretched

out. He finally acquiesced, coming to my level. He did the one-arm stiffy around my shoulder. Finally, the group hug with Clint still between us present and accounted for.

Checkup

A couple of weeks passed. I hobbled into the patient room, pushing the stroller for Mya's follow-up appointment with Dr. Wong. Me being on crutches and Mya in a back brace made my mother-load twice as heavy. Dr. Wong, petite, spry, and full of energy, came in immediately gushing about Mya having a fan.

"Your friend, the attending physician at Jackson Memorial, really thinks Mya is special." Her smile tightened. "First I thought he was an overbearing jackass, asking how my patient was doing, making recommendations for Mya's follow-up care as if I didn't graduate from the top of my class. Then, he says, 'I'm Venus Johnston's friend. Very good friend.' 'Who?' I said. 'Mya's mother,' he said. 'Oh,' I said, 'that makes more sense.'"

Dr. Wong maneuvered past my extended leg still bundled in the cast from my knee down. "Your friend, he started to sound good to me. I was tempted to ask him on a date, but I thought, he's got to be married. The good ones always are. How are you doing, Miss Mya? Let's see what's going on here." She lifted Mya's little arms and instructed her to hold them up for a moment. Mya was quick to touch her head like she'd learned in our Mommy & Me class, her normally wobbly body erect from the steel armor around her back.

Dr. Wong moved Mya's head from side to side, back and forth. More baby talk to make sure she was distracted before popping the brace off. It happened quickly. No scream. No pain. "Tough and beautiful, can't beat the combo."

Mya smiled on cue to the word *beautiful*. Early programming.

I bent over and picked up the brace. "What do you do with . . . stuff like this?"

"Return property to the issuing hospital. Jackson Memorial is one hospital we make sure to give their stuff back. That place is three seconds away from closing. The county board of health is threatening to shut them down."

"Really, that bad?"

"That bad. Mishandling patients is one thing, but money and medicine—" She shook her head. "—that's going to cost them. Nurses were accused of stealing patient's meds to peddle on the street. Medicare funds being mishandled. One woman was six feet under and the hospital was still charging the government for her stay."

"Shit," I mumbled, not just from the story but also from the sharp pain crawling up my knee.

"So your friend has his work cut out for him." She made Mya wiggle her fingers and grab for the rubber ducky she held out of reach. "As for you, I'm surprised you came alone. You shouldn't be driving yourself."

"My husband is in the waiting room."

"Thank goodness. You don't look good." Dr. Wong didn't believe in superlatives. The best thing about people who spoke English as a second language was they left out the niceties and got down to business. "Let me take your blood pressure."

I stuck my arm out. She strapped the black pad tight and pumped till the little needle couldn't go any farther.

"Good grief, woman. Are you breathing? Low blood pressure, just as dangerous as high blood pressure. Who's your doctor?" she said, reading the dial as it inched down to 90 over 50.

"You gonna rat me out?" I eyeballed her then took my arm back.

"Yep."

I believed her. "Then I don't have one."

"Exercise and take some iron. Mya, you take care of your mommy." Dr. Wong looked back at me before going out the door. "You have to have a physician. Who is attending your broken bones? You planning to see your doctor friend at Jackson?"

"I . . . hadn't . . ."

"Watch yourself and be good." She winked and started out the door.

Jake was coming in as she was going out. He said hello to Dr. Wong and went straight to Mya, picking her up, kissing her about a dozen times. She kissed him back. Their union was a remarkable miracle I witnessed every single day.

I came and stood next to them, feeling as pitiful as Dr. Wong said I looked. The ibuprofen had worn off, and I was tired. Once we were in the car, Jake turned to me. "I think we need to hire someone for Mya until you feel better."

"My mom is helping." I reached in the back and checked to make sure Mya's car seat was secure. Since the accident, it was my habit to check and recheck the belt straps to make sure they were locked and in place.

"Your mom comes over and visits. I'm talking about all day, and into the evening. I heard Dr. Wong tell you how tired you look and about your blood pressure."

That made my blood pressure rise for sure. What else had he heard? Maybe the part about Dr. Ex-Lova being a fan, of Mya not me. He turned onto the freeway and sped into high gear.

"Jake, baby, you need to slow down."

I could see the muscles tighten in his neck. He disliked me correcting him on any level. He shifted in his seat and eased off the gas slightly so it wouldn't be obvious he was doing it at my request. "So you want to tell me why Dr. Ex-Lova was calling to check on Mya?" He said it so slowly, I was still reading his lips when he finished the question.

"What were you doing, standing outside the door the whole time? Why didn't you just come inside and have a seat?" I turned to look out the window at the brown hillside along the Los Angeles freeway, destined to rise up in flames after someone flicked their cigarette butt out of a speeding car. Fire season. Earthquake season. Clint season. "Mya was his patient, remember?"

"Long as he doesn't make any house calls," Jake said, turning toward me.

"Are you serious? I mean really. Are we having this conversation?"

"The question is, would we be having this conversation if you hadn't lied?"

"What did I lie about?"

"You know what I'm saying."

"So now I have to deal with your eavesdropping, listening for innuendo that isn't there because you think I deceived you in some way?"

"Face it, Venus. You have a history."

"I have a history? Okay, this is getting sillier by the minute. I see an old friend, who happens to be in charge of Mya's medical treatment, and now you're accusing me of what . . . what?" I shook my head. "I knew this day would come." I rubbed my throbbing head.

And here it was, the day Jake would use my past, *our past,* against me. Iron-clad proof that I was no good. Yes, I'd cheated on Airic with Jake. Yes, I'd lied to Airic on a few occasions, but . . . okay, I lied and cheated. But it was all for a great cause. I loved Jake more than anyone I'd ever loved in my life. I reached out and touched his hand. He released the gear and settled both our hands in his lap.

"I'm sorry," I said. "I really am, okay." I squeezed his hand. He had to know. The love I felt for him could flood the parched valleys and drown the surrounding mountains.

Something of a smile formed on his face before he turned his attention back to the fast-moving traffic.

Rap Star

If anyone had predicted I'd be married to a rapper (an ex-rapper—nonetheless, the title still sticks), I would've slapped him or her for the insult. Dating a hip-hopper was equivalent to dating a drug dealer with sagging pants, backward hat, gold teeth, and all the bling-bling one could reasonably stand. Serious cause to run in the other direction. How were they expected to support you if the rapping thing didn't work out?

Then there was the small problem of hoochies lined up to get the goods when the hard work finally paid off. I pictured Jake with women, many women, all beautiful and barely covered, with big butt cheeks and high heels. No, he swore it was all lights, camera, and fantasy. His brief, vigorous brush with fame brought the women to his door, but he swears he opened it only a few times and hated every minute of it.

Okay, whatever.

Those days were over. Short of a few not-so-super-models, a Grammy-winning songstress as a spokeswoman for his women's line, and on occasion a couple of groupies who couldn't quite remember why he looked familiar, he was all mine.

Jake turned around. "What do you think, too much

going on up here?" He brushed his hands against the red, blue, and orange felt patches on his chest while he faced the mirror.

I sat in bed with my cast propped up on a pillow, enjoying the impromptu fashion show. The best part, the only good part, was when Jake undressed in between changes. "Love it," I quipped when I was really looking at his solid thick arms, the width of his chest, and the lines of his true six-pack.

"It was Shaun's idea to put the patches. First I thought it was a little played . . . but it'll work."

"Oh yes, Beverly's outdone herself. Did she think of those little buckles on the shoulder, too?" When Jake first mentioned Beverly, his senior designer, he referred to her as Shaun—his right-hand *man*. So imagine my surprise when Shaun (Beverly Shaun) turned up as a flawless beauty. No magical airbrushing. For Beverly it was all real. She wore little makeup, her face, neck, and chest were a blanket of brown silk. Her eyes danced with fascination with any subject discussed, thereby making anyone and everyone in her presence feel special and pretty damn lucky to be near her. Yes, one of those women.

Still, as beautiful as she was, I didn't find her a threat. I trusted her relationship with Jake as purely platonic. Jake was a no-nonsense businessman. He didn't play at all when it came to JP Wear. If anything, Beverly Shaun may have felt a little overworked and underappreciated so I tried to give my support whenever possible. Especially knowing what kind of taskmaster Jake could be. His inability to accept excuses and total refusal to cut slack to those who weren't carrying their weight made him seem hard and on edge most of the time, not conducive to office romances.

"I saw an old friend." He said while he finished the

last snap closure on the yellow, black, and white plaid shirt.

"You see Beverly every day."

"I'm not talking about Beverly. I'm talking about Trina, somebody I grew up with, and went to elementary and junior high school with. She takes care of children for a living. I was thinking she could come help out with you and Mya until you get your cast off. She's a good person—she just had a series of unlucky breaks."

I sensed danger in this Trina person, but the killer itch traveling up my shin overpowered my train of thought. I began looking around for something to scratch the itch. I grabbed the pencil next to the notepad where Jake had asked me to take notes on the clothing line and eased it down my cast. Still no luck. I looked around the bedroom for something longer.

"You want this person to take care of Mya? Why would . . . never mind, what kind of unlucky breaks are we talking about—drugs, prison, a couple of murders thrown in for good measure?"

He pulled the jersey over his head and reached for another shirt. "Trina's a good person."

"You're in the zero category for judging what's considered a good person. Example *A*, Legend Hill, your best buddy and my worst enemy."

"Legend rubs every female the wrong way. I don't know why you take it so personal."

"It's always personal," I said, unwinding a wire hanger. "You're not instilling much confidence, here. So what's Miss *Trina* been doing all this time?"

"Taking care of kids, other people's kids. I saw her when I went to my mom's last week. We talked, she's working for a family, the kid is autistic and the parents are doing nothing for him. She thinks if she quits, they'll have to find him a school or someone better qualified to handle him. But she can't quit until she has another job lined up. I told her we were looking for someone to take care of Mya." He paused, facing me after buttoning his next shirt. "What do you think?"

"I like it," I said, funneling the hanger down the side of my leg, almost there.

"Cool, so I'll tell her she can start."

"Huh? No. I meant the shirt."

"What are *you* doing?" He caught a hold of my wrist before I reached the magic spot. The hanger stuck out of my cast where it was wedged against my skin. He eased it out.

"You're going to scratch a hole in your skin, get an infection, then your leg's going to swell up and have to be cut off. You want that?"

"If it would stop the itch, then yes, that would be fine."

Jake shook his head, his wife's irrational behavior never ceasing to amaze him. He went to the bathroom and came back with a wad of toilet paper. He wrapped it around the end of the hanger until it resembled a small animal's paw. "Here."

I worked with MacGyver speed to push the hanger to the flaming spot. Relief.

"You back with me?" he asked, standing over me bare-chested and sexy.

"Yes, you have my full and undivided attention." I kept focus on his tight abs.

"But seriously, I really think Trina will work out. Plus, I want to pay her a little more than she's used to, see if it helps her get back on her feet."

"I don't know, Jake. Sounds like you've known her, but you don't know her. People change. Or sometimes don't," I said quietly.

"She's cool people, Venus. Trust me."

"Things aren't that bad around here. I don't need help." I peered around at the unfolded laundry. I thought about the garbage bags full of baby diapers stacked near the garage door. The kitchen sink held mildly crusted sipper cups I'd been meaning to soak. Still, my housekeeping was no indication of my caregiving ability. I was a good mother and a good wife. Everyone was clean and fed, the basics covered. I hadn't left my child on top of the car and driven off or anything.

I relented. "I should at least meet her."

"Of course. I wouldn't do what you and Dr. Ex-Lova did to me. Oh yeah, by the way, this is Mya's doctor, and did I mention my ex-boyfriend," he drew out playfully, though a small trace of hurt was still in his voice.

"So you and Clint are ex-lovers?" I said, horrified.

He pointed a chastising finger. "Don't even try it. You know exactly what I'm saying."

"I know, I know. I've apologized and I will keep apologizing until you feel better."

"Hey, I'm over it. Like I said, long as Dr. Ex doesn't make any house calls, I'm cool."

I scooted out of bed and hobbled up to him. I pushed my hands into his back jean pockets, kissing and inhaling his smooth chest. "Is the fashion show over?"

"Yeah, I guess so. My audience of one has left her seat."

I unbuttoned his jeans and pulled the zipper down. "I'm still here. Great show, by the way."

"Glad you enjoyed it. Did you happen to take notice of the actual clothing?"

"Yes, I did." I gave his jeans right along with his boxers an even push to his ankles. I felt around to what I knew was waiting at firm throbbing attention.

He stepped out of the clothes and reached underneath my nightshirt, grabbing my plump cheeks. "You're not wearing any panties."

"They're kind of hard to get on over a cast." I pressed my naked pelvis against his.

"So you've given up panties until the cast comes off. I think I like this injury." Our tongues swirled in a kiss.

Before hitting the mattress I remembered, "Mya's going to be up any minute."

"Keep it quiet, then." He pushed his fingers inside me and worked them in and out.

I took a hold of his thickness and squeezed gently before straddling him. He let out a soft groan.

"You're the one better keep quiet." I slid the length of him, pretending to take control. The truth, I couldn't stop moaning from the second his lips touched my body. He stretched wet kisses across my neckline, pulling up my nightshirt. He tasted the milk that still leaked from my breast. His tongue encircled the thin center of my navel. My entire body was awash with the wetness from his tongue.

I did my best to suppress the grunts every time Jake pushed deeper inside me.

The precise moment my toes started to curl, I heard Mya's faint cry. Her soft whine blended with mine, then continued like an echo when I was through.

"Told you not to make all that noise." Jake kissed the center of my moist chest, threw on his boxers, and went to fetch Mya from her crib.

Nanny Love

Jake was right. Trina Simpson made our life easier. I suddenly understood the hubbub in Utah, where polygamy was an acceptable practice. Having an extra wife (without sharing the marital bed, of course) was the greatest idea since family-share plans for the cell phone. I commended Jake on his excellent idea and relished each day Trina arrived, ready to make my day go smoother.

Monday through Friday she let herself into the house with the key. She started coffee precisely at 7 A.M., not a minute late. She cooked. She cleaned. She took care of Mya. On occasion we had good conversations. She liked to tell funny stories about when she and Jake were kids. Although, I can't remember laughing. In fact, I thought it a little tragic holding on to recollections with such detail, hanging on to the past and all. But I humored her and asked the requisite question now and again.

"So Jake was the shy type, huh?"

"Oh yeah, every time I turned around, he was getting chased home by some girl claiming he was her boyfriend. This one girl, Helena, she threatened to beat him up if he didn't come out and kiss her. His mama came out instead and did her own threatening. Jake's mama was something else back then." Trina's eyes squinted with memory, "Oh . . . and there was this one time—"

"All right, I can see where this is going." Jake breezed into the kitchen, dressed for work. He leaned near my ear and whispered, "Don't believe anything she says. I was a saint."

Trina coughed out a laugh. "Right."

"You don't want to start exchanging war stories." Jake shot Trina a look that shut her up pretty quick.

"Yes, sir, Mr. Parson. Can I get you your coffee, sir?" she mocked.

"I think I can manage." He poured his own fresh cup. "But you can bring me the newspaper."

"We don't take the paper," I helpfully interjected.

Jake and Trina chuckled, looking to each other like I was the only one who didn't get the joke. Mya even grinned, showing her wet teeth and gums covered with half-eaten Cheerios.

"All right, I'm out of here. Have a good day, babe." Jake kissed Mya and then me. On his way out, he squeezed Trina's shoulders. She shrugged him off. I wasn't concerned about the playfulness I witnessed. Lately Jake wasn't in the joking-around mood, so seeing him light and happy was a relief. Trina was hardly a threat, at least from a physical aspect. And for good reason. Girlfriend could use a makeover. Then again, so could I. But their friendship was obvious, the kind built from growing up together, the foundation of childhood memories.

"Okay, Miss Thing, let's get you cleaned up." Trina wiped Mya's hands and mouth before scooping her out of the high chair.

"You need to stop taking advantage of Trina, little

lady." I took Mya out of Trina's arms and set her on her wobbly two feet. "She needs to walk. Come on, pretty girl, Mommy will get you dressed." I started to walk Mya, holding her two small hands while she stood between my legs. Instead of taking off like she usually did, she craned her neck followed by her entire body, looking for Trina.

My cast had been off a whole two weeks, but I still moved like I was carrying the weighted stump. "Shhh, Mya, let's go."

Trina picked up the remote and turned on the TV, doing her best to ignore the mother–daughter tussle. The morning news came to a full screen of picketers holding up signs. OUR COMMUNITY OUR HOSPITAL. A little girl used both arms stretched high above her head. Her sign read, I WAS BORN HERE.

"There he is. That's him." The television cameras followed the picketers to a group of men and women dressed in staid business attire.

"Why are you trying to shut down our hospital?" A thick older black woman spoke out. "Many of the people in this community have no cars, no transportation. Where are they supposed to go for their medical care? What happens when someone is shot and bleeding in the streets? We're supposed to wait an hour for an ambulance to take us to the other side of town?"

"Our investigation is not conclusive." The well-dressed woman with large teeth and stiff hair lifted a hand with calm, demanding control. "The county wants to make assessments and put this hospital back on its feet as quickly as possible. Our goal is to keep this hospital operating at full capacity. Please go home and let us do our job." The camera spun around to the shouting picketers.

"They can't hide forever. We'll be waiting when they

come out," the lead picketer vowed. The crowd behind cheered.

The newscaster turned her face to the camera with a grave tone. "As you can see, the Los Angeles County Board of Health is cracking down on the hospital. An investigation committee has been assigned to evaluate the affairs at Jackson Memorial. For some time they have been under investigation, and sorry to say, this might be the end of the Jackson Memorial Center, which has a deep history in the African-American community. I'm Delores Stevens, in Los Angeles."

"Did they just say they were closing the hospital?" Trina and I were both straining to hear over Mya's consistent wail.

"Mya. Stop it."

Trina went around me and scooped Mya up. "It's okay. What-sa-matter with that baby, huh?" She poked her head past Mya, who was now relaxed against her chest. "I can't believe they're closing the hospital. Where're people supposed to go?"

I took Mya out of Trina's arms *again*, set her down and shot a look that said, *Don't you dare.*

Trina turned her back and pretended to be busy. "You hungry? I'm fixing eggs," she spoke over the ever-rising volume of Mya's cry.

"No, no thank you. Mya, let's go."

I inevitably picked her up myself duly defeated.

I could see Mya's outstretched arms reaching over my back for Trina. I cringed and out of spitefulness I swung around and simply handed her over. It was supposed to be a test. Mya was supposed to fret and panic over the separation. Instead she did the opposite, gladly migrating against Trina's chest, forgetting I was in the room.

I gave it a few more minutes and said something

caustic like, "Mommy is leaving. Okay, Mommy is saying bye-bye, Mya."

Mya went on to play with the cross hanging against Trina's worn out Super Bowl T-shirt. I left the kitchen and went upstairs and closed myself in the bathroom. I sat on the closed toilet seat for a brief me-oh-my tirade. In the beginning, I cherished every moment I had away from the pressures of work and office politics, now I felt like I was wasting away.

The knock at the bathroom door shook me from my pity party.

"Venus, uh, you all right in there?" Trina's brassy voice came through like she was standing next to me.

I snatched some tissue off the roll and wiped my face. "I'm good. You need something?"

"Well, no, I just heard . . . you sounded like you were throwing up or something."

"I'm fine."

"Okay, well, I'ma take Mya to the park. You sure you okay?"

"Yes." I said through seemingly gritted teeth, although I meant to smile.

I heard the distant steps and then the bedroom door close.

"Wendy, hey girl," I tried to talk above my plugged nose, then realized I probably sounded A-okay. The countless times I'd dialed Wendy after a good cry probably made this time sound tame and normal in the world according to Venus Johnston. Johnston-hyphenated-Parson, my driver's license read. I was a missus now.

"Want to go to lunch?" I asked like the old days when we were cubicle buddies at Mayer Advertising, where we first met eleven years ago.

"You in town?"

"No. I'm still in L.A."

"Okay, what happened?"

"Nothing, absolutely nothing. Just a little time on my hands," I said, extending my legs and stretching my toes to see if one leg might really be longer than the other since the cast came off.

"Girl, you know nothing would make me happier than you coming to visit. But whatever has got you under the bridge is still going to be there when you get back."

"Lunch," I said. "I wasn't planning to stay for a week."

"So you're going to fly out here just to have lunch with me, then you're going to get back on the plane and go home. Is that what you're telling me?"

"Ah-huh," I said with a good sniff.

"Good grief, what'd he do?"

"Jake. Ohmagod, are you kidding? He's perfect."

"Nobody's perfect," Wendy exclaimed, never having been a fan of Jake the rapper. Though he did get points for being fine as hell and extremely polite.

"Jake's perfect," I said brightly.

"Then what's wrong?"

"I'm bored. I know this is the life I asked for. Wife and mommy status was like winning the lottery, and now I'm bored out of my gourd." Another sniff attached. "I worked so hard before. Now I feel useless. I feel like everyone is moving forward and I'm standing still."

"Okay," she said, satisfied with the answer. "When are you coming?"

"Now."

"Now? Well hate to break it to you, sweetheart, but we'll be having dinner instead of lunch. It's already eleven o'clock here. . . . East Coast, baby, see you tonight."

I called Jake and explained Wendy needed me. It

was an emergency. Mya and Trina were fine and I'd be back the next day. Jake was in the middle of threatening his manufacturer in Thailand and simply said, "Hurry back."

"I love you," I said before the phone went silent.

Free at Last

One thousand dollars and five hours later, I was standing on the curb of the Baltimore airport. I could hear Wendy scream out, "Heyyy!" but couldn't see her coming from any direction.

I spun around one more time. I cupped my hand over my mouth when I realized where the voice was coming from. "Girl, no you didn't."

"Yes, I did."

"No you didn't."

"Yes, I *did*." Wendy spun around to give me a full view. My sister friend who hadn't missed a month in the relaxer chair since I'd known her was standing proud with her Miss America hair gone, cut down to the natural baby-fine root. Her dark skin, high cheekbones, and light brown eyes were accentuated to the fullest.

"You look awesome" was all I could say once the shock wore off. "Amazingly beautiful."

"You like it? Really?"

"I love it. Really." I hugged her fiercely tight.

"I was going to tell you. I mean your coming out here was a surprise. I thought, why not surprise you back. So here I am. Pulled a Venus Johnston. Cut it all off and daring somebody to say something ignorant. Just daring 'em."

"What does Sidney say?"

Her eyes watered slowly. "Well, there you go . . . that's ignorant." Her big amber eyes captured the reflection of light just enough to show how sad she truly was. "You don't know. You forgot." She shook her head like she was disgusted. "Get in."

I pulled on my seat belt and snapped it locked. "Wendy, when I cut my hair, the first thing you said was, 'What does Clint have to say?' It was the first thing out of your mouth. Now when I ask, what does Sidney have to say, I'm crazy. It's a real issue. Black men do not, I repeat, do not like their women cutting off all their hair. They rather you walk around with a Diahann Carroll wig flipped up on the sides than see you in a natural short cut."

She started up the engine. The car pulled out, garnering a few honks from drivers she'd nearly swiped. "You should know more so than anybody—this is not about Sidney, or what he thinks. This is about me."

"Okay, you're scaring me."

"That bastard has been screwing the babysitter," she blurted out. I stayed silent in shock. We drove to the restaurant without another word spoken. I was too busy praying we got there safely. She was too busy trying to see the road through her tear-swollen eyes.

The hostess seated us outside underneath the clear black sky. A tall steel gas furnace sat next to our table, pumping out heat. The airplane ride had been unbearably cold. I was still fighting off the chill.

After the bread was left and the water was poured, I reached across and grabbed Wendy's warm hand. "I'm sorry about Sidney."

"I didn't want to tell you. I knew you'd say it was

partly my fault, especially with your . . . it-takes-two-to-tango philosophy."

"No. I wouldn't have said it was your fault. No. I mean, I do believe in cause and effect. You get what you give and all that, but when it comes to a man, all bets are off." I pulled my hand away after I felt eyes staring. It dawned on me that the table next to us thought Wendy and I were a loving couple. Wendy's new short haircut. Mine pulled back in a frizzy cottontail as I sat whispering words of solace that may have looked like a lover's apology.

Then I reached out and took both her hands, not caring what people thought. "So tell me, are you enjoying your new freedom? You like the way you feel, because I think you look amazing."

"I do. I feel good, I mean when I'm not thinking about what Sidney did. I saw it with my own eyes. Her mouth was wrapped so tight around his—"

"Are you two ready to order?" The waitress held her pencil up, ready for action.

"Water for now." I wanted to hear the rest of Wendy's details. *Scoot!* The waitress went away quietly.

Wendy decided to whisper this time. "Eighteen. The girl is barely legal. I swear if she'd been one year younger, I'd have his ass arrested. Too bad screwing around on your wife in your own home isn't a crime."

"It is a crime, just not one punishable by a jail sentence."

"Let me tell you, I walked in, turned around, and went right back outside and shut the door. Then rang the doorbell. He answered, and that's when I socked him square in his big nose. He didn't know what hit him."

I busted up laughing. "I'm sorry. That's not funny."

"It is funny. It's ridiculous. It was like watching

something from real far, far away. He didn't even look up when I first came in. Why does a blow job make a man lose consciousness? I swear, I can chew bubble gum and figure out an algebraic equation with Sidney's mouth on my crotch. I want some of whatever good-sense blockers are released in a man's brain when he gets a blow job."

"I am sorry. What do the kids say? How are they taking all of the drama?"

"They'll live. What's important is that I stop living in a fantasy world. Sid and I have been wrong for a long time. No renewal of the vows or marriage therapist is going to fix it this time. Really, I'm good." She used her napkin to dab her eyes. "You're the one flew all day to get here. What happened to you?"

My episode of loneliness felt petty and small compared with what Wendy was going through. "Nothing. Just needed to get away."

"Do me a favor, don't feel bad for me. Feels like a weight has been lifted. I have to beat the men off me, girl. Your little theory about men and short hair is way off. Way off." She leaned in and whispered, "I already met someone."

"Well, why didn't you say so? This calls for a celebration." I flagged the waitress back over. "A bottle of Moët, please."

"Oooh, for little ol' me?"

"To you and the new life that awaits." When the bottle came, we lifted our glasses for a toast.

"You know the best part about all this: I feel so entirely free. It took something tragic to make it happen, but damn if the price wasn't worth it."

We turned up our glasses and went through the bottle like it was water. Before it was over, there were three bottles of Moët on the tab. Through my blurry eyes, I kept questioning who drank them, but from the looks of us both, we were definitely the guilty party.

"Ladies, would you like a cab?" The Asian waitress had four dimples, two faces.

Wendy and I must've seen the same thing because we both cracked up.

"No, ma'am. We're not quite ready to leave yet," I said, trying not to laugh.

"Okay, but if you don't mind, I'm going off shift in a few minutes and would like to clear this bill."

"Oh, yeah, sure." Which sounded more like, *Oohy-eahshooore.* I pulled out my gold card and laid it on top of the bill. The waitress was quick to scoop it up. "She don't have nowhere to go. She just wants to make sure I pay before I fall into the harbor," I said, still seeing double.

Wendy laughed and slobbered at the same time then stopped abruptly. "What? What are you staring at?"

I followed her eyes to the couple that had been watching earlier. A black man and a white woman. They quickly averted their eyes.

"Act like they ain't never seen no fine sister girls. We do exist, you know. Sorry, I was busy before, but I'm free now. Want a date?"

I grabbed Wendy's hand that was pointed in their direction.

"Did I mention the babysitter was pregnant?" she said, quieting suddenly.

I shook my head.

"Yeah. Sidney's. So she says." She downed the rest of her champagne.

My eyes watered right along with Wendy's. My head throbbed, and then I ran to the bathroom to throw up.

Stupid Women Tricks

My disappearing act didn't go over well with Jake. I explained how I'd forgotten my phone charger and how the battery died before I'd even reached Baltimore. So why didn't I use Wendy's phone? he raged.

Then I went with the truth, thoroughly explaining Wendy's crisis, and our drinking until we couldn't see straight. How time got away from the two of us. Nothing seemed to squelch Jake's anger.

I admitted I was wrong, and frankly, I was sick of making amends. Each morning, the day started out with Jake interrogating me. "What are you going to do today?"

My answer had to be detailed. "I have Gymboree with Mya at ten. Meeting my mom for a late lunch, then I'll probably go to LA Fitness and work out."

"Are you coming straight home after the gym?"

"Yes."

Believe it or not, this is what my already tedious life had come to. I was left feeling more stagnant than before.

After Jake left for his studio, I lay in bed. I rolled over, reached for the remote, and clicked on the TV. The sleek flat screen opened up to the picketers going strong in

front of Jackson Memorial Hospital. The restless crowd
had grown, doubled in size from the last telecast. A press
conference was about to take place. The camera swung
to the empty podium, waiting for whoever would take
the mike. A heavyset woman finally arrived, shuffling
notes, not sure where to start. She shook her collar a little to cool off, but still perspiration sprang to her armpits,
making wide dark circles on her lavender suit.

"As you know, there have been many allegations about
the efficiency and care given at this hospital. Outra-
geous rumors and nothing more. The list of problems
is long but comes from lack of resources, not lack of
caring professionals."

"Is it true you're closing?" The question came out of
the crowd of reporters.

The woman looked at her stack of unorganized papers. I waited for the answer that would set us all free.

"No," she said. "Any other questions?"

"I've heard the neonatal unit will be closing first." Another reporter fired, "Of all the facilities in the hospital,
why do you think that department was pinpointed?"

"Money, why else? Isn't this what it's all about? Forget about saving lives." She waved a hand as if she'd
had enough. "Forget about the people of this community since they can't afford good health care. Thank you
and have a good day."

I clicked the TV off and thought about what I'd just
heard. The cost of running the neonatal ward was
bankrupting the hospital.

All I could think about were those innocent babies,
each and every one of them, with tubes coursing in and
out of their bodies with barely a fair chance to survive.
What would happen if they didn't have Jackson Memorial? Little brown angels with nowhere to go. Who
would care for them?

I knew it was a long shot, thinking I could pick up the phone and reach Clint on the first try, but I wanted to talk to him and tell him I wanted to do anything I could to help. He was my friend after all, regardless of how badly he'd broken my heart. Most important, I knew I could help . . . at least trying would be better than wallowing in too much free time.

"Dr. Fairchild, please." I chewed on the inside of my jaw. "Yes, I'll hold."

The line picked up to another receptionist.

"Hi. I'm calling for Dr. Fairchild."

"He's unavailable. May I take a message?"

"Please tell him Venus Pars . . . Johnston called and would like to speak with him. It's urgent."

"Regarding?"

"Um, the hospital. The closure. Public relations," I said, tapping my short nails on the desk, wondering why I had to explain anything to a receptionist in the first place.

"Venus Johnston?"

"Yes." I began to spell the last name.

"That's not necessary, Venus. This is Kandi, Clint's wife. I didn't realize you were in Los Angeles." She patiently waited for a response.

I had none. I swallowed hard and forced myself to speak. "I didn't realize you were in Los Angeles either," I lied.

"This is where my husband is, so naturally I would be with him."

"Naturally," I said, noticing I'd drummed my fingertips numb and stopped.

"Is there anything else?"

Tension filled the telephone line.

"Umm, he has my number."

"You take care," she said, reminding me of the day

I'd first set eyes on her. Bambi lashes and spear-arched brows, her broad shoulders covered with overflowing hair. Female perfection. Large breasts, childbearing hips, and still insecure.

Anyone else would have seen this as a warning, a danger sign with a large detour arrow pointed to take another route. Surely there was another worthy cause, a building to save, a fur dealer to shut down, maybe a political party to campaign for, something not involving my ex-fiancé and his she-whore wife.

I called and left a message for the administrator of the hospital requesting a meeting, explaining Dr. Clint Fairchild of Pediatrics and Neonatology referred me. I pictured my magnificent entrance, strutting through the hospital doors wearing a suit that screamed diva with an exclamation mark, pointed-toe Via Spigas and a matching shoulder bag.

I had a fabulous career before succumbing to mother and wife-hood. I had an office that overlooked the Potomac River. I had a staff of three that reported to me and occasionally hung on my every word. In the words of the great Martin Luther King Jr., *"I am somebody."*

Or at least I was.

Entering my walk-in closet I realized it was past tense. My business attire, all dated and ill-fitting, hung dusty and worn. Motherhood T-shirts and plenty of yoga pants hung where my good stuff used to be.

"You throwing all that stuff out?" Trina stepped into the closet doorway. She held Mya against her hip.

I raised up with a handful of hangers with heyday blouses and rayon-blended suits. "Yep. You know you don't have to carry her around all day. She can walk."

"You mind if I take a look before you throw that stuff out?" she said without so much as loosening her grip on Mya. She and Jake had gone to school together, same age, nearly ten years younger than me, which would explain her stamina. Carrying Mya around all day was a workout.

"Sure, but, most of them are fours. Some sixes." I didn't want to state the obvious.

She flagged a hand for my assumption. "Not for me. I have a friend."

Trina put Mya in the playpen nearby and rushed off. She came back with lawn bags. Plenty of them. Mya stacked blocks in her playpen and sang songs that didn't exist. When we were through, nothing hung on the closet rods except a couple of sundresses picked out by Jake on our honeymoon. Sentimental value and the fact I'd never worn them kept me from tossing them out.

"What about the shoes?" Trina asked, looking up at rows upon rows of shoe boxes.

"My feet haven't changed."

"You sure?" she said. "Most of my friends agree, once you have a baby, your feet grow at least one size bigger."

I resisted the urge to snarl. I pulled down a pair of my favorite slingbacks as a test and stuck my foot inside. Pain rose up, sprouting through every pore on my scalp.

"Tight," Trina confirmed.

"Tight," I agreed. I pulled down a few more shoes. A few more. Before long I was left with one single row of shoe boxes. None of which were my favorites.

I stepped over the mess, grabbed my purse, and told Trina I was going shopping. For backup, I called Jake and told him, too. The mission would go far into the night hours, I didn't want him putting out a search posse.

"Shopping where?" Jake breathed into the phone when I thought I was doing a good deed by at least telling him where I was headed. A change in my usual plans, no Gymboree, no grocery shopping. I had to count to five not to scream in his ear, *Stop asking me where I'm going every five minutes*!

"The Galleria, sweetie," I sang out instead. "I can swing by and pick you up if you'd like. We can shop together."

"No. Just wanted to know."

"Okay, then."

"Hey, Venus . . ."

"Yes, dear?" I said, sarcasm dripping from my every pore.

"Thanks for checking in with me." Jake's sweet sexy voice deepened. "You know it's just because of the accident. Ever since then, I get nervous when you're out all day. I don't want to ever lose you."

Moistness built up in my eyes, and my bottom lip quivered a bit. "I know I scared you when you didn't hear from me while I was off to see Wendy. It was stupid. Thank you for putting up with me. So I'll see you tonight, okay. I'll have a surprise for you."

"Oh yeah, I like your surprises." His voice fell softer.

I wasn't sure if he was going to like this one. But enough was enough. It was time to get my career back on track and moving again.

Two Sides

Jake shoved the profit-and-loss statement he was reading to the side and leaned back in his large leather chair.

Beverly Shaun leaned in, knocking lightly. "You don't look good."

"Thanks."

"No, I'm serious. You look like you might have a fever or something." She sat at the edge of his desk, close enough to brush against his leg. She placed a cool hand against his forehead then moved it lightly from cheek to cheek.

"I'm fine." He nudged her hand away. "Did you get the production schedule straightened out?"

"Yep." She tossed her silky mane from one shoulder to the other. Her top barely covered the sparkling diamond in her pierced belly button. "Is that what's bothering you?"

"I'll tell you what's on the brotha's mind." The voice of reason came from Legend, who'd just plopped his well-dressed self into the leather chair. "Too many women, not enough time."

"What's bothering him . . . not your horny ass." Beverly moved off Jake's desk and took a respectable seat next to Legend. "And stop looking at me like you haven't eaten, 'cause I am not your next meal."

Legend leaned in and stared harder. "You dress like that because you want me and every man within viewing distance to look at your goodies. Now if they're not eatable, you need to wrap 'em up and put 'em away."

The antics of Beverly and Legend put a smile on Jake's face. They were the three musketeers. It felt good to have them by his side, especially while things were tough.

"Somebody bring me some good news. That's all I ask." Jake folded his hands over his chest.

"The new line is selling. What else do you need to know?" Legend leaned forward. His dark heavy locks were tied back, showing off his baby-fine side burns.

"I need to know why I'm still losing money."

"I didn't major in accounting, my brotha. That's our boy Byron Steeple's department."

"You went over budget on the marketing. Byron's a number cruncher. He's not responsible for how it comes in and how it goes out."

"Marketing and advertising are a mainstay. You can't cook without fire. You try to cut back on face time, you become invisible."

Beverly rolled her eyes, twice. "Don't look at me. I can't cut back any further or the pants will be closed with Velcro instead of zippers."

Legend stood up and adjusted his tie. "All right, then maybe it's the—" Something caught his attention out the large picture window. He clapped his hands together, his stark white teeth showing his enthusiasm. "Since when can number crunchers afford Bentleys? Should've been an accountant 'cause brotha man is rolling."

Jake and Beverly both rushed to the window. Byron

Steeple got out of the large shiny automobile with his briefcase, looking like he'd won the lottery.

"Mr. Suspenders is looking mighty happy." Legend cut his eyes toward Jake.

Jake went back to his chair, leaned back, and tried not to panic. His heart was racing.

Beverly sat back down, too. "I know what you're thinking. Byron wouldn't do that. He's been with us from the very beginning."

Legend laughed. "Good thing you're pretty, 'cause you're not too bright."

Beverly was gunning up for something evil to say, but Jake interrupted. "I got things to do. You mind taking your little love–hate thing out the door?"

Legend stood up and extended his hand. "After you."

Beverly sidestepped his assistance. "I'll be downstairs if you need me, Jay." She pushed past Legend as they both left quietly.

Men were simple creatures. They needed two basic things in life: sex and money. Two big hands washing the other. Just paying the bills wasn't enough to inspire a man to hit the ground running each and every morning. He did it for one reason: access to good lovin'. If he didn't have legitimate means, then he'd steal for it, bottom line.

After a few minutes, Jake picked up the phone. "Byron, come talk to me for a minute, man." Jake reached inside the drawer and pulled out his inhaler. "Yeah, I'll be waiting."

Jake studied the statement, looking for any clues that he may have missed. He was being robbed right underneath his nose but couldn't prove it. Where else would Byron get a hundred-thousand-dollar vehicle? Jake himself drove a sports coup Lexus, and he made sure he got a good deal. He wasn't the extravagant

spending type. He wore a carat in each ear and his wedding band, the extent of his need to shine. Other than that, he took care of business and family first.

Byron entered Jake's office, nervous, closing the door behind him. "Was I late for a meeting or something? You sounded upset."

"Yeah, you could say that." Jake pushed the profit-and-loss statement across the desk to Byron. "Why is my shit still red?"

Byron put up both hands. "You know I only report. Don't shoot the messenger," he said, attempting light-hearted humor.

"This can't be right. This is the third quarter in a row. Sales are strong. I've got more orders than I can handle, and the numbers still show me losing money. I want you to go through the accounts, find the problem, Byron. You know what I'm saying."

"I'll do my best."

"That's all I ask," Jake said calmly, but he wanted to get up and throw Byron's ass out the window.

"I'll get right on it," Byron said as he closed the door.

"You do that."

Bigger Bully

The interview at Jackson Memorial was scheduled for the late afternoon. I arrived wearing the soft pink Donna Karan suit I'd purchased on my shopping spree. My hair was smoothed back in a tight bun. I was ready to put on a good show. It'd been years since I had to interview for a job, be put under scrutiny and assessed by someone—always less qualified than myself, as it turned out.

I did a quick scan of the hospital lobby. Floors shined, plants watered, and sprawled bodies cleared from the waiting room floor.

"I'm here to see Morgan Taylor, the Deputy Administrator. I have an appointment."

"Administration. She's on the second floor." The receptionist paused. "What channel are you from?"

I shook my head. "Channel?"

"What station? You're a newscaster, right?" She used her long acrylic nails like extended fingers and handed me a guest badge.

I put the plastic clip on the hem of my jacket, not wanting it to interfere with my newscaster ensemble. Not sure if it was the look I was going for, but it was better than housewife-starting-over.

I took a long deep breath before entering the elevator. Certainly, I was qualified. Getting the job seemed like a slam dunk until I entered Morgan Taylor's office. She was the woman who'd given the botched press conference on the news.

She extended a straight arm without pleasantries. "Have a seat." Hair pulled back in a tight chignon. Pearl drop earrings hung a small distance from her neck, resisting movement. No lighthearted swing. "Dr. Fairchild has told me good things about you. I'm almost ready to move past the formalities and offer you the job." She sat upright in her fabric-covered chair, pushed all the way to the desk, ramrod straight. Which could explain the stiffness in her voice and demeanor.

"That's a huge compliment. Thank you."

"But of course, that would be wrong and unfair to the other candidates." She poised her pen over a yellow tablet to take note of anything of interest I said.

Other candidates. I did my best to look unfazed. I unclasped my hands, reached down into my leather case, and whipped out my résumé. I attempted to hand it to her.

She waved it away. "I've seen your résumé, Mrs. Parson, and I'm quite impressed. But the experience you have does not tell me whether or not you could handle the pressures of Jackson Memorial."

"Please, call me Venus," I said, feeling the distance growing between us. "I know I'm capable of doing this job. I have an MBA, and with my emphasis in marketing . . ."

"As I said, I've read your credentials. This hospital needs someone who can reach out and be heartfelt. We're on the television just about every day for one mishap or another. The county board of health is on a fierce campaign to shut us down. This hospital needs someone as close to a heavenly saint as we can find. Someone approachable and as sincere as they are knowledgeable, and I know for a fact it's not me. Every time I set foot at that podium, I want to hurl myself at those crucifying monsters, claws and fangs ready for battle. Who do they think they are, condemning us? This hospital has done so much good, and no one wants to acknowledge that. This hospital stands for something. We will not be ridiculed any further." By this time her eyes had turned into steely dark balls, her mouth tightened in a frightful straight line.

She pulled a Kleenex from the box on her desk and patted moisture from her neck.

I was afraid to speak. "I know I'm capable," was all I managed to say. I felt rusty and out of sync. I tried to focus on what I'd already rehearsed and not let her high frequency interrupt my original intent. I took a short deep breath and told myself, *Go.* "I've researched every detail of this hospital and its history. I see a void and know I'm capable of filling it. This hospital established itself in the black community as the primary caregiver in 1965 after the Watts riots left hundreds of injured on the streets with nowhere to go. Jackson Memorial is an institution, a landmark in history. It can't close or be threatened with closing every time an unfortunate incident takes place. The same kind of common errors happen in hospitals all over the country. I believe this hospital is receiving the wrath of righteousness due to the fact that it's in an area servicing only people of color, staffed by a majority of black doctors and nurses. There are people who believe it's not up to par. We know that's not true. It's time to let them see a stronger front, staff and administrators who won't be bullied anymore."

"Really, and how does one stop a bully?" Morgan Taylor relaxed a bit in her chair.

"Find a bigger bully, someone to back us up. Privatizing with a solid backer. Move from underneath the local government's wing."

"Who's going to be our bigger bully? No one will speak up for us, not the county board of supervisors, not our so-called black leaders, no one."

"For now we make one up just like the days on the school grounds. When you're a kid getting stomped on at recess you have to start talking about the crazy uncle or big brother who coincidentally just got out of prison."

A surprising snicker came from Morgan Taylor. I was winning, gaining speed.

"For now we pretend. Keep implying the message, a threat to privatize. Do a little PR magic. Image is everything. Once we look stronger, more stable, we'll look like a viable company and I promise others will want to stand with us."

Morgan Taylor smiled and shook her head. "You're on the ball. I can see that. But as I said, there are other candidates." She paused, as if she wasn't sure about trusting me. "Well, one candidate," she said truthfully. "I'm in a dilemma. The person who wants this position is the wife of one of our doctors. A doctor who has done a great deal for this hospital, and I feel obligated to give her a shot out of loyalty."

My heart sank, my well of confidence suddenly filling with disappointment. I picked up my leather case and set it on my lap. "Thank you for your time," I said with a genuine appreciation for the dress rehearsal.

She stood up. "Wait a minute. Really, give me a day or two before you approach another employer."

"Sure," I said, knowing to leave while I was still ahead. I shook her hand and marched off in my wobbly new heels feeling slightly off-kilter.

Before the end of the day, Morgan Taylor called. I

answered the phone, already prepared for the letdown. No biggie, I was thinking. Jake would have killed me anyway if I took the position. No loss.

"Helloooo," I sang out, preparing myself to say something polite after the disappointing news.

Morgan's voice was filled with delight. "Venus, I want to welcome you aboard. Come in tomorrow, we'll get you situated. Get your office set up and begin our search for a bigger bully."

"Yes. Thank you. You won't regret your decision."

But I would. I hung up the phone. What had I done?

Ultimatum

It was an exquisite setting, complete with a view of the city, fine dining, and a killer little black dress. I adjusted my back to a nagging itch several times until I finally reached back to find a tag still attached. I snatched it off and crumpled it in my hand.

I'd called Jake and told him to meet me for dinner at his favorite restaurant. I had great news. His response, "I'm finally getting my little JJ?" Referring to his wish for a Jacob Marcus Parson Junior. We'd talked about it on and off. I knew in the long run Mya needed a baby brother or sister. I just wasn't up to it anytime soon.

"No, sweetie, no JJ for now. Just be there. Reservations are for seven."

When he walked into the restaurant, I wanted to get up and run in the other direction. This man, serious and remarkable, complete in his duty as a husband and father, had no idea what I was going to say.

I waved, then turned my head toward the twinkling lights of the city skyline. He bent over and kissed me on the cheek. I grabbed his hand while he sat. "Hi, baby."

We were immediately accosted by the male waiter with overwaxed brows. "Sir, what can I get you to drink this evening?"

I hung on Jake's decision, figuring if he ordered a hard-hitting drink like Remy and Coke, I'd go straight with the truth. After the first sip, he'd be too numb to feel the pain. If he ordered something light and fruity, I'd have to dance around the truth, lie, using my story of coincidentally meeting the hospital director while I was laid up with the broken leg. No mention whatsoever of Dr. Ex-Lova.

The waiter stood patiently at our side as if we were his only customers, though the restaurant was filled beyond capacity.

Jake still hadn't decided.

"Water for me." I swallowed a few times, wondering when my tongue would loosen up.

"Apple martini, without the apple," Jake said.

Great. This would take all night. But then again, he'd left out the actual fruit. So it wasn't technically light and fruity. Martini: two parts gin, one part vermouth, shaken with ice and a dash of sweetened syrup.

"Wonderful choice." The waiter still lingered near Jake. "And can I bring you an appetizer, sir?"

"The bread . . . what's it called?"

"Yes, sir, I know exactly what you want."

Jake folded his hands in front of him. His jacket fell away to the sides. His crisp collar no longer held the tie I'd seen him wearing at the start of the day. "So what are we celebrating?"

I grabbed his soft firm hands over the table. "Well, I got a job."

He slipped his hand out of mine.

"Okay, let's start over. Hi, baby—guess what, I got a job. And you say . . . That's wonderful, sweetheart. I know this is what you want and I'm going to offer my full support," I choked from making my voice too deep.

He shook his head. "You do a lousy impersonation

of me." He leaned past the table and placed a soft thick kiss on my lips. "So where's this great new job?"

The waiter came back and turned the crystal goblet in front of me up, then poured the bottled water. I grabbed the glass and took a short sip.

"It's going to be great. I'm very excited. Jackson Memorial," I continued, carrying on the conversation with myself. "The hospital is in dire need of someone who can put out a good message. I mean, the place will close if they don't do something soon. I'm going to be their new public affairs spokesperson." I looked up briefly, fearing Jake had actually left me sitting at the table alone.

He continued staring at me dead-on, making me fear the moment when he eventually did speak. His dark lashes fanned with a few hard blinks, as if trying to discern my speech pattern. "I think I missed the first part, and the last, and everything in between." He leaned forward. "Especially the part about you working where your ex-boyfriend is centrally located. You want to go over that part again?"

"Ah-huh," I said, looking around briefly. Everyone was in their own world, laughing and talking. Dim lighting kept the focus on the person directly in front of the diners. The volume of chatter alternated between highs and lows with a large party closer to the back, where I wished we were. I was about to go into my speech before he put up a hand.

"No. Don't bother." Jake leaned back in his chair and shook his head. "It's looking real clear to me that you think I'm completely stupid. You must—there is no other explanation."

"What? I—"

"Nah, we can end this conversation right here."

"There is another explanation. I actually thought you'd be mature and—-"

"Oh, okay, so I'm immature now." He laughed unexpectedly. "So you're all of a sudden the smart, mature, do-the-right-thing older woman? And I'm the pull-anything-over-on younger dude you happened to marry? The one naïve enough to let you walk into that hospital every day and work with a man you lived with and loved, and even planned to marry at one time? Accepting that would make me mature, is that what you're telling me?" He made some kind of gurgling sound, a cross between a laugh and clearing of his throat. He picked up a piece of bread and dipped it into the olive oil. With calm ease he sensuously slid the piece into his mouth and chewed lightly. He took a sip of his martini. We sat for a solid minute without eye contact.

"How could you be so insecure? You go to the JP Wear studio every single day and work with Beverly Shaun. I know about the two of you, your history. Do I worry? No, because I trust you. Are you saying you don't trust me?"

"I don't trust the situation. The difference is simple. Beverly and I have been working together for the last four years. There's no lost-love scenario. No rekindling, or trying to get back what was once taken away. We see each other almost every day. She's like my sister. With you and the doctor in the hood, there are a lot of loose ends. I'm not going to sit back and watch you try to tie them up."

"You're accusing me of doing something I haven't even thought about, let alone, plotted and planned. And Jake, as a side note, you don't screw your sister."

He rolled his eyes, ignoring my tactic of bait and switch. He leaned into the table and gently picked up my hand and kissed it. "I'm saying it doesn't have anything to do with you . . . or him. It's the situation. If it was different, we'd be having another discussion, but it is what it is."

"I'm taking the position. I start tomorrow," I said flatly, taking my hand back.

"So right here, right now, we're renegotiating the terms of this relationship. Is that what you're telling me?" He pointed a finger on the table. I detected a hidden threat.

"I'm not renegotiating anything," I swallowed, tempted to back down. "There's no reason for you to feel this way. None. I love you. I want to spend the rest of my life with you. It's that simple. Taking a job, whether it's at this hospital, or anywhere else, has nothing to do with our relationship."

"Why all of a sudden do you want to work for Jackson Memorial, which by the way *is* shutting down? It doesn't even make sense for you take a position there, unless it's to pack boxes."

"Exactly, I want to try and save the hospital."

He started to laugh. A raucous, deep, hearty laugh. No hint of faking it out of spite. Here he was genuinely amused and slapping the table and swiping his eyes for good measure.

"What is so funny?"

"I'm sorry . . . I'm sorry. It's—" He attempted to stifle his amusement. "Baby, I think it's a noble plan. Your heart is in the right place, but this thing is bigger than you and your magic. I know what you're capable of, but this seems a little out of your range."

Oooooh-no-he-did-nt. "I'm going to take the position. I can help them. You didn't see what I saw. That place is taking care of people who otherwise would be dying on the street. There are babies there that can't breathe or eat on their own. They'd already be dead if Jackson Memorial wasn't right there in the community."

He no longer thought the situation was funny. "The community? The area of town you didn't want to be caught in after sundown, and practically snapped my head off for leaving you and Mya there at Jack the Ripper? Now it's power to the people and all that. Unbelievable. I know what this is about." He glared.

"Okay, you found me out. It's about me taking a position right up my alley and being able to do some good at the same time."

"And the good doctor has nothing to do with it?"

"Jake, his wife works at the hospital, for goodness' sake. I mean, truly, this is about me starting my life again." What did I say that for? It came out completely wrong. Jake stood up and didn't waste another minute trying to listen to what I had to say. He stormed out of the restaurant.

I followed right behind him. "This hospital is important."

Jake handed his ticket to the valet and refused to look in my direction.

"You can't tell me where I can work, Jake. That's ridiculous. I'm not after Clint Fairchild. I couldn't care less about him. I'm trying to get back on the horse. You said yourself that's why you fell in love with me . . . because of my spirit, my ambition."

"Then find another hospital you want to do such great works, find any place, I'll pay your fucking salary."

We'd had our share of passionate fights, but we both agreed on the rules. Spewing out four-letter words was just as dangerous as brandishing sharp knives. Cuts healed but always left scars. As soon as he realized he'd broken code number one, he suddenly softened. "How do you expect me to feel when you say you want to start your life again, huh? I'll tell you, like I've been a side note for the last two years." The shiny red two-seater arrived. He peeled off a twenty and handed it to the valet. "I'll see you at home." He sped off while I stood in the cool night air freezing in my little black dress.

In the time it took to go back inside the restaurant and cover the check, then get home at my *Driving Miss Daisy* speed, the house was settled and dark. Jake had already sent Trina home and tucked Mya in for the night. I slumped to our bedroom, where he pretended to be asleep with the covers pulled close around his broad shoulders.

"I hate fighting with you." I waited for him to face me.

He stayed in position, refusing to give in so easy. "Just tell me yes or no. Are you going to take this job?"

I kissed him near his ear. "I'll do whatever you want me to do." I waited patiently for the reverse psychology to kick in. A few more seconds, and I let the heat of my breath slide down his neck. Jake had a few tender spots, places where I could send him over the edge within minutes. I teased with my tongue then slipped my hands under the covers to the rim of his shorts. "Whatever you want, baby, I'll do," I whispered.

He rolled over with a boat-sized erection. I shoved the sides of my black dress over my thighs and strad-dled him. He reached underneath and moved my thong out of the way. He slid deep inside me.

"Um, *yesss*." I was sure by morning the entire issue would be resolved.

Love, Honor, and Obey

I think I've wanted to be a married woman all my life. When I was a little girl, I practiced saying my vows in the mirror with a towel draped over my head holding a handful of folded-over toilet tissue for my bouquet. My Ken doll sat on the edge of the sink, bright eyed and all smiles, wearing a multicolored vest over his white turtleneck and pants that, had Ken been anatomically correct, could be classified as crotch crunchers.

In a deep southern preacher's voice I asked, "Do you Venus Johnston promise to love, honor, and obey?"

"Why, yes, yes, I do," I'd respond like Scarlett O'Hara. I meant it, too. Then why in the world, you're probably asking, would I put it all in jeopardy over a job?

I woke up with the question imprinted on my mind, listless and hungover, though I hadn't ingested one ounce of alcohol. I rolled over to see Jake's side of the bed empty. I heard him stirring around in the bathroom, using his overpriced face washes and exfoliating shaving creams. When the water stopped running and the drawers stopped opening and closing, I knew he was headed my way.

I curled up and tried to stop my eyes from moving underneath my lids. I felt him standing over me. I couldn't pretend any longer. I opened my eyes when I figured he wasn't going to budge. "You awake?" he asked, though it was obvious with my eyes blinking for focus.

He stood a lickable distance away, wearing only loose boxers stopping at his firm muscular thighs, his arms folded over his bare chest. I felt like purring and wondered if he was ready for round two. The fight at dinner led to the perfect makeup sex, the kind that left me useless till noon.

"What did we decide?" He asked slowly, as if I were under a hypnotic spell. He didn't know he was the one victim to my magic.

"We decided, I'm a grown-ass woman who won't be told what to do." I rolled over, smothering my face in the pillow.

"Noooo, that's not what *weee* decided."

I flipped back over, facing him. "All right, what did *we* decide?"

He squatted at eye level. He slipped his hand under the cover and trailed to my middle. He rubbed lightly, sending me into tiny quivers. "We decided that you *could* take the position. The minute, the second, you put this job before me or Mya or have any irrational behavior, you quit."

"What did *we* classify as irrational behavior?" I said, fighting the urge to reach out and stroke the fine hairs of his carefully shaped goatee.

"Irrational behavior would be, um let me think, anything I say is irrational." His dark long lashes swept closed then back open again. "All I want is for you not to get carried away." He pulled his fingers out and put them to his lips. "It's just something to keep you busy—it's not a livelihood. I take care of you, that's all you need." He held out his pinkie.

I looped my pinkie finger around his. "You know, a lot of men would appreciate their wives getting off their ass and bringing home a paycheck."

"Are we clear?" he asked, squeezing the blood to the top of my pinkie.

"Yes, sir, Captain JP, sir." We shook on it.

"Hey—" He kissed me deep and hard. "—better not be late for your first day."

"Be gone," I moaned, feeling like I'd run a ten K and wanted two or more laps from deliriousness. The woman myth about having an overactive sex drive starting around midlife was true, and Jake knew it. He, being a younger man, made us evenly matched in the getting it and giving it department. I liked sex a lot. Not in general, per se, I should make that clear, but with Jake. I wasn't a desperate housewife. I wasn't trying to make the bag boy at Gelson's Market my love slave or anything. I was completely satisfied in the pants-down department. Besides, the only other men who'd crossed my path weren't very appealing. I grocery-shopped once a week and stood in line with husbands sent there by their wives, obvious by the six-pack of beer, diapers, and sanitary napkins. I went to Mommy & Me and Gymboree classes three times a week. All the dads there were either gay or laid off and pretending to like their new jobs as househusbands. There was a man in my Pilates class who came with his wife as if there were a gun to his head, and he moved accordingly. There was the mailman, the UPS man who delivered all my Babyland items. I had a special tingly feeling when I heard the delivery truck pulling up with the special honk just for me. There was the seventy-year-old handy man, Jim, who unclogged my drains, caulked the windows, and hauled away my baby junk after Mya lost interest. I admit I felt a certain little something for the old guy, more like hero worship.

I could see where Jake could be concerned: I'd basically been cut off from all possible attractions. Now here was the main attraction, the show I never saw the ending to—Dr. Clint Fairchild.

But it wasn't about Clint, I kept telling myself. I was happily married with a kid. It was about keeping myself whole, not squandering my mind on pet peeves such as toothpaste spilled in the sink and left for me to rinse away. Or going into the bathroom with half a sheet left on the roll, or giving up the remote and letting Jake turn the channel even though I was in the middle of a trial on Court TV. Pet peeves could become monsters if studied for too long. I didn't want to be that kind of wife.

I just wanted to feel good about myself. I admit my first reasoning for wanting to take on Jackson Memorial centered selfishly on being a thorn in Kandi's side, but the more I thought about it, the more I became committed to helping the hospital stay open and to having a purpose. I knew I had a calling, one that I would not take lightly. Jackson Memorial deserved a second chance. Don't we all?

Introduction

First-day excitement fluttered in my belly along with the double-shot espresso I'd drunk on the way. Arriving at the hospital at eight sharp, I found the entrance peacefully surrounded by tall healthy green palms silently greeting me like guards at attention. The picketers hadn't arrived yet for duty. I was walking on air, my heart beating so heavily, I didn't hear my name being called.

Morgan Taylor stood erect with arms extended. "Come. Welcome." She gave me a stiff hug.

"I'm really excited. Thank you for this opportunity."

"It's an honor having you. Come, I'll show you to your office." Morgan led, and I followed. "There is something I want to tell you before we go on."

I waited for her to stop, but she didn't. Her pace, in fact, picked up a little.

"This position is very important to the hospital, the staff, we're all depending on this person being able to turn things around. That's why I had to bring you both on board . . . just to allow me the chance to make the right decision."

"Both?"

"There she is."

I followed Morgan's line of vision to none other than Kandi Treboe, now Mrs. Fairchild. But not to confuse, we'll just call her She-whore . . . okay . . . *She* for short.

"Were you looking for me?" The voice from countless nightmares landed directly in front of me. I was practically staring up her nostrils. I'd forgotten how tall She was, a full-fledged woman, all right. Picked up a few extra pounds in the breast department—something she didn't need.

"Kandi Fairchild, this is Venus Parson."

I took a noticeable step back when She extended her claw . . . I mean hand. "It's good to see you, Venus."

When I realized there were no secret weapons attached, I shook her hand. "Good to see you, too."

"Both of us will be vying for the same position?" Dry gasps followed. My mouth was still open, but nothing was coming.

She smiled wide with the sides of her mouth turned up like the Joker in *Batman*. "I thought it was a perfect idea. Two candidates competing toe to toe for the same position."

"I guess I'm a little in the dark." I looked to Morgan for clarification, but she'd found something more interesting in the opposite direction and refused to look my way.

"You both get to handle PR. The person that exudes the best qualities will get the job. Sort of like a trial period for both of you."

I felt my right eye twitching. I swallowed and adjusted my tone, remembering that She was probably enjoying my reaction. "Great. I'm up for the challenge."

"Excellent." Morgan looked satisfied, as if she were actually in control of the situation. She reached out and touched Kandi's hand and then mine. "I really appreciate you two going along with this. It's unusual, I know, but I already like what I see. Kandi, please show Venus to her new office. I have a nursing staff meeting I need to look in on. Then we can all three sit down together at noon for an all systems go."

We watched Morgan's heels pump away at high speed. Left alone, we dropped the pretense energy.

She faced me. "This should be interesting, don't you think? Us working together, I mean. Who would have thought?"

"Not in a million years. I didn't know you had a background in public relations. I guess working with third-graders may qualify?"

"I've worked here at this hospital for the last year. I've prepared most of the press releases for Morgan since all of this media hype broke out." She wasted no time getting to what really mattered. "From what Clint told me, you've been doing the housewife thing for the last couple of years."

"Right, yeah. Loved being at home, but it's time to get back to work."

"I'm sure your baby and husband are going to miss you. He's a rapper, right? JP . . . Juicy hips . . . luscious lips. I remember him. He only had that one song, right? Like a one-hit-wonder kind of thing. So is he covered head to toe in bling-bling?" She covered her mouth to stifle her fake amusement. "Do you guys know P. Diddy?"

I attempted to answer at least one of her stupid questions, but she was faster.

"What's that like . . . being married to a—"

"—successful businessman," I spoke over her. "I'm sure it's nothing like the calm peaceful life of being married to a doctor." I held my breath steady, trying not to let on she'd pushed every one of my buttons. "JP Wear is a multimillion-dollar company. I'm sure you've heard of it."

"Right. And yet you still feel the need to work?"

"Same as you, I guess. I didn't know doctors' wives needed extra income." I kept my focus and calm. In a different setting, she would've been eating my pointed-toe slingback.

"Of course I don't need extra income, but I like feeling needed, having goals and purpose."

"Exactly, I couldn't have said it better. Sounds like we're on the same page." I was still breathing shallowly. Her perfume was doing a number on my sinuses. Seems the doctor's wife should've been able to do better than Lady Stetson.

"You know what, I can see where all this conversation is going," I said, swallowing my pride. "It's going to be awkward, us working together. But honestly, the past is the past. I wish you nothing but the best." I had no reason to be bitter. She got Clint, and I got a great life.

She seemed relieved. "We never really got to know each other back then, you're right. Let's start over." Her hand extended, poised for a shake, then suddenly drew to her belly. She circled and rubbed as if she had a tummy ache.

"Are you all right?" I asked, only slightly concerned.

She held up her claws in truce. "Oh, yes, fine. I'm in my first trimester. The nausea gets to me sometimes."

"You're pregnant." I, too, felt nauseated. "Congratulations."

I followed Kandi into an office no bigger than my walk-in closet. "Here you are." Her hand lifted like a *Price Is Right* model. The small space was filled with file boxes stacked against the wall with dates felt-penned on the sides. The prison shade of gray on the walls told me it probably was used for storage at some point.

"Knock, knock." A short stocky man came behind us and stood in the doorway with another box. He moved past me and shoved it on top of the others then offered to shake my hand. "I'm Jasper Callaway."

The shiny dome on the top of his head caught my attention. At five feet two and a half, I didn't usually see the tops of many people's heads. "Welcome aboard." He put out his hand, onions, garlic—possibly both—emanated from his breath, skin, and, well everywhere.

"Thank you."

"Jasper is my assistant. He can answer any questions you might have." She turned and left with a crawly wave of her fingers.

Jasper closed the door. "Nice lady. I've worked at this hospital for twenty years, and she's the most pleasant of additions."

"You've been here twenty years?"

"Actually, twenty-three."

"And you're an assistant?" I said, visibly mortified.

"I've had a variety of positions at this hospital. Assistant is a general term."

"Great. Well, I'm glad we'll be working together. Someone who's been here that long will definitely be an asset." I walked to the door and pulled it open. "I'll give you a shout if I need anything." I stood off to the side, waiting for him to use the door I'd opened for him.

"No problem. I'm right here with you. I'll help you get organized." He took a seat behind a stack of boxes.

"No, really, you don't have to stay." I peered over, surprised to see a desk and chair set up with a telephone and a tiny plaque that said, JASPER CALLAWAY.

"Jasper. Is this your office, or mine?"

He looked up, adjusting his flat square glasses. "Ours," he said somewhat amused. "We're sharing. Mrs. Fairchild is in charge of office space assignments. She decided we should share."

This wasn't happening.

"Execuse me. I'll be right back." I moved swiftly to the door and outside to a maze of cubicles filling up as the morning progressed. I made my way down one aisle, then up another, looking for any seat open. Bingo—a cubicle devoid of family photos or dead-flower-filled vases from three birthdays ago.

"Is anyone using this space," I asked the young woman sitting on the other side.

"That's Tammy's desk. She's on maternity leave," the young woman said without looking up.

"I am," a voice called from a short distance away. Kandi came gliding toward me. She slid into the cubicle and sat down, crossing her cinnamon stick legs that extended far past her skirt.

"Don't you have an office?"

"I do," she said gleefully, "but I wear many hats around here, and I need a place to spread out."

Spreading out was her forte, as I recalled. The affair she'd had with Tyson Edwards, while seeing Clint at the same time was proof she was very good at spreading herself out and around. I'd told Clint about her affair with Tyson Edwards, a married man: *"Hello, she was messing around on you."* Clint didn't want to hear what I had to say on the subject of Kandi back then, and I was sure nothing had changed.

"This is the last empty space." She scooted closer to the desk.

"I can't share a space with Jasper. That won't work out for me."

"I definitely understand where you're coming from. It's like he's wearing garlic around his neck or something." A pruned smile rose on her face.

"Jasper just told me you were in charge of office

spaces. I think it's a little strange you would have me sharing such a small space with him when there's a perfectly good open space right here."

"We really are limited on space around here." Her voice was like fingernails scratching down a chalkboard. She let her hand slide to her belly. I refused to let my eyes drop to what she wanted to be the center of attention.

"I have an idea," I blurted out, needing to shut her up, "why don't we share, just like the old days. You remember how to share, don't you?" I winked and backed away slowly. "See you around."

I felt the rush of air as she sucked in a gasp. *Water under the bridge, my foot*, I was thinking as I did my best switch and stroll. She had no idea what kind of hidden fury lurked underneath my mild-mannered suit. The soft pink must've given her the impression I was cotton candy. Wrong. Let the games begin.

Catfight

I took my shoes off in the car and drove home feeling like I'd boxed thirteen rounds with Laila Ali. I was boiling mad at the thought of the She-whore running around like she owned the entire hospital. I wanted nothing more than to show her up, prove once and for all who was the better woman . . . for the job, of course.

Jake's car was parked and still a bit warm when I pulled into the garage. The house was quiet and dark. Music trailed from our bedroom as I took each stair with great labor. Jake was just getting out of the shower.

I debated on telling him how my day went. Somehow I knew he would not be amused.

"Hey, baby." I kissed him softly on his moist nose. He drew me in for a full tongue exchange. I was thinking what a far better kisser I was than She. Not that I'd kissed her myself, just an educated guess—with her mouth so wide and those juicy sticky lips, fine, if you like that kind of thing.

I gently eased off Jake's bottom lip, thinking this was how it's done, simple, pleasurable, not too messy.

"How was your first day?" Jake sputtered the magic question.

"Great. Where's Mya?" I backed up gently.

"She and Trina are having a bath."

My eyebrow raised.

"You know what I mean." He dropped his towel exposing his naked bottom and headed toward the closet. "So you plan to let me in on your day, or what?"

"It went well." I began undressing. I sat on the edge of the bed, peeling off my pointed-toe shoes and vowed never to wear them again. My big toe pulsed as the blood rushed to the pinched skin.

"Did you see the doctor?"

"There's lots of doctors. I'm working at a hospital, remember?"

"Okay, let me be more clear. Did you see Dr. Ex-Lova?" He came out buttoning a pair of his nicer trousers.

"No. I did not. If you want to know how my day went, ask about My Day. None of this is about *him*. How many times do I have to tell you?"

Jake's shoulder had a small tattoo barely the size of a quarter with his initials, JP, in a delicate swirl. I pulled him down toward me until the small tattoo was at eye level. My lips lingered before I put a moist kiss against the spot.

He softened immediately, sitting down next to me. "I'm sorry." He lifted my legs over his lap and began to rub and knead the tension away. I rubbed his shoulders simultaneously so we were wrapped around each other.

"Seems I'm in a competition for the job. The PR director's position is up for grabs between me and someone else. The administrator isn't ready to just hand it over. She wants to see some kind of showdown, a battle for the ultimate job. I've never been in this kind of situation. It feels weird."

"You mean competing for the same job openly?" He grinned from ear to ear. "Are there cameras following you around like *The Apprentice*? Have you met the other person?"

"Yeah," I said, leaving out the part where the woman who'd married Clint right under my nose was my actual competitor. I knew there was something really wrong with this situation, yet I couldn't pull myself away.

"Is it a female?"

"Why do you ask?" I said, feeling like there was an information ticker on my forehead.

"Girlfights can get a little nasty." He scratched at the air. "Want me to teach you some moves, baby?"

"You're enjoying this way too much. I'm going to jump in the shower." I made a swift exit before the truth spilled out of me.

When I came out, Jake was fully dressed as if he had a date. I squeezed more water out of my hair with the towel then wrapped it good and tight. That was one thing I could say for Trina, she knew how to make a towel as soft as cotton candy. Something I could never do, no matter how much fabric softener I poured in the load.

"You washed your hair? You knew we were running late." He stood before me with a loose linen shirt exposing the right amount of smooth pecs with the silver cross hanging from his chain. Modern bohemian, it worked for Jake with his slim goatee and finger-combed hair.

"Running late, for what?"

"You forgot." Disappointment shrouded his face. "That's okay. That's cool."

"What did I forget?" Then it hit me. He was having a buyer's party, an excruciatingly boring mixer where he fed and watered the people responsible for getting his clothing on the retailer floors. "It's tonight. Oh, baby, I'm sorry."

"No, really it's cool."

It wasn't cool. I could see the way his lips tightened up to one side then released.

"Let me get dressed. Is Trina going to stay with Mya? I'll just pull my hair back, throw some gel on it. I'll be ready in fifteen minutes."

"Nah, fifteen is going to turn into thirty, and I can't be late." He attempted to move past me without so much as a kiss.

I grabbed his sleeve. "I'm sorry, really. Go on ahead and I'll come soon as I'm dressed."

"Don't worry about it. Stay home, get some rest." He kissed my forehead and left.

I sat on the edge of the bed and reasoned that it was probably for the best. I was exhausted. Not to mention he hadn't invited me to one of his mixers in months. Many months, to be exact, which led me to believe I was invited only after I'd complained that he left me out of everything concerning JP Wear. Suddenly, now, it was important that I be by his side. I pitched myself underneath the down comforter and closed my eyes to the muffled sounds of Trina and Mya in the next room. Mya's tickled laughter put a smile on my face. I had every intention of relieving Trina of her duties—that was until sleep knocked me over the head, sending me into dreamland.

Inside and Out

Jake arrived late. He blamed his wife. If he hadn't sat around listening to her work tales, he would've been on time. Still he couldn't keep from smiling, inside and out. He was betting she wouldn't last a week. A week and two days, max.

"J-man, over here." Legend nursed a sparkling blue martini that matched the eyes of the woman standing next to him. "I want you to meet Fenny Maxwell. She's the new buyer for the Rocknell department stores."

"Nice to finally meet you. I'm a big fan." Fenny Maxwell may have had blue eyes and wild spiraling blond hair, but she was a soul sista through and through. Her soft sandalwood complexion glistened from too much California sun. Her voice was thick and sultry. "You're every bit as handsome in person as you are in all those magazines I've seen you in."

Jake extended his soft manicured hand. "Thanks for the compliment. So you've replaced Deon. What happened to him, promotion or demotion?"

"I ate him." Fenny Maxwell laughed at her own joke.

Jake and Legend grinned for sales' sake.

"No, really, he's moved on," she said. "He's repping for FUBU. I told him he better be nice to me or that crap won't see the light of day in one of our four hundred stores." She winked. "I'm on the barter system." Wetness slid off her glass, and she licked her finger lightly.

"My goodness," Legend chimed, figuring the overtures were up for grabs. "A fair exchange ain't no robbery." He moved closer to Fenny Maxwell.

She moved an arm through Jake's. "So tell me about this new line. Kind of high risk going straight, don't you think?"

Legend watched, temporarily mystified as the two slowly marched arm in arm toward the bar. Let Legend tell it, Jake was hopelessly pussy-whipped, hen-pecked, and stupidly satisfied with his wife. When he saw a woman go stir-crazy over his friend, he simply shook his head. "Another one bites the dust."

Jake saw it merely as an opportunity to pitch his new line. "Eventually these boys are going to be men. They're going to have to get real jobs, paying real bills. They can't do that with their pants sagging. And they sure as hell aren't going to start wearing Dockers or Nautica. Those pants were made for men without the proper equipment."

"Sounds like someone's bragging. Do you have the right equipment, Mr. Parson?"

Jake gave her his slanted smile. "I'm just saying, you check any college campus and you see these cats running around with their pants still banked at their knees, shirts still five times too big. All of a sudden, they're graduating, they're ready to hit the world serious, and what are their choices? They need an urban contemporary line to bridge the gap. I've got the entire implementation planned out from the production to the marketing. Better get in," he said, satisfied with himself.

"Sounds like we should talk about this further." Fenny

Maxwell was coming for him. A woman with confidence and beauty was a dangerous combination.

"We're talking about it now," he said.

"Well, maybe we can talk about it . . . alone."

Jake wet his lips and thought about his choices . . . and there were always so many choices.

For the better part of his life, since he was thirteen, fourteen years old, he continually had to make the choice. The pressure never relented. In high school the girls threatened to tell everyone he was all show no go, a pretty boy who probably preferred other pretty boys. In his music career, not much had changed. Only then the silent threats came from women who had the power to go public, in the spotlight with their reasoning for why he wouldn't play along. *He has to be gay.* Not gay, just extremely sick and tired of women who thought that's all they were good for.

"Four hundred stores," Jake said, mostly to himself.

"Opening eleven more by the end of the year." Fenny blushed as if she were a schoolgirl who'd finally convinced the boy next door her parents weren't coming home for another hour.

"Sorry to interrupt." Legend stepped between them. "Your other fans await." He stepped back so Jake could see the gathering of retail buyers, men and women, appropriately watered and fed.

"We'll pick this up later."

Fenny nodded. "Can't wait."

"I can definitely take over where he left off," Legend offered.

"Don't worry yourself. I'm a patient woman." She moved into the crowd.

Jake moved to the center of the room. "I'd just like to thank you all for making JP Wear the success that it is today. I see new faces, but most of you have been in my corner from the very beginning. This evening is dedicated to you all. Thank you, and enjoy the evening."

The crowd lightly clapped then went back to the lavish spread of hors d'oeuvres and free-flowing martinis. Jake pushed his way past, landing outside of the group. He observed who was talking to whom, what alliances had been formed over the years. His eyes landed on Byron, who rarely came to such events, calling it work beyond the call of duty. Jake started toward him before seeing Fenny Maxwell come into the picture. They shook professionally, but the twinkle in Byron Steeple's eyes gave off more than networking interest.

"Better run while old blue eyes is busy. I see Byron's good for something." Legend smirked.

"Yeah, I was headed out."

Beverly joined the two men. "You're leaving, Jay?"

"Been a long day."

"I'll walk out with you. I don't like going to my car alone."

Jake shook Legend's hand. "Keep an eye on our boy," he said, nodding toward Byron.

"Don't mind me—you two run off while I tap dance. Let me just get my white gloves and my bow tie. Just don't expect to see me in the A.M."

Jake and Beverly were already gone before Legend could continue his rant.

Best Actress Goes To

If I were logging days into my diary, I would have written, *Dear diary, I woke up this morning with good intentions. I would be a better mother to Mya. A better wife to Jake, and possibly a better woman by going into the hospital and telling Morgan Taylor I'd changed my mind about competing for the public affairs position, a job that wasn't worth the complete demise of my self-worth. Having to deal with Kandi and her smugness. Having to face Clint on a daily basis. Letting Jake down by not being there for him. Feeling like I was losing on both ends of the stick.*

But when I walked into Morgan Taylor's office, who did I see but the She-whore sitting in a chair holding tissue in her hands, dabbing dry tears. I immediately felt satisfaction. Maybe Morgan was giving Kandi the boot. Life was already looking up.

"What's going on? Is everything all right?" I reached out and gave a patronizing pat on Kandi's wide back. She nudged my hand away. I gave Morgan a perplexing look, letting her know I had no idea what was going on. Mostly I was vexed by the fact that She-whores could cry real tears. There was my true puzzlement: Kandi's eyes were red and filled with glistening sadness. Not even Meryl Streep could pull off this kind of performance.

Morgan Taylor leaned forward on her desk. She clasped her hands in front of her and talked with schoolteacher concern. "I had no idea there was going to be this much conflict between you two. Of course, competition of any kind will breed contempt, but on this level, I'm shocked."

A conflict? Who has conflict? And shocked, that would be me. The She-whore sat as the innocent victim, refusing to look in my direction, her shoulders rising and falling in spurts.

Morgan Taylor cleared her throat to get my attention. She continued, "If I'd known there was a history between you two, I would never have brought you on. There are issues that need to be worked out, or I don't see how I can keep you here."

You was obviously me.

"I would like for both of you to stay here and talk for a minute. I'm going to leave the room and when I return, I expect resolution." I watched Morgan leave her office and close the door gently.

Kandi turned to me on cue. "I'm sorry to have to bring all this out in the open, but I had to tell her about you and Clint."

"Me and Clint?"

"I understood clearly what you implied yesterday, loud and clear, and let me tell you, I'm not going to put up with it. Clint is my husband, and if you haven't heard, we're about to have a baby."

My mouth dropped. "Honestly, I didn't mean to imply anything. I'm here for only one reason and that's to help this hospital. I swear, Clint and I are beyond history. If you met my husband, if you saw my daughter, you would know, I have way too much going on in the present to care about the past. I have nothing but best wishes for you two, and let's not forget baby makes three. Really, you have my word, I'm not out to harm you or your relationship in any way."

Oh, Dear Diary, you should have seen me. In rare form. Oscar caliber. Julia Roberts eat your heart out. I apologized for making She feel uncomfortable. I hadn't meant to offend or project hostility.

"I was hoping after all this time you and I could finally be friends," I said, just in time for Morgan, who was entering the room. She eyed us both, expecting to see one of us holding an ax dripping with the other's blood. I told her we were fine, all a misunderstanding. Kandi nodded in agreement then rose from her chair like the Queen of England, grasping her tissue to her bosom before making a grand exit.

Morgan smiled under duress, waiting patiently until Lil Miss Crybaby was out of earshot then leaned toward me in a conspiratorial whisper. "Dr. Fairchild is very important to the hospital right now. Actually, all of the doctors are prized possessions at this point, and if they start leaving, it's just one more obstacle we have to overcome. We need to keep our staff happy. And you know how a wife can pressure a husband," she said.

I smiled and nodded my head like this was nothing more than a blip on my busy screen. I rose from my chair and reached out for a womanly handshake. "Don't worry. I'll stay completely out of the She-whore's way. She won't even know I'm here." (I'm pretty sure I used her real name.) I also added another brief amendment to the apology: I would be more careful knowing of her mental collapse. I understood about those pregnancy hormones, making a woman emotionally unstable. Morgan Taylor appreciated my compassion. I left her office with my head tilted to the side, humbled with a touch of confusion. Outside in the hallway, I threw my fists wildly in the air. I wanted to hit something, throw something. How dare she? If I had access to Jake's inhaler, I would have used it. My breathing was shallow, low, and strained from adrenaline pumping out of control through my veins.

Diary entries are private, so I wouldn't be ashamed to say I hated Kandi Fairchild. Using my long-ago and forgotten artist skills, I would have drawn her with spiked hair and black eyebrows shooting upward with a rectangle body and large droopy tits that scraped the ground when she walked. Mrs. She-whore wanted to play. Dear diary, I'd give her a game she would never forget.

I sat in my office still fuming over the morning's escapades.

I'd spent the last few hours on an assignment given by Morgan to take past incidents and spin them into something more positive. A man whose leg had been amputated, the wrong leg. A woman who'd spent three days in ICU though she'd been faking just to have a nice soft bed away from the usual concrete where she'd made her home. Then there was the accidental—and I must say proverbial—scalpel sewn into the belly of a woman who'd had an appendix removed. The only spin I could add was, "These things happen." I scratched the words out as soon as I'd written them. A strange vibrating sound caught my attention. The noise was coming from my purse.

When I answered my cell phone, my breathing was still erratic. I strained to hear over the thumping blood in my ears.

"You think we can meet for lunch?" Jake asked. "I have a situation over here I need to talk to you about."

"Oh, sweetie, I can't." I looked at the stack of files

staring me in the face. I was seriously angry that I'd been derailed by Kandi's escapades. I was also chewing on the rough fact that Jake had stayed out far later than any other night he'd given his mixer. If I brought it up, he would say "the buyers," using it like a magic wand that washed away all unanswered questions.

"I really need to talk to you."

"Jake, I'm sorry, but I'm swamped here. It would take me almost an hour just to get on your side of town, and there is nowhere around here I'd want to eat."

"Maybe we can—"

"I'm sorry, can I call you back?" I inhaled, preparing myself not to breathe when I saw Jasper coming toward the open office door.

"Venus," he said, trying to get a hold of my runaway brain. "You all right? Remember what we agreed on."

"I'm fine. I'm just saying I can't come all the way over there."

"No. I understand." Jake paused. "Is this really what you want to do? You're supposed to be fulfilled, remember?"

He was mocking me. "What?" This made the fine hairs on my arms stand like prickly fiberglass poking out of my skin. "What? You can't expect me to just fall into a sweet spot, Jake. Work is still work. I'll find my balance—I'm just getting started."

"Okay, okay, calm down. I'm just pointing out the fact that this was supposed to make you happy, and right now you sound a bit pissed off."

"I'm not. Really, I'm fine." By this time, Jasper was rummaging through boxes. He adjusted his glasses and looked in my direction. I gave him a friendly nod . . . still holding my breath and counting the seconds when I could breathe again. He found what he was looking for and left.

"You don't sound fine. Maybe this isn't the job for you. Maybe you should keep looking. It's not like you have to accept the first thing offered. You don't have to be so desperate."

"Desperate!" I slammed the small phone closed and went into a silent growl.

Never hang up on your husband. This is a law, not a rule. As soon as the phone left my hand, I tried to call him back but he wouldn't answer . . . for the rest of the day.

Eyes Are Watching

You all right over there?"

I looked up to see Jasper standing in the doorway. I thought he'd gone. "Just trying to clear my throat," I said, hoping he didn't realize it was a bona fide growl he'd heard.

"Would you like something from downstairs, water or a Diet Coke?"

"Yes, sure, that'd be great, and one of those macadamia nut cookies if they have them." I reached in my purse and handed him a five.

I dialed Jake's number again, accepting that he wasn't going to answer. I could apologize on the voice mail. "Call me when you get a chance. I'm really sorry for being so rude. You know I love you."

"Love you, too," a voice mimicked from my doorway. I looked up to see Clint.

I closed my phone and hoped Clint's voice didn't get picked up on the message. "I guess you didn't get the memo." I stood up and moved swiftly to the door.

Clint smelled fresh, giving off a minty coolness. "What memo is that?"

"You're supposed to stay one hundred yards away at all times." I pushed the door closed. "Kandi told Morgan

Taylor that I was rude to her. She also went on a tirade about our past relationship, implying I'm only here to be next to you."

Clint shook his head. "We had a fight about it. I told her not to start with that insanity."

"What's insane is you failed to mention the part about your wife wanting the same job."

"She only wanted the job after she found out you were interested. The phone call, the message you left kind of tipped her off."

"Can't you talk to her? Really, this is going to get out of hand. You know Kandi doesn't really want this job. And Ms. Taylor is under the impression you'd leave if she doesn't give the missus a fair shot. Which doesn't make any sense after you're the one who recommended *me* for the position." I sensed I was whining, though I couldn't hear it completely. My ears were still stuffed with the early morning's rage. "Can't you explain to her she's only causing strain and confusion? I mean, really, we should be about the business of keeping this hospital open, not dealing with an in-house catfight."

Clint rubbed his slick head. "I'll try, but don't do anything rash, like quit."

"That's the last thing on my mind." I left out the fact that I wanted to crush Kandi with everything I had. I took his shoulders and turned him around. "Time's up. I have major work to do. And secondly, I don't want to get into any more trouble from the mean principal."

He rolled around to face me. "Morgan, she does kind of remind you of the mean principal in school. Promise me you're not going to quit," he said.

"Quit what? I haven't even got the job yet." I turned him about-face.

He spun back around. "Seriously, promise you're not going to walk out of here busted and disgusted."

"I promise. Even though you lied to me. What was that all about?"

"I lied?"

"Kandi, being pregnant."

His eyes dropped. "You didn't ask."

"Oh, but I did, specifically, the first night I saw you. I asked if you and Kandi had any children."

"And I said we were working on it. That's an honest answer."

"Yeah, but . . ." I had to let it go. I placed my hands on his chest to turn him toward the door. "Go, Dr. Fairchild. We don't want any rumors to get started."

"Promise you won't quit, and then I'll leave." He turned around again. "Please . . . don't let her bother you."

"Go," I said without making any promises. Funny how easy the word *please* fell from Clint's lips these days. When I'd known him, loved him, he never liked asking for anything. At least not of me. Years ago, Clint told me I emasculated him by expecting so little of him while we lived together. It's hard to expect anything of someone who doesn't have a job. I was just trying to help, that's what people do when they're in a committed relationship: support one another. Little did I know we were not committed. Had I known, I would have made him pay his share of the rent, the food, and the utilities.

My record stands undefeated of having men in my life with an image to maintain. Machismo, chest stuck out, must be man, I must be woman. All strange, considering I wasn't the rescue-me type. Not like Kandi, who cried foul when things got rough. I at least had the decency to do it in private, holed up in a bathroom or closet, somewhere no one could witness.

Then there was Airic, my fiancé of two years right

after breaking up with Clint. He said I was impenetrable. What did that mean? Like a new kind of superhero made of Teflon. I didn't understand how he could make that statement. I blended, molded, and reshaped myself to be by his side. Had I not met Jake, who loved me—supercoating and all—I would probably still be with Airic, pretending everything was hunky-dory. I could be the good docile type if required. Which reminded me, where was Jasper with my damn cookie?

Jasper had been gone for nearly an hour to chase down a pastry. The more I thought about food, the hungrier I got. I headed out to get my own.

I rounded the corner and saw Jasper rushing my way, cookie-less, walking fast, head down with that shiny bald spot aimed like a missile. He rammed right into me.

I rubbed my shoulder where he'd connected at full speed.

"Stay out of my way." He looked directly at me, but it was as if he'd never seen me before.

"Jasper, are you all right?"

"Excuse me, I have to get to the restroom." Perspiration covered his face. His hands hung by his sides, balling in and out of tight fists. He blinked a few times before removing his glasses and swiping his shirtsleeve to dry his face. "Move!" he burst.

I pushed myself up against the wall, letting him pass. I watched him walk away and turn the corner before I felt safe enough to move a muscle. What just happened?

That's when I heard all the commotion. Footsteps moving quickly. The swishing of polyester rubbing thighs pushing in stride.

"Four at one time. How does something like that *just* happen? I'm telling you, there's a ghost running around here trying to put us out of business." Two nurses dressed in green scrubs hurried past, pushing a cool breeze.

I caught up and double-skipped to keep their pace. "What's going on?"

"Who are you?" The nurse with one line of plucked eyebrows barely looked my way. Neither of them slowed their step.

"I'm new in public relations, Venus Johnston." When they turned the corner, I turned, too, nearly being run into the wall.

"Four incubators were unplugged. Four." She held up four fingers and shook her head as if she'd take the number to her grave.

"Are the babies okay?" I wanted to stop and go the other direction, where I knew Clint would be.

"So far, so good." They continued marching until landing into a crowd of nurses filing into a large lecture room. Rumblings of foul play and conspiracy moved between their conversations.

One nurse shot her hands upward and shouted, "This wouldn't have happened on my watch! Let me catch someone that don't belong, let me catch 'em," she threatened.

Mostly women and a few men were all riled up and ready to take action. This was war as far as they were concerned. I backed off and watched as they mumbled forms of attack and retribution.

"Whoever did this needs to be hung by their nails."

"Yeah, then see how they like it with a bag over their head so they can't breathe. See how they like it."

"Please, hurry, this meeting has got to be quick." The head nurse tapped her microphone. She waited impatiently with her hands resting on the podium. Her hair was pulled on top of her head with a long waterfall wig attached, making her eyes sharp and slanted. When she was sure everyone could hear, she began, "I'm going to get right to the point. Someone messed up. We don't have time for this, ladies and gentlemen. I'm not going to waste my breath by asking what happened. It had to have been an accident. Easily, anyone could have tripped over a cord, relocated an incubator, and accidentally unplugged the rest. I can see it being an accident. But if it wasn't—" She leaned into the microphone and lowered her voice. "—know this: You are messing with the wrong crew."

The crowd clapped and cheered, yelling out in agreement. "This is a family. We are united in caring for those who can't care for themselves. I put it out to you like this, anybody who doesn't feel the same way needs to find a new home. Pay more attention. Be more responsive. If you see someone doing something that looks questionable, step in. Take responsibility. Ladies and gentlemen, this is our home. When someone comes through those doors, they are not patients, they become part of this family. Those babies upstairs, each and every one of them are our babies."

A short woman with full gear, gauze hair netting, and face mask marched down the aisle and up to the podium. It was Frieda. She moved to the head nurse and whispered in her ear.

The head nurse put her hand over the microphone while they whispered back and forth. She let out a deep sigh then announced, "The babies are fine. All their vitals are back to satisfactory." The crowd clapped and sent out mini praises and thank-you's to Jesus.

"I know many of you are wondering why you're here. You're saying to yourself, That's not my floor. Not my problem. I'm here to tell you, every floor is your floor. Open your eyes and your hearts and know that our jobs are on the line here. Lives are on the line here. How many more unnecessary mistakes need to happen before you understand, this is serious?" She blinked slowly as if it hurt to do so. "I want everyone in here to raise your right hand, raise 'em. Repeat after me: This is my hospital. This is my house. These are my patients. This is my life. I will be alert, responsive, and caring at all times, so help me God."

I found myself repeating the words, feeling like I was in a Sunday church service. "By the grace of God, those babies are doing fine. Remember that. Each and every one of you, we can't win this war alone." She walked off the stage, and the rest of the nurses clapped and mulled over the words of inspiration. The nurses came out of the meeting charged, ready to put a hurting on anybody who threatened their good name.

"There you are." Morgan paced hurriedly outside my tiny office. "There's a mass of hungry media wolves out there. We need a statement prepared, pronto."

"Okay, okay," I said more to myself so as not to panic.

She continued to pace. "How could all those news reporters be here and know about the incubators? How? It's as if someone tipped them off."

I sat down at my desk and fired off a quick monologue, almost citing verbatim the rah-rah speech I'd heard in the nurses' meeting. Lots of *we*s, an abundance of *our*s, and a pinch of the truth.

I handed Morgan the printout. She scanned the page and then handed it back to me. "Perfect. You're on."

"I'm on?"

Morgan escorted me by the elbow. Our heels moved in sync, striking against the tiled floor. As we approached the double glass doors to the entrance, it struck me she was right. This kind of news frenzy didn't happen by accident. A mass of cameras and microphones stretched from the concrete to the grass and near the street. Near the entrance, a podium was set up. I saw Jasper adjusting cords and microphone height. He showed no traces of crazy. Sure I wanted to work and get back on the fast track, but not putting my life in jeopardy with some smelly nutcase. Jasper glanced my way and gave me a thumbs-up as if all was right with the world. The crowd impatiently waited as if a rock star would descend the stairs at any moment, but it was only me, staring blankly into their engaged faces.

The questions blasted toward me.

"Is it true four infants nearly lost their lives today?"

"When is the hospital closing for good?"

"How are the babies? Might there be brain damage from lack of oxygen?"

The questions were fired from every direction. The statement I'd prepared shook to a blur in my hands. I laid it flat so I could make out what I'd written.

"Our mission at Jackson Hospital is to provide our community with excellent health care as well as compassion, honor, and peace of mind. We want the community to know we are here with pride and dignity, knowing that every precaution is always made to provide a safe and healthy environment. We are happy to report the infants are doing well; heart rates and oxygen levels are excellent. They are completely out of harm's way and remain in the capable hands of our loving, caring staff." I folded the paper neatly as if I'd just given a valedictorian speech.

I caught a glimpse of Kandi standing off to the left, away from everyone else, her arms folded over her heavy breasts. I could swear she was sneering, her lip hiked up in disgust. I didn't have time to concentrate on the drama queen. The questions continued to be fired from all angles. I finally had the strength to point, signaling to a journalist who held his pen in the air. He was nice enough looking, a tempered face with a long comb-over extending from one ear to the other. He gave the impression of someone who knew how to report the unbiased truth.

"Incidents of this nature seem a little excessive for one hospital. Do you suspect sabotage, maybe one of your own staff?" His question landed squarely in my face, causing short-term blurriness.

"All possible explanations are being investigated."

"Possible explanations for putting people's lives at stake? That means you have no idea what's happening in your own hospital?" The journalist tilted his large comb-over to the side.

I ignored him and made a note to self: There was no such thing as an unbiased reporter, no matter how modest and humble they appeared. I pointed a finger to an attractive newswoman with her camera crew focusing on her good side. The camera swung around to me after she asked me to introduce myself.

"Yes, of course. I'm Venus Johnston. I'm the public affairs spokesperson, a position I'm most proud of at this time. This hospital represents a bold history of achievements and will continue to do so." From the corner of my eye, I could see Morgan Taylor lift her hand in a small fist. A few others started clapping. I figured it was best to end on a high note.

Before I could close out the press conference, the newswoman continued. "Thank you for that wonderful introduction," she said into her microphone. "Now if you could briefly touch on the past few incidents surrounding the hospital. The patient who was given a near overdose. The male patient who was prepped for the wrong surgery." She lifted up a yellow pad. "Then there was the woman who'd actually died in Jackson

Memorial and the next of kin was never contacted, though billing continued for the deceased's care for nearly a week. Needless to say, she wasn't good for it." This comment brought about a few chuckles from her fellow newshounds.

I took the opening quickly. "The incidents you are referring to have yet to be fully investigated; therefore, you are relying on hearsay. I assure you, Jackson Memorial is operating to the highest degree and, match for match, we are as well run as or better run than any hospital in the Los Angeles area. When Cedar Crest lost a patient for well over twenty-four hours, no one was there requiring a public explanation. When Grossmont removed the spleen of the wrong patient, I don't recall it being on the six-o'clock news. As for the interest in Jackson Memorial, we're flattered. Knowing all eyes are upon us will make us even more efficient. I want to thank you all for this opportunity to introduce myself. The next time we meet, it will be assuredly under better circumstances."

I caught a glimpse of Clint standing in a small group of doctors. He winked and put his thumb up.

"So you're saying there are future changes under way for the hospital?"

"I'm not able to comment at this point, but I can say that once these changes are made, Jackson Memorial will no longer be under threat of closure. Thank you, and have a good day."

Morgan was my own private cheerleader when I stepped down from the podium. "Venus. Thank you. Perfect. You handled them—you truly handled those vultures."

The crowd dispersed slowly. The picketers went back to their circular march. Somehow I made it back to my office, shaking knees and spotty vision. I closed the door and sat down with a dry cotton ball mouth. I thought about each and every word I'd uttered, wondering if I was really cut out for this job. I spun around in my wickedly crooked chair and sank into the moment, finally allowing myself to take a deep relieving breath. It was scary and exhilarating all at the same time. All those cameras pointed at me.

Eventually I stopped patting myself on the back and thought about the reality of what just happened. Babies' lives were endangered. It could have been a real tragedy. Worse, *It's as if someone tipped off the media about the incubator incident before it even happened.*

"You did an excellent job out there."

Jasper was only a few feet away from me. "Thanks." An uneasy feeling swept over me. I clamped my armpits down to stop the stream of perspiration.

"Couldn't have done better myself," he said, taking off his glasses and wiping them on his blue-and-white-striped dress shirt, the kind with a white collar and white cuff. It was unfitting of his style, like he'd bought it at a used clothing store with impeccably good taste. Far calmer than earlier, he cocked his head before speaking. "I thought the question about sabotage was interesting."

"It was the furthest thing from my mind."

"I think it's a fair question. Definitely possible. There are a lot of people who feel mistreated in this hospital. People who have unjustly been accused of negativity all because the administration has needed a scapegoat." The edge of his voice cracked. He stepped completely inside and closed the door.

"Like who?" I suddenly felt like sprinting out of there. The air was at a minimum when Jasper was around, but this was something else. Fear. I slipped my shoes back on underneath the desk. I spied my purse hanging on the hook near the door where I'd thrown it haphazardly before meeting the press.

"I'm not going to mention any names. It would be unfair to continually persecute someone who hasn't been proved guilty." Jasper shoved his glasses tight against his face. "Lest he not judge who does not want to be judged."

"All right, yeah, I can see your point." I stood up. "I think I'll call it a day." I moved with efficiency to grab my purse, but it didn't budge. I snatched it, pulling the steel hook out of the wall.

Jasper faced me with concern.

"Must have missed a stud when they installed it," I said, picking up the hook and tossing it in the trash. I moved to get away as fast as possible.

Big News

Jake stood over me at the kitchen table where I'd been working on my laptop with the sole purpose of not waking him. But there he was in his boxers at midnight, standing over me. "How's it feel to be a superstar?" He leaned over, giving me a proud papa kiss on the forehead. "You're on every news station." He opened the refrigerator and pulled out the OJ.

"You'd think there was something else more pressing going on."

"That's what happens when you give a good performance. Now I understand why you couldn't meet me for lunch."

"I'm so sorry about that." I looked up and gave him my sincerest eyes.

He leaned in and kissed me again. "I understand, babe." He wedged a kiss in my ear and slid his hand down the front of my sleep T. "I think it's time," he whispered, cupping both of my breasts and squeezing gently. The tingling swirl of heat landed between my legs.

I nudged his hands away. "Give me a few more minutes."

He massaged my shoulders, kissed my neck and whispered, "Now, baby."

Jake was in serious love mode. He reached around and circled the tips of nipples that completely disagreed with me. *Yes,* it was time, they screamed, budding against the thin cotton, but I needed a few more minutes.

He slipped his fingers through my hair and pulled the band loose, allowing the mass of thickness to break free. Jake inhaled then began planting a wet trail of kisses along the curve of my neck as he worked his way to my mouth. He sucked my bottom lip just lightly enough to get my juices flowing.

"Just five, I promise, five more minutes," I said, prying my face out of his grip, ignoring the warm spasm centered below my belly. I squeezed my thighs tight, letting the fabric of my nightgown gather between my legs. Five more minutes, I had to tell my own body, *Just hold on.*

Jake let out a sigh of defeat. He grabbed his glass of orange juice and left without a word.

I couldn't help it. The imagery of Jasper sweating and nearly delusional kept creeping into my mind. I wouldn't be able to rest or make love properly until I'd surfed the Net clean of every story about Jackson Memorial dating all the way back to the 1970s, still nothing associated with Jasper Calloway.

I pushed my reading glasses high above the flat ridge of my nose. The computer light picked up the taut angular shape of my cheekbones. I could almost see my entire face in the reflection of the screen from leaning in so close. All the information I needed had miraculously appeared.

By this time Jake was back. He pulled up a chair next to me. His arms folded over his bare chest. It was nearly two o'clock in the morning. He reached out and pushed the laptop closed. "Come to bed, babe. It's late. Whatever you're doing can be finished in the morning."

I lifted it right back up then held up one finger, indicating *un momento*.

Jake stood up, taking my hand, lightly pulling my palm to meet his lips.

I snatched my hand away. "Okay, just three more minutes. Did you know you can find anything about someone for thirty-five dollars? Everything—their credit report, marital history, criminal history. It's a crying shame, but amazing at the same time."

"Take your time," he said, walking out of the kitchen.

A while back, Jake told me he'd been rejected by a woman twice in his lifetime, both times had been me, which was irony in itself. He'd married the one woman who'd had the restraint to say no to him. In both cases, I made it up to him later. I planned to do so again.

I typed in my credit card number and within seconds I'd downloaded every aspect of Jasper Calloway's life. I ran to Jake's office, where the wireless printer was already rolling. Thirteen pages. I read each and every page. Before long, it was three in the morning.

By the time I got to bed, Jake was secure in dreamland. I scooted next to the warmth of his body and tried to shake the cold fear. It had to be Jasper, I thought before sleep shrouded my mind. It had to be him.

C-A-T, Kat?

The next morning I awakened pinned underneath Jake's thigh with his arm draped over my chest. The alarm clock was going off, but I couldn't budge to turn it off. Finally he shifted position and I made my escape.

I grabbed what I'd planned to wear and headed for the bathroom but changed directions when I heard Mya's morning banter. No complaints, just talking to herself.

"Hey, Miss My-My. How's my baby?"

She smiled when I entered the room, standing up against the crib with her stuffed SpongeBob in her hands. I picked her up and inhaled her soft scent. Even with a wet diaper, she smelled of baby powder and mineral oil. The heaviness of her diaper weighed her down. "You've got to start going on the potty, little lady."

She shook her head.

I set her down on her two round feet while I went to the closet to get the Fisher-Price potty. She started pitching a fit. I picked her up to shush her. I sat her down on the blue plastic and handed her SpongeBob. She threw him across the room. SpongeBob landed on his square head.

"Okay, okay, but if you sit on the potty, Mommy will

make you Happy Face pancakes, with little sprinkles." She adamantly shook her head, probably remembering the last time. More like scary-face pancakes after I'd burned them and went a little heavy on the whipped cream eyebrows. I kissed her and hugged her. "I don't blame you. I wouldn't want them either, sweetie."

Every time I sat her on the potty, she got right back up. "Stay there," I ordered.

After the tenth time, I gave up. I changed her into a fresh diaper, securing it tight around her thick thighs. I grabbed the cute one-piece terry jumpsuit that was my favorite. I'd bought it before she was even born. Jake had laughed at all the baby clothing in boxes stacked ceiling high when we'd moved in with him. Mya was no more than doll size, but I had enough clothing to start her first day in kindergarten. "A girl is nothing without a wardrobe," I told him.

It shocked me when I couldn't get the pink terry sleeve over her shoulders. The bottom kept unsnapping whenever I made headway. When did this happen? "You're growing so big, My-My. I bet you can say *ma-ma*. Say *ma-ma*," I repeated while I found something else for her to wear.

She shook her head. All the books I'd read made it clear there were no true timetables for language development, but I was sure at this age, a child was supposed to know how to say *mama*.

"Good morning?" Trina sang out as she came into the room. Daybreak had turned the walls a pale orange where they appeared gray before.

"Cattt," Mya sang out.

I clapped softly. "Good job, My-My. Trina, would you mind writing down Mya's activities during the day, maybe keeping a log of some of the things she does and . . . maybe start her on the potty."

"Sure. But the potty . . . I think she's a little young," Trina said over her shoulder.

"No. All the books I've read say potty training should start as early as possible. If she can walk, she can go to the potty."

Trina dumped an armload of toys into the white wood chest. "Sure, no problem."

"Cattt," Mya did a little dance against the railing of her crib. This was more excitement than I'd seen out of her since she got to squeeze Mickey's nose at Disneyland over the summer.

I was excited, too. Besides *no* and *Daddddy,* she hadn't expressed a desire to talk. "Oh my goodness. Yes, *cat.*" I pointed down to the big picture book opened to the animated Garfield.

Mya pointed to Trina. "Caattt."

Trina turned around. Her smile showed a mild gap between her teeth. "That's right, sweetie, Kat. I taught her how to say the first part of my name, Kat . . . from Katrina. I know the Trina part is too difficult." Trina lifted Mya out of her captivity. "Go on, get ready for work. I got her."

"Thanks." I said, "Thanks a lot." I guessed a lot of children learned how to say *cat* before *mama*—they just weren't referring to the babysitter.

Trina walked in holding Mya dressed in her yellow pajamas and squeezing her SpongeBob doll. "Well don't you two look like the power couple?"

Mya's little arms reached out for me then pulled back when I was about to take her—*psych.* Already we were having mother–daughter drama and she was barely in toddlerhood.

Trina handed her over to me anyway.

I kissed Mya quickly and shifted her into Jake's

arms. He kissed Mya then handed her right back to Trina.

"See you later, babe." I kissed Jake in musical chair fashion and made a quick exit into the heavy coastal fog. I didn't get far before realizing I'd left my brief-case. I did a modest U-turn, still driving like I had Miss Daisy in the backseat.

The house was quiet when I walked inside. I went straight to my leather case on the breakfast nook. Trina and Mya were nowhere to be seen. I peeked down the hall then headed for the garage door, feeling a clean break. The sound of Jake's voice stopped me. He did a lot of *ah-huh*s and *ummm*s when on the phone. In be-tween a "right-right," I took the extra steps and waited directly outside his closed study.

Not only was it his telephone voice, but it was the soft melodic tone reserved for . . . me. "You know how I do things," he said. "This just isn't a good time. Aha, right. What do you want me to say?" He paused. "All I'm saying, aha, aha. This is something I have to do in my own way."

"Hey, Venus, I thought you were gone."

I jumped, startled by Trina catching me with my face pressed against Jake's door. "I forgot my briefcase."

Trina freeze-framed, holding a balled-up Huggies like it was a grenade about to go off.

Jake opened the study door. "She came back because she forgot to give me a good-bye kiss. It was meant to be." He took a hold of my face and gave me a long pas-sionate kiss.

I refused to ask Jake who he was talking to even though it was killing me. Instinctively nosy, always needing to know what was going on, but if I asked, it would start a new precedent, a rule eventually turned on me. Having my conversations monitored would be the last and final straw, so I kissed him again, this time softly, and left with my imagination in full throttle.

I already had enough to contend with. Loving someone like Jake was like walking around with a pristine white fur coat and hoping it never got dirty. Women and sometimes men stared at my husband as if I wasn't by his side. I used to think it was recognition from his valiant fifteen moments of rap fame. In the grocery store, at the mall, in the popcorn and soda line at the theater, I would glance up and see hardcore interest in the sexy man on my arm. Jake always pretended he didn't notice. I pretended I didn't care.

Eventually I became immune and accepted being ignored and invisible. Not to say I was chopped liver. You couldn't attract a man like Jake, have him fall madly in love with you without a few redeeming qualities of your own. Cute, I got a lot. Pretty, a close second. Sexy, something I hardly had to work at.

For most of my life, my hair was the ward of the flat irons, gels, and wrap scarves. I forbade any man to mess with the do while in the heated throes of passion. With Jake, it was part of the ritual. He took handfuls, grabbing and pulling, directing my every move.

It's the one thing I could depend on—glorious beautiful, hot, thick, luscious, and sometimes dangerous lovemaking. We did it everywhere humanly possible. The shower being one of Jake's favorite locations, which never would've happened if I'd stayed straight. So while the high-maintenance snooty pants stared and wondered how I landed such an expensive perfect fur, I simply stroked and purred, knowing I had secret powers. Whether he strayed or not wasn't big on my list of worries. I considered myself through with the whole jealousy thing. I knew what kind of man I'd married. A man, nonetheless, and if he felt the need to roam the sugar walls of another woman, I knew there was nothing I could do to stop him.

I put the thought of Jake's mystery phone conversation out of my mind and entered Jackson Memorial Hospital with my game face on.

La Vida Loca

Morgan Taylor stood outside the hospital talking to a full-figured woman wearing an orange poncho and green pedal pushers that made her look like a pumpkin. I tried walking discreetly by, making a wide half circle around the entry and between the tall white pillars.

"Venus, there you are."

"Good morning, Morgan." *Damn.* I waved, still moving in the opposite direction.

"I thought you should meet Deidre McKinley, have a sit-down." Morgan fanned me toward her. "Deidre McKinley is one of our strongest advocates. She's a councilwoman for the Thirty-seventh District and strongly opposes the closure of Jackson Memorial."

When I got close enough to offer my hand, I realized she was the outspoken leader of the picketers. I shoved my satchel and purse under my arm and shook the woman's hand. "So good to meet you. You've been diligent in fighting for the hospital. Really good to meet you." I looked at my watch.

"And you're the new speaker at the podium. You handled those newshounds with style. About time we had someone say what needed to be said. I'm at your service—take my card." She patted the cell phone attached to her hip. "Call me, let me know when you're ready to talk, I'll come right up."

"Thank you, I will." I rushed toward the entrance.

"Let me know when you're ready," she called out again, adding a dash more pressure.

I entered the hospital and had to immediately slow down, waiting for my eyes to adjust from the early morning sun to the dull indoor lighting. The Southern California rays zapped unprotected skin and corneas like laser beams. I was becoming impatient, needing to see better, walk faster. I needed to talk to Clint and in a hurry.

My cell phone rang as I stepped onto the elevator. I reached inside my purse and flipped it open, ready for Jake's voice, the one that was meant for me.

"Venus."

I did my best to hide my disappointment. "Hi, Mom. What's up?" My mother who never called anyone just to say hello sounded tired and a wee bit on edge.

"Ruby said she saw you on the news last night. What's that all about?" she asked, not wanting to let on her excitement. Having a daughter on TV might put Pauletta back in the good graces of her hairdresser of thirty-three years. My mother's status had been seriously weakened with my digression from Black American Princess–dom. Having a daughter who cut off her chemically straightened hair and "let herself go" was a definite blemish on one's royal report card. I refused to go back to the chair no matter how many times my mother emphasized she hadn't raised me to be some wild child.

"I got the job at Jackson Hospital, Mom, doing PR. I told you about it."

"P-what?"

"Public relations."

"That's great, that's nice. When were you going to tell me you're working? Who's watching Mya?"

"Mom, you know we have Trina. She's been working for us for a few months now."

"I thought that was temporary while your leg healed."

"Temporary turned into permanent. She's good with Mya. Mya loves her, so I took the opportunity to go back to work." I scooted out of the way of the throng of nurses coming onto the elevator carrying hot coffee and dry pastries.

"Venus, have you lost your mind?" Pauletta sounded eerily like when I was in the second grade, the day I'd declared myself black no more. I'd reached a point of kiddie stress that sent me storming to my mother's side with a list of reasons why I was no longer going to be a *black girl:*

Black girls couldn't play in the sandbox.

Black girls couldn't go over to Linda Gay's house to swim.

Black girls weren't allowed to work up a sweat in the sun outdoors.

Black girls had to stay behind after school when it rained so someone could pick them up instead of walk and play splash with the other kids.

When she was through laughing, she took me into the bathroom and held my father's belt under my nose and whispered, "You let me hear you say something crazy like that again, you hear. Just one time and see what you get."

"What?" I said back to her, trying to figure out if the last thirty years of my life had been a dream or if I was still seven years old being scolded for thinking outside myself. The elevator was suddenly packed. The light on the number runner above wasn't working, so you couldn't tell what floor you were on unless you were up front or over six feet tall, of which I was neither.

"Venus, you don't let another woman run your household." My mother sucked her teeth in an exaggerated drag, one more thing I should've learned from Pauletta's house of rules.

"What are you talking about, Mom? I'm running my household," I whispered, but still got the knowing glimpses from the female populace on the elevator. The age-old question—who's watching the children?

"Listen, you know I don't like to tell you anything, 'cause you don't want nobody telling you anything, but trust me, this is not the way to handle your business. Just because you and Mr. Jake over there are living *la vida loca* doesn't mean you gotta start acting like you don't have any good sense. If you want Mya to be watched during the day, I'll watch her."

"Mom, you still have chemotherapy. I know how tired it makes you. I couldn't ask you to watch her all day, every day. She's a handful."

"Then put her in a good day care. Having someone come there, to your private space every single day taking over your home, your responsibilities, that's not right."

"Mom, there's nothing wrong, I assure you. Trina's the best thing that ever happened to us."

"Um-hum."

"If it wasn't for her, I wouldn't have this job. I wouldn't have even thought it was possible. I mean really, Mom, women have been helping each other run households since the Dark Ages. If anything, it's the most natural—"

"There's nothing natural about it. Adam had one woman—Eve. You don't mix up things bringing another woman into your home. Didn't you just tell me something about Wendy's awkward situation? Her husband and the babysitter," she added to her final analysis.

"Jesus," I whispered, feeling eyes on the back of my head as I pushed myself forward past the crowded mass.

"Don't take the Lord's name in vain."

"Then ohmigod," I said, nearly fuming. "Is that better?" I was determined to get off the elevator regardless of what floor I was on. I raised my voice when I was free at last. "That has nothing to do with what's going on in my house. Of course I'm not going to hire an eighteen-year-old babysitter with a tattoo on her ass and wearing jeans low enough to show it. Now that is crazy. Trina is nothing like that."

"All right."

"Mom, it's not like that around here. You've met Trina, seriously, no way." The doors opened. I stepped off, not believing my great timing and luck. I was on the pediatrics floor.

"All right, Venus. I'm just letting you know that I'm available to watch my granddaughter. The only grandchild I have. I certainly wouldn't mind spending time with her."

"Is this what this is about, you're jealous?" I spun around, not sure which direction to go for Clint's office.

"Child, you are about as stubborn and hardheaded as they come."

I sighed heavily to send the message, conversation over. I had to find Clint. It was urgent that I tell him about Jasper. "I'll talk to ya later, Mom." I hung up and threw the phone back in my purse. My mother's cryptic premonition of doom hung over me like a black cloud. She had no idea what was going on in my life. I had real dangers that didn't include the threat of a babysitter. Serious dangers like a madman trying to poison a hospital, a She-whore that was trying to get the job I was meant for, and worse, a husband who might feel slightly neglected—a lethal cocktail, I certainly knew.

Baby Blues

Surprisingly, no one stopped me when I stepped into the neonatal ward, where only days before, nurses were stationed outside like the militia. I peered into the glass enclosure and saw Clint sitting alone in a corner chair holding a small infant in his arms. I tapped lightly with my knuckle. His startled look quickly turned warm and inviting. He motioned his head to the side entrance. I pulled on a fresh robe and tied a face mask on with the skill of a surgeon before going inside.

"Do you sleep here?" I said quietly enough not to disturb the sleeping infant.

"If there was an extra bed, I would." He barely looked at me. He placed tiny drops of watery milk to the baby's parted lips, keeping his hand steady. The liquid rolled down the side of the baby's cheek.

I took the seat next to him. "Let me help." I took the dropper and laid it against the side of the infant's mouth and waited for the involuntary wave of sucking to start. Like a timer, all babies had it from the time fingers and toes were formed in the womb, the natural instinct to suck. I waited again for the next wave and put the dropper against the cheek. We continued as a team until the feeder was empty.

Clint saw my concern. "She's full, trust me," he said as he lifted her gently and patted her back with two fingers. A barely there sound of gas escaped her lips. I remembered Mya's thirst when she was a tiny baby, slurping and gulping milk from my breasts until they were no longer swollen. This one could barely hold a teaspoon of liquid.

"You did a good job with the press," he said.

"I'm just glad they're all right." My eyes searched the wall for tangled cords and outlets, wondering how they could have come unplugged. "Do you really believe it was an accident?"

Clint's head rested against the thick pane of glass behind him. "It's crazy, I know. One thing after another. I feel like I'm in the Amityville house of horrors." His Adam's apple bobbed up and down like he couldn't finish what he wanted to say.

"I think I know what's going on."

"This isn't how I pictured it, V. I never thought I'd be holding a baby that barely weighed a few pounds, and I never ever thought my job would be threatened by some bullshit. Being a doctor used to mean security, prestige, something close to royalty. Now it's like . . ." He trailed off, focusing on the small baby sleeping on his chest. "Now it's like I'm a shift worker like my father. Dispensable. Like I didn't go to school for ten years, busting my ass, humping sunup to sundown to make something of myself."

He stood up, cradling the baby with all the love and care, but anger and frustration crowded his face. He paced. "Do you know how many times I wanted to give up? It was never easy. I wasn't raised in a house with a single parent. Worse, I had no parents. So essentially, I'm a self-made man. And what's my reward? Sometimes I wonder if Kandi was right. I never should have come here." He paced, shaking his head.

By this time, I was prepared to take the baby from his arms. "Clint."

"Did you hear that?" He stopped in his tracks.

Besides the pumps and fetal monitors, I heard nothing. I looked around, eyeing the colorful mural on the walls, the row of tubular housings where the other tiny babies slept with soft warm light filtering down on their bodies. "Hear what?"

"She made a baby noise," Clint whispered in amazement, answering his own question. "That's huge. She was dreaming . . . which means active brain synapse. That's huge. She'll be going home soon," he said, completely turned around from his turmoil. He carried Baby back to her bunk. "Could you get the handle?"

I slid close to him and opened the door. He laid her down on her stomach. She was in a peaceful slumber. We stood watching for a few silent moments. "I always could talk to you about anything." He lifted an arm and draped it around my shoulders. I slipped it off, feeling uneasy. I stepped to the side and put safe distance between us.

I stayed a few moments longer, arms crossed over my chest. I turned quickly, looking over my shoulder, unable to shake the odd feeling of someone watching. No one was there. The glass windows were thick enough to feel like bulletproof barricades but couldn't stop piercing eyes.

Clint had already moved on to the next incubator. A boy I assumed by the soft blue cap on his head. He put the shiny stethoscope to the baby's tiny brown chest and listened with love.

"I have some information about Jasper Calloway. Do you know him?"

Clint held up a finger for a moment of silence. He moved his stethoscope to another area on the thin beating chest, then another. When he was finished, he followed me out. We both pulled our face masks down at the same time. I picked up the file and placed it in his gloved hand.

Nancy Drew Who?

"I think I know what's going on around here." Outside the neonatal ward I could speak louder.

He scanned the top sheet. His face scrunched up, making his exhausted eyes fall into smaller slits. "What is this? Why do I care that Jasper Calloway has a four hundred score on his credit report?"

"Jasper Calloway was a doctor. Happened to be a very well paid doctor right here at Jackson Memorial. Now he's an assistant. Does someone that used to make life-and-death decisions voluntarily go to low-level admin? I need to know what happened, why he doesn't practice medicine anymore."

"Okay?" Clint said, still not getting my point.

I took a breath. "He was the head of Pediatrics. The job you now have." That got Clint's attention. He took the papers back and focused on the second page. Jasper Calloway, MD. Graduated 1979, Loma Linda University. "I replaced him?"

"Bingo. Doesn't that sound crazy to you, the makings of someone hanging around just to cause havoc, vengeance on a hospital that busted him down in rank?"

He smoothed a hand over his head. "I still don't get

what you're saying. You're trying to say Jasper unplugged the monitors?"

"It makes perfect sense. This man is going around flogging this hospital. It's him. He's trying to shut it down."

"How can he be responsible for everything? The billing discrepancies? The surgeries gone wrong? The lady who was dead for a week before anybody filled out a death certificate? Those things happen." He shook his head and handed the papers back. "It's a stretch."

"I'm not saying he's done everything, but seriously, Clint, you have to admit, it's creepy. If I used to be running around with a white coat, filled with the arrogance of being a doctor, I certainly wouldn't hang around and be demoralized as someone's assistant."

"It's always about you, isn't it?"

I used the file and popped him with it.

"Since when'd you become so violent?" He rubbed his shoulder as if it really hurt.

"Well, stop acting like this is a joke. You know what I'm saying. If this guy is responsible, he's dangerous. I need your help to get proof."

"Sorry, Nancy Drew, I don't know anything about spying. I got my hands full."

"Yeah, well, if you don't help me, your hands are going to be empty, looking for a job." That time I hit a sore spot without throwing any real punches. "I'm sorry. I'm just trying to get your attention. I have better things to do, too, but I'm nervous around this guy. I know something isn't right. Too many coincidences. Right around the same time when the incubators were discovered unplugged, I saw Jasper. He came out of nowhere, dripping with sweat, nervous, very suspicious looking. I didn't make the connection until later when I saw all of those news people out there. How would information like that get out without someone leaking it? Literally picking up the phone and calling with the information."

"Okay, V, that still doesn't prove he's the one."

"Then help me get proof."

"What do you want me to do? I mean, seriously, what would you like me to do?"

I gave in to the fact that there really wasn't anything he *could* do. "Fine, you're right. We'll just have to wait until he strikes again. Hopefully no one will be hurt seriously and he'll be caught in the act."

I pulled the paper-thin robe off and grabbed my bag. I was about to leave when Clint grabbed my hand. "Wait. I have to tell you something."

"What?" The energy in his fingers wrapped tightly around mine, causing me to momentarily forget what our conversation had been about. Wait, he'd said, wait for what? Had he finally come to his senses and wanted to admit he'd chosen the wrong woman? *Too late,* my eyes screamed.

"You're right. I left the part out about Kandi being pregnant for a stupid reason."

I pulled my hand out of his. "What's going on here is what's important. You and Kandi are not my concern. Seriously," I begged. "Focus on what's important." His confession would have to wait.

"There're cameras all over this place. I don't think they're on, but I know where the video equipment is."

"Show me."

We took the elevator down to the basement. The doors opened up to a dimly lit hall. Clint led the way to a door with a sign overhead that read *KEEP LOCKED.* Obviously a rule no one followed, as Clint simply turned the knob and we were inside. He flipped a heavy switch and fluorescent lights hummed and bounced on and off. Eventually they decided to stay on, revealing steel filing cabinets and stacks of boxes.

"They use it for storage, but through there is the security station."

I stayed close behind as Clint led the way.

Inside were two televisions side by side. "Okay . . . this is like from 1970." I flicked the button on and off. Snow formed quickly on the screen. I turned the dial back, and the screen went blank again. "I'm sure I can get someone to hook them up. If I recall, you were pretty good with that kind of thing, right?" I attempted to sound demure. I reached in the back of one of the screens. "I bet it's really simple. If I could just reach this line."

"Move, V. I see what you're up to." He stepped in my place, brushing against my arm. He twisted the back panel around to face him. Wires were attached and some weren't. A set of green, red, and yellow wires stood out like orphans with no place to go. Right before he was about to experiment, buzzing from his hip vibrated with an echo. He reached at his belt and pulled up his phone. "I can't get reception down here."

"I'll wait, go on," I said, waving him off. As soon as he left and the door fell closed behind him, I thought I saw something move from the corner of my eye. I waited a minute, paralyzed, thinking if I moved, whatever giant rodent I'd trespassed against would attack with territorial vengeance. The only sound I heard was my own blood pulsing through my ears. I waited for the rat, probably big enough to eat a good chunk of my face, to jump out with teeth barred.

A box tumbled and I leaped for the door. The knob turned, but the door stayed put. It wouldn't budge.

I twisted the knob then beat the door. "Clint!

Somebody, help!" I waited, I listened, and I beat some more. "Please, somebody!" I fumbled with my purse on my shoulder, feeling for my phone. No bars for reception, not one. "Please, somebody open the door. Help!"

I heard movement, feet shuffling on the other side. Then a muffled voice—"Stand back."

I got out of the way just in time. The door swung inward. My mouth dropped. "Jasper."

"I heard you all the way upstairs, in our office. Must be the air vents." He stepped inside, giving enough room for me to pass.

"I have to get out of here." I swept past him. When the elevator didn't open right away, I headed for the stairs and didn't look back.

I went straight to Morgan's office. "Jasper Calloway is crazy. I think he's the one who unplugged the baby's units, on purpose."

Morgan shifted uncomfortably in her chair. "Please don't repeat that to anyone else. The liability of your statement could cripple us. It's one thing to fight accidental ineptitude, but blatant negligence, or premeditation, we'd be shut down for good."

"My point exactly. If he's a liability, why keep him around to do more damage?"

"The stress is already getting to you," Morgan said, matter-of-factly.

Kandi knocked on the open door. "I have the statement about the fiasco yesterday. I wanted to let you see it before I faxed it to the newpapers." She came inside and put her back to me as if I didn't exist.

"The fiasco, as you call it, nearly killed four innocent babies."

Kandi turned around as if surprised. "Oh, I didn't see you."

"Morgan, I think we need to take action."

"I think you're right. We'll pick this up tomorrow. Right now I've got a meeting with Pastor Michaels and Deidre McKinley. An administrator's work is never done." She tried to look busy.

Kandi and I both left her office and went in opposite silent directions.

Guilty

Jake didn't have time to worry about anything outside of the JP studio. He was a master of making everything look easy.

"Find anything?" Legend entered his office and eased down on the thin leather sofa.

"Whatever he's doing, he's doing it well. I can't find a trace." Jake rubbed the fine hairs on his goatee.

"Exactly. But the facts speak, my friend. There is a thief among us."

I need more than a car, Jake was thinking. Something real. Concrete. Bank transfers. A witness. "How does ten million dollars just disappear into thin air?"

"He's obviously good at what he does or you wouldn't have hired him. I say you put his ass out on the street."

"If I get rid of him, I'll never know the truth."

"The proof'll be in your bank account. Close the leak, man." Legend got up and straightened out his suit. "Twelve o'clock we've got lunch with our fair lady, Fenny Maxwell. Four o'clock we've got the interview with Carla Terry, host of *Hip-Hop Vibe*."

"I'll meet you at the TV studio for the *Vibe* show."

"Is that a fact?" Legend stopped in his tracks. Intrigue filled his eyes. "I'm impressed."

"Don't be. Lunch," Jake said before rising from his desk. "Four hundred stores. Need I say more?"

"Four hundred and eleven," Legend corrected, pulling something out of his breast pocket. "Send my regards."

The small square package landed on Jake's desk. "I don't think so," Jake said.

"Oh, you riding bareback these days? And don't give me that 'I'm married' crap," Legend mocked.

Jake picked the condom package up by its edges and slid it into his drawer. "Whatever."

"Whatever is right," Legend called out behind him. "She's a freak."

Precisely, Jake was thinking. He'd had his fair share of freaks, women who pretended they were above it all only to start swinging from the chandeliers the minute the lights went out.

The truth was he was sick of women, period. At twenty-eight years old, he was sick and tired of the whole game. The very reason he'd married in the first place. He was tired of putting his life on the line for a fake piece of ass. What if the condom broke? A thin piece of plastic was supposed to make it all right. Every day he thanked God he was still alive. He'd slept with well over two hundred women. That was just a round figure averaged out over his short adult life. But each and every one lived in his memory, breathed in his soul and weighed down his spirit.

Caprio's restaurant was in a refurbished old warehouse downtown. Jake was grateful for the open space of the place. Glad he wouldn't be suffocated by her heavy perfumed scent. She wore a jeans jumpsuit with the zipper open, revealing a heavy dose of cleavage. Each step was the longest. When he got closer, he saw the man sitting in the sleek wood-paneled booth.

"Saul Levine." He stood up next to Fenny, rising to her shoulder at best. He extended a hand to Jake covered with heavy rings in gold and diamond settings.

"Jake Parson."

"I know who you are—I was once a fan."

Jake heard it often enough, but something about Saul made him believe it was true. Young white boys had been his biggest fan base. Saul Levine had to be barely drinking age.

"I'm glad you agreed to the meeting." Saul leaned against Fenny's shoulder enough to send a message of territorial claim. Jake laughed on the inside and did his best not to smile.

"Actually, I had no idea anyone else was going to be here."

Fenny's mouth curved in a smile, but her eyes gave her away, the type of woman who did nothing for the joy of it. Everything boiled down to win or lose. She was there to win. "I wanted you two to meet, and I knew if I told you why, you wouldn't come," she said.

"Okay, this is getting interesting."

Saul took over. "Consolidated wants to buy JP Wear."

Jake's eyes darted between the two and then clouded over with a confused haze. "JP Wear is not for sale. Never has been."

Fenny touched Jake's hand. "Consolidated stores are your largest distribution channel. It only makes sense. We want JP Wear exclusively at our stores. I think it's a huge honor."

"Right, we're not trying to take the company, just share in the growth." Saul winked.

Jake was still taken aback. "I . . . um . . . JP Wear is my life. I mean, this is definitely what I call flattering, but I can tell you the answer is no."

"You do realize if Consolidated stopped buying JP

Wear for the Rocknell stores right now, you'd go under." Fenny's voice sharpened. "We're fifty percent of your sales and ninety percent of your profit. Your company will see red within six months if you don't take this deal. Or should I say more red than you're already seeing."

Why did she know this? How?

"So now I'm being blackmailed. Why would you want JP Wear? There's a hundred different lines you can take and call a private label. I'd think the fact that I'm losing money would concern you."

"To the contrary. JP Wear is doing phenomenal sales in our stores. It would only make sense that we get involved, control the price points—fix whatever's broken and everybody wins."

"You walk away with twenty-five million in your pocket," Saul added. "All yours."

Jake stood up. "Saul, I want to say it was nice meeting you, but I'm having a little problem with that right now. Fenny, we'll talk soon." Jake worked hard to keep it together. When he made it outside the restaurant, the façade crumbled. It felt like someone shut off the oxygen to his world, unplugged his only source. He waited for a moment, talking himself out of collapsing. He'd fought asthma all his life. Triggers were obvious, like allergies and bad perfume. And stress, let's not forget trying to contain the urge to kill somebody. When he could move, he took a few steps. Ridiculous, he was thinking. Just a bad dream. His cell phone shook him to reality.

"Yeah," he said with labored breathing.

"Jake," Fenny said lightly. "We'll need an answer by Friday—otherwise we pull JP Wear off the floor and cancel every existing order."

He closed the phone and fought the urge to throw it

as far as he could. *Son of a bitch.* He wanted proof;
now he had it. Byron Steeple not only was stealing
from him, but he'd also given Fenny Maxwell a direct
line to his business affairs. Blind rage was the only
way he could explain what happened next. All he could
do was pray for forgiveness.

Picture Perfect

When Jake came upstairs that evening, I was determined to end the silent fighting. I wanted to know how his day went. I'd been so busy trying to save an entire hospital that I was losing one man.

I sat on the closed toilet while Mya splashed her blocks in the warm tub of water. Contentment glowed over his face as he reached out and rubbed Mya's mass of curly wet hair then placed a soft kiss on my forehead. I inhaled a scent that wasn't his or mine. The soapy fragrance was precise and exact as if placed there just for me to find, so I did the bigger thing and ignored it.

"You guys look so peaceful." Jake kneeled beside me. The picture-perfect scene of his wife taking care of his child. Safeness, security, and hope. I felt it, too, a rare moment when you're actually grateful for what you have. Mya took a handful of bubbles and put them on her head. She grinned with a fresh top row of baby teeth. She splashed the water and sang out, *"Daddee."*

"She's growing so fast. She's so smart," I said, stroking and playing in Mya's hair. "I miss you," I said, quiet and unexpectanly. I took a hold of his face and kissed him heavily, not letting an ounce of air get between his mouth and mine. I ignored the scent that still traveled around my good senses.

In his arms I was soft and fragile. All the fight exhausted out of me. The day's frets and observations falling away. The solid muscle of Jake's arms encased me as he leaned me backward in a tango kiss. The very same moment I felt a slam against my forehead.

"Kaaaaat, Daddeee." Two words or one, Mya stood at the edge of the tub. The plastic block she'd used to pop me on the forehead rolled off to the corner. She reached for it, nearly slipping out headfirst.

"Mya, no!" Jake caught her like a vase before falling and shattering into pieces. He scooped her dripping butt out of the water. He wrapped a towel around her. Her big eyes blinked with innocence and peacefulness like, *Did I do that?*

"Beddy-bye time for you, young lady."

I began to pick up all the toys and wipe up the puddles of water around the tub.

"Leave it, babe. Trina can get it tomorrow."

"No. I should do it. It's a mess in here."

"It's all right. C'mon. I'll put Mya to bed." He put his hand out for me to grab. I gave a quick glance to the demon child looking for baby weapons.

Jake pulled me up by my arm. He took the rubber ducky, blocks, and assorted squeeze toys out of my hand and threw them back in the pile on the floor. Mya contested with a growl. He carried her off to her room and closed the door. I went to our bedroom and climbed into the cool sheets. I could hear Mya gearing up for her usual night cry. Listening to her exhaustive wail, I stuffed a pillow over my head.

When Jake came to our bedroom, he was no longer superdaddy, more like Super Fly Mack Daddy. His eyes were lowered, glossy. He tossed the covers back, exposing me to the cool air.

"Hey, sweetie," I said, a little concerned about what was in store.

He pulled me by my ankles, separating my legs so I was directly in front of him. He pulled his belt loose and his zipper down with one sweep of his hand. His pants dropped to the floor. He was completely naked within seconds, and I knew instantly this was no ordinary playdate.

I inched away to the center of the bed. He pulled me forward again before I could get away. I was face-to-face with his elongated hardness. He made sure there was no misunderstanding, holding himself with one hand and using the other to gently grip the back of my neck. I took his weight with my mouth and immediately knew it wasn't my imagination.

No ordinary playdate.

With each tantalizing motion of my tongue, he grew thicker. He pulled away, ripe and glistening from my saliva. I took a hold again, wanting to feel him against my throat. He pulled away, threatening to bust if I held on any longer. He moved swiftly, pushing me onto my back. He kneaded my wetness until he was satisfied it was enough.

I wanted to tell him to slow down, to take his time. No words escaped my lips, only a gasp when he pushed himself inside my moistness, working his way to the center. He swirled his tongue against the length of my neck and chin.

I felt the grip of his hands around my hips, flipping me over. I was on my stomach, bearing his full weight. I was afraid he'd push us both over the side of the bed with the power of his thrusts. A steady moan trickled with the heat of his breath in my ear as he grunted, pushing deeper, hungry and determined. He shoved every inch of himself inside me.

"Baby, wait." I tried to shift with his rhythm but couldn't catch up.

His slick hardness drew in and out faster, harder, filling me with heat. He grabbed my hair, pulling my head against his chest. The tension eased while he kissed my neck and ran his hands down the front of my thighs. But the romance was only temporary. He pushed me back down on the bed, stretched under his full weight.

"Baby, please," I begged quietly.

"Please, what?" he groaned. "Please, what?" He pushed even harder.

I held on, eventually giving in totally and completely. He slipped out, starting over. He pushed his fingers inside me and out, then landed on the soft point that grew hard and alert with his touch. He fingered me until I reached a state of frenzy. I sighed a pant of relief and joy, but quickly realized it wasn't over. He was revving me up for part two. I had nowhere to run. He sank back inside me, taking up where he left off. He let out a hoarse cry as if disappointed he couldn't go on forever.

He rolled over, his chest rising and falling. I placed my hand on his heart, and then followed with my head resting against the rhythms pounding under the layer of muscle. I knew the workings of his body. I knew how many beats per second meant danger. I listened until the rhythm of his heartbeat matched mine.

"I love you, baby."

He didn't answer back. I lifted my head to see his face. Sleep, I assumed, until I saw his eyes blink under his lids.

"You want to talk about it?"

Still no answer. I wrapped my arms tight around his waist and waited patiently. Soon enough we both fell into deep and grateful sleep.

Stop, You're Under Arrest

I was ready for the day to end, and it had barely gotten started. My mind was filled with images of Jake making love to me. Whatever was troubling him resulted in some kind of magic lovemaking that stole the soul and mind and inhabited the body to the point I could hardly keep my eyes open from dreaming about his touch. I visualized his tongue, his hands, his wide chest pushed against my face suffocating me with heart-pounding thickness.

One would never know my husband's hands were caressing my breast, moving down, kneading the smooth hairless skin above my pubic line, and eventually fingering me into completion. One would never know, especially while I managed to have a full coherent conversation with Morgan Taylor where she sat only an arm's distance away. Kandi, too, who was far easier to ignore. The entire day had been spent playing some kind of match-for-match game. Morgan was throwing out scenarios that we were to quickly give our spin, changing a catastrophe into a rosy positive light. Was this the extent of the public affairs duty, to spray air freshener instead of cleaning up the mess?

How do you make a positive situation out of a man

being wheeled on a gurney to have X-rays, then forgotten about for six hours, just long enough for him to have an aneurism and choke on his own spit? It was disgusting, and I kept asking myself why didn't I just throw in the towel and go home, find Jake, and make love to him again and again.

Because I needed purpose, I kept telling myself. Loving up on my husband can last for only so long. One hour, maybe two. Though I couldn't shake the memory or the feel of him all day.

"Your turn, Venus." Morgan Taylor nodded in my direction with her spine erect waiting for the next mini-presentation.

"Um, yes, a man collapsed in the waiting room and still was not seen for four hours. My spin . . . Mr. Caldwell received immediate attention as soon as he was discovered incoherent and without a pulse." I felt like I was at a spelling bee. Incoherent. *I-n-c-o-h* . . . then the buzzer going off signifying the wrong answer.

Kandi snickered. Her last two were easy. Who couldn't put a good spin on someone with dilated pupils that wouldn't recede for nearly two weeks? Then the one with the lady having a scalpel left underneath her buttocks, a simple mistake. Maybe it shaved off a few butt hairs.

Morgan tilted her head slightly. "Okay, well, I wouldn't go with the part about finding him incoherent. Sounds a little harsh."

"Right, I was thinking the same thing." I crossed out the word.

"Maybe we should call it a day, pick up where we left off tomorrow." Morgan must have sensed my delirium.

Kandi crossed her legs. "I'm not tired in the least. To some of us, putting a rosy light on things comes natural."

Before I could clear up what came natural for She-whores, the loud sound of a bullhorn sent us all reeling from our seats.

"What was that?" We rushed to the window, crowding for a spot. Below was a clash of picketers and police officers. I staggered backward. "What in the world—Who would call the police on the picketers? They're on our side." I turned around, looking for Morgan's response; she'd already bolted from the office, leaving Kandi and me alone watching the melee from the window.

"We should go, too," I said, not sure why I needed Kandi in tow.

"If you haven't noticed, I'm pregnant. Last thing I need to do is be in a violent mob fight." She rubbed the silk chemise, where I still couldn't see any visible sign of this magnificent pregnancy.

"Violent mob? They were picketing, nice and quiet, minding their own business. Why would someone have called the police?" I immediately thought of Jasper. He'd been a no-show all day. After he'd rescued me from the basement, I did my best not to accuse him of any wrongdoing.

"Not so nice and quiet now." She folded her arms over her chest and lifted one of her already overarched brows.

I arrived outside just in time to see a police officer throwing a young woman down to the pavement. The police officer lifted his arm back, holding a small black gadget like a remote control. I realized it was a stun gun.

"What are you doing? Stop." I grabbed his arm. He gave me a shove with his elbow. The pain rose through my chest. I lost my balance and landed on my butt bone. I got up, angrier than I'd started, and lunged in his direction. I was grabbed before I could sink my nails into the officer, which, looking back on things, wouldn't have been a good idea with the Taser in the police officer's hand ready to do some testing.

"Calm down." I felt a grip tighten around my waist while I kicked and struggled. Clint was holding me back.

"Why are the police here?" I huffed. "Who called the police?"

"I don't know. But you getting arrested won't help. Calm down."

"This is crazy. I need to talk to someone." I raised my voice. "To whoever is in charge. Who is responsible for this?" I screamed.

"V, back up. Stop it." Clint pressed a firm hand around the back of my neck like I was a puppy being carried off by a doggy parent.

"No! This is crazy. Someone did this. Someone is trying to destroy this hospital." I instinctively looked up to see Kandi still in the second-floor window. Before I could say what I was truly thinking, I felt my wrists being grabbed.

"Ma'am, you're going to have to take a seat over here."

Clint quickly intervened. "Hold on, now, she didn't do anything."

"She attacked an officer." The thick-chinned policeman wrapped the plastic tie around my wrist and pulled tight.

I gritted my teeth and tried hard not to say another word. A television camera was headed in our direction. The officer sat me down near the others on the entry curb. I put my face down as far as I could hide, pushing my chin into my chest. We stood idly by as protesters started being cuffed with plastic bands around their wrists.

I recognized the newscaster, the woman with the red

hair and rosy cheeks to match. She stood off to the side and said a few words then led the camera to scan the embattled faces.

"Do you think this protest will help save Jackson Memorial?" She put the microphone to the face of the young man sitting next to me. He didn't respond. "What about you, miss? Do you mind answering a few brief questions?"

I didn't look up but felt the camera angled over my head.

"Miss Parson, right? I believe you handle public relations for Jackson Memorial. You mind explaining what happened here today?"

I prayed hard for her to go away. Being caught on film like a detained prisoner was not good PR.

"I'll answer any questions you have." I heard Clint looming over us both.

"Yes. And you are?" The newscaster flew to his attention like red meat cast in an ocean full of sharks. She was determined to eat him alive first before the others picked up on it.

"I'm Dr. Fairchild, the Department Chair of Pediatrics and Neonatal." He started off slow and meticulous. Then the tone changed to fast and passionate. I was tempted to look up, wondering if this was the same man who only days ago had given defeat the upper hand. "This hospital has saved more lives than any other facility in this county. The doctors here are dedicated to their community and know what it's like to have grown up without decent health care. None of us want to see that happen to the many children in this area." Shark meat he was not.

I finally got the nerve to lift my head. Three or four cameras were pointed in Clint's direction, and he was ready for round two. One camera was pointed at me. I stared into the black lens only a second before putting my head back down. All I could hope was that Jake wasn't watching the news. This was definitely going to fall in the irrational column.

Sounds Like Mail

We were a battered bunch. Everyone sat hunched over in chairs, on the floor, or standing against the wall. The holding cell was one big room with a tiny window and a posted sign in black and white, GIGI'S BAILBONDS AT AFFORDABLE RATES. The barred gate that should have been closed and locked was slid half open. Our group wasn't a flight risk. By the looks of things, no one was headed anywhere. We were honest criminals, if there were such a thing, the kind that paid their fines and scooted over to make room for new inmates.

The phone rang forever it seemed before Jake picked up. He answered on a bad connection. "You're a snail?"

"No, I said in *jail*. . . . Where are you, why can't you hear me?"

"You've got mail?" He was beginning to sound facetious, and this was no time to play around.

"Jake, I need my ID. I've been arrested."

"You're in jail?" he said, finally getting it.

"Yes."

Silence followed on both our parts. I refused to speak again. Not until I heard what he was thinking.

"How in the world?"

"I'll tell you later. I have to get out of here, and they won't let me leave until I can show some ID."

"You'll tell me now."

"There was a commotion at the hospital. I stepped in to help a girl who was being harassed by the police."

"You interfered while someone was being arrested."

"No. Well, yes. Absolutely. The police guy was twisting her arm and shoving her. When I tried to help, he turned around and arrested me."

Silence.

"I can't leave until I show them a picture ID. I left my purse in my office at the hospital." I was doing my best not to get choked up. "Can you bring my old ID, or my passport?"

"Too busy getting arrested?"

"Yeah, okay, too busy getting arrested. Can you just bring it?" I heard a voice in the background. A female voice. "Where are you?" I asked, this time really wanting to know.

"Jake," I whispered when he didn't respond. The phone went dead. I pushed the button to dial again. The phone was gently pried from my hands.

"There's a line." The skinny police officer with bad acne all over his chin nodded past me. I followed his vision to the endless line of first-time offenders.

"I have to call my husband back . . . really quick. We got cut off."

"Sorry, it'll have to be after everyone else has had their chance."

"But . . ." I moved out of line and sat down. Next to me was the young woman I'd like to think I rescued. She had no visible signs of damage, but she held her wrist cradled against her chest.

"You all right?" I asked.

"It's twisted, not broken."

"Why in the world were they trying to arrest you? I just can't figure that out."

"I can't figure it out either." She stared straight ahead and shrugged her thin shoulders. We weren't doing anything. Most of us were there to get credit in our Pan-African Studies class. We were supposed to find a just cause and participate in effective change." She rolled her eyes.

"So why were the police called?"

"I don't know. We were minding our business, quiet as church mice. All of a sudden the police pull up in full riot gear and everything. We stopped to stare. Anthony was with us—he's in my class. He dropped his sign and started booking. We're all like, Why is Anthony running? The cops swooped on him and dragged him back like a runaway slave. I will admit, when they brought him back with a busted mouth and giant knot on his forehead, some of us got a little rowdy."

"So they came after him."

"They couldn't have. All that was after the fact. Up till then, there was no reason for a team of police to be there. And Anthony, he's just like that. He's afraid of LAPD. He thinks they're out for one thing, to serve and protect, and break a black man's neck," she said almost to a beat. I looked around and hoped no one else heard even though it was a consensus the police department would never live down after the Rodney King debacle.

"He didn't do anything except run. They didn't have to beat him up like that just 'cause he ran."

I nodded.

"Thanks again. I mean, you didn't have to step in like that."

"No problem. I'd do it again if I had the chance. I wouldn't change a thing." I bit the inside of my jaw.

Maybe I'd bring my purse next time. Use pepper spray instead of trying to jump on an officer's back. Then he couldn't have seen me. Better yet, maybe I could've screamed in her defense instead of physically jumping in. Pain was creeping up the center of my spine where the officer had practically slung me down on my butt.

"Shavonda Miller!"

The young woman I'd been speaking with stood up. The lady officer with a huge beehive bun on top of her head waved a hand forward. "Shavonda Miller, you're free to go."

"See you around," Shavonda said.

Something told me it was quite the opposite. I wouldn't be seeing her ever, at least not on the picket line. "Take care," I whispered, since she was already gone.

I let my head fall in my hands and decided sitting in jail overnight might be better than dealing with Jake's attitude. Seeing him smirk and hearing "I told you so" would be torture.

"Venus Johnston-Parson," the loud woman with the bun yelled. I stood up like a jack-in-the-box.

"Me. Here. Yes." I moved quickly, expecting to see my husband looking perturbed but forgiving.

"You're free to go." The female police officer pointed me to the exit sign. She stamped my hand and told me to show it to the officer at the exit. The red ink said, FREE. I had to stop myself from cracking up. I was far from free; I was in a pot of scalding hot water.

"Venus."

I turned around confused, shuddering from the loss of balance. It was Clint who took a step toward me, holding my purse at his side. "You okay?"

"Thank you. How did you know I needed my ID?"

"I called the station." Clint handed me my purse. "They said they would let you go on your own recognizance if you could prove who you were." He tilted his head. "I figured your purse had to be in your office."

"Right. Thank you." I clutched the bag to my chest, wondering if he'd seen the nasty note I'd written about Kandi inside. Not so much a note, but scribbles of evil defeat and doom. At least I'd folded it up in tiny origami squares. It would've taken a bit of energy on his part of open it up and read. "Thank you. Thanks a lot." I walked fast, showing the police officer my stamped hand. I pushed past the double doors with Clint right on my heels.

"I better get going."

"I'll take you. You need a ride, right?"

"No. I better not. I'll get a taxi."

"Let me give you a ride, V."

I thought about it, looking up and down the dark city street, wondering if Jake was on his way.

"I better not. Thank you, though." I watched Clint go, then craned my neck up and down the street, looking past cars like a child waiting for her late parent to pick her up. After waiting nearly an hour, I finally called the Yellow Cab Company.

Inside the house it was freezing. The air conditioner running on full blast while it was even colder outside. I moved cautiously to Mya's room, stopping on the way to adjust the thermostat in the hallway. Most homes near the beach had no air-conditioning at all. Jake made sure his house was filled with every bell and whistle, including the cameras angled on each entrance. Paranoia, I'd called it. He called it security.

Another chill rushed through me. This time it was fear. A strange instinct came over me that made the hairs rise on my arms. I pushed Mya's door open, and the hall light beamed on her. She lay asleep on her back. I moved closer and watched her chest rise and fall with each breath. She was at an angle with her head touching the corner of her crib. Her long shiny lashes fluttered but stayed closed. Such an angel when she was sleeping. My angel. I pulled the cover up around her shoulders. I wanted to pick her up and kiss all over her face, so grateful to be home, but I knew one thing for sure. If I woke her, she wasn't going back to sleep.

As I pulled her door closed, Jake was coming up the stairs.

"I see you made it home," he said.

I heard the door close downstairs, Trina leaving. I didn't see her anywhere when I'd come in. Jake went straight to our bedroom, tossing his keys and wallet on the dresser. He sat on the edge of the bed to take off his shoes. "I went to the police station." He pulled out the blue leatherbound passport and held it up. "By the time I got there, you were already gone."

Guilt nudged me to take a step toward him. "I waited over an hour. I thought you were too mad. I didn't think you were coming."

"And what, you thought I'd leave you there?" He sucked his teeth and took a long deep breath. "I'm going to bed."

The rest of the night was a wordless tango. A silent fight. Tossing and turning under the covers. Low heavy deep breaths. I lay awake, staring at the back of Jake's head, wondering what I'd say when he eventually would ask, *How'd you get your ID to be released?* I walked, I ran, I flew, back to the hospital, the little witch that I am, just hopped on my little broomstick and flew. A far better answer than saying Clint rescued me. Things were out of control.

Duty Calls

I woke up ready to tackle another day at the asylum. I jumped out of bed loaded with determination. Things were going to change around Jackson Memorial, I vowed to myself. I tiptoed toward the bathroom.

"Where you going?" Jake asked, as if the last couple of weeks had all been a bad dream.

"I have to go to work," I said. "Remember, I have a job."

He rose up on his elbows, his bare chest beckoning me to climb back into bed with him. I did just that. I straddled him then traced his firm sculpted lips with my finger before meeting them with a kiss. His hands worked diligently, positioning himself for entry and not bothering to test for clearance. From the urgency of my kiss, it was obvious the fire was already lit. He plunged inside, sending ripples of desire up the curve of my spine. His hands cupped my hips while he thrust deeper without warning. I tried to pull back to release some of the pressure.

"Don't," he said, grasping me tighter.

I gripped his shoulders, preparing for the bull ride. Each slow thrust moved deeper and more tantalizing than the first. Jake sustained the rhythm, making certain

I knew who was in control. It didn't matter that I was the one on top. He wanted it absolutely understood.

"Look at me." He grabbed my wrists and pulled me down chest to chest. I clutched the nape of his neck and wrapped my mouth against his, tasting the light salt from his perspiration. I controlled as much movement as I could with the muscles in my pelvis, but it was nothing compared to the dance Jake led.

He flipped me over on my back, not missing a beat. I stared into the solid wall of his wide smooth chest, preparing myself for the strength and power of his passion. The total package, full, warm, strong, and graceful. He unleashed pulsating thrusts riveting through my body. I was in a dizzying state of arousal and then he suddenly stopped.

"Have a nice day at work," he whispered. He slipped out, wet and glistening.

"But . . . wait a minute." I was a babbling fool. "Honey?" I watched as he got up and went into the bathroom. The shower came on, and I was still in a state of disbelief.

I got up and followed him. The frosted glass still revealed his perfect brown body. He soaped up his hair and stuck his head under the blast of water.

"Jake, what was that about?"

"Nothing. I didn't want you to be late for work," he said over the sound of water.

I swallowed hard. "No, honey, really, what was that about?"

The water shut off. The door slid open. I was a dizzy mess, staring at his hard body, dripping wet. Shame on me, but I was still ready to pick up where we'd left off.

"Like I said, you're a working girl now. You have priorities." He wrapped himself with a towel and moved along as if I wasn't standing there. And soon enough I wasn't.

* * *

"Good morning." Trina was fresh as the morning. Her usual loose-fitting jeans were replaced with a cute hoodie track suit. She stood in the middle of the kitchen watching the early-morning news. Every station started with the same story. Jackson Memorial was the subject of an emergency review by the county board of supervisors.

"I thought you were turning things around over there."

"Getting there." I was already dressed and ready to head out. My pantyhose felt itchy and my skirt hugged too tight. The day was going to be long.

Jake walked in carrying Mya. "Look who I found awake."

"They keep showing you on the news. Look, there you go again." Trina picked up the remote and punched the level of volume. It was the press conference the day after the picketers' arrest. Me standing at the podium looking like I was playing dress-up in my mother's clothes. It was difficult to hear and watch. I thought I looked nervous and unsure of myself. My words shook like small afterquakes. My eyes were wide with false confidence.

"You look good up there. I'm proud to know you." Trina moved around faster than usual. She quickly poured a fresh-squeezed glass of orange juice, then a cup of coffee.

"Yep, you look like you know what you're doing, sweets. A few more of those press conferences and you could run for mayor." Jake was fast on his comebacks, always had been. Smart. A smart-ass now, it seemed.

"Eggs coming up, Jay."

I switched the channel to cartoons. Wilma Flintstone was telling Fred she was going to work whether he liked it or not. Caveman days were over!

Trina set the toasted bagel with an over-easy egg in front of *Jay*. She placed the glass of orange juice next to the plate, then disappeared with Mya, claiming she needed to get her cleaned up and dressed.

The kitchen was immediately sapped of energy without Trina. I sat next to Jake but not too close. There was a serious barrier between us. "Tell me what you want me to do, and be honest. I just can't believe you're this angry about me getting arrested. It was serious. The girl couldn't have weighed more than ninety pounds, and this policeman was going to use a stun gun on her."

His only response was to take a sip, letting the hot steam swirl around his blank eyes.

"All this animosity is all about me, Jake. It doesn't make any sense. You're really scaring me." I cautiously reached out and touched his shoulder. "I'm here for you. No matter where I work or what I do, I am one hundred percent your wife, your friend."

He bit into his bagel and chewed a moment before speaking. "I don't need any more friends," he said. "I just need my wife. Go to work, sweets. I want you to be happy and fulfilled." He made a quick smile then continued chewing.

There was a magic rabbit hiding underneath his statement. Use of the proper buzzwords, *happy* and *fulfilled,* scared me like I was walking close to a huge cliff while he waited patiently for me to fall off, landing on jagged rocks below.

"I love you," he said, this time with more sincerity. "That's the bottom line. I don't want you to feel inadequate in any way." He drank his coffee, picked up the remote, and clicked the channel. Once again a fresh round of stations showing Jackson Memorial in various stages, my original press conference, followed by the arrests of innocent picketers, including myself. Right before the camera panned on Clint restraining me by my waist, I reached over Jake and clicked the power off. I gave a cautious glance to see if he'd noticed. He blankly stared straight ahead, unfazed.

I, on the other hand, was fuming. "You want me to quit? I'll quit," I said, really meaning it. I was beat. Exhausted on the battlefield. All the work I was putting in seemed to be netting no results. The neonatal department still had a close date within two weeks. Where would the babies go? Which department was next . . . until it was nothing more than a clinic offering shots for STDs?

"Nah, too late for all of that. I can see you're needed. Do your thing, sweets."

The better part of me wanted to sit by his side, and I did, for an extra five wordless minutes. Then I checked my watch, a huge mistake.

"Don't let me keep you," he snapped.

I stood up, pulled my keys out of my purse, and took my happy, fulfilled self to work.

Try Me

The morning sun was still hiding behind the San Gabriel Mountains when I left the house. I cried all the way to the hospital, wondering how to fix the mess I'd made. Quitting wouldn't solve the real problem.

I'd asked for this life, begged and prayed for it. I'd wanted to be married with babies with the ideal man by my side. Then the universe and God collaborated and had given me the full picture, not one item missing from the list, and yet I couldn't have felt more lifeless. Maybe it was the independence I was afraid of losing. Not once had I ever asked anyone to take care of me. Working at the sweet age of sixteen, I did clerical duty for an insurance company three days a week after school. On the weekends I babysat. Money earned I saved for nothing in particular, only the joy of not having to ask anyone for a dime. The joy of knowing my mother would have no say in my choice of back-to-school clothes. Proud I didn't have to have a consulting war with Pauletta on the overpriced Bongo jeans with rips on the knee. "Why pay sixty dollars for tore-up jeans," she'd asked, disgusted. "You can get those down at the thrift store for three dollars." Straight out of high school, I even bought my own car. A beat-up Honda painted with four different shades of blue. I bought the gas that went into it and even chipped in on the insurance costs. It felt good. Right. Decent.

When I met Jake, I was an independent woman. At least financially. He respected the fact that I had a career, even admired the work I'd done as a marketing guru, seeking out my services specifically for JP Wear.

The emotional landscape was a completely different story. I'd just found out my mother was diagnosed with breast cancer. Airic, my fiancé at the time, was charged with securities fraud by the SEC. I'd had a run-in with Clint that tossed me back in a black hole I'd worked diligently to climb out of. A wreck is what I was. An emotional glob of instability. Jake fixed me. Simple enough. He applied direct healing on every wound and he fixed me.

The very reason I fell in love with him—he wasn't afraid of anything. He had the strength and resolve, to make everything all better. It didn't matter that he was younger than I. He was truly the most mature, loving man I'd ever known besides my own father. I pulled inside the hospital parking garage. I had the pick of the lot, right between a handicapped space no one ever used and the cinder block keeping people out of the loading zone. I dabbed my eyes, preparing to get out of the car and deal with the other problems I seemed to have wrought upon myself. The rest of the hospital staff would be along shortly. I walked a few quick steps then realized I hadn't locked my car. I stopped and pointed my key ring in the direction of my car and pushed the button. The echo of the alarm being set twisted in my ear, much louder than usual from the emptiness of the concrete housing.

Then the echo of another sound kicked in, punching,

hitting. Sounds of someone getting a good old-fashioned ass-whuppin'. Moans with each connecting blow.

"Next time . . . Ah, what am I saying, won't be no next time." The heavy voice barked, "Cash and carry, muthafucka. I want what I paid for."

One last slap for good measure. I swallowed the lump in my throat. I pushed myself against the thick concrete column to become invisible. Footsteps headed in my direction. I scrambled inside my purse for my cell phone. Before flipping it open, I stopped myself. The digital voice would ask loudly, *"who would you like to call?"* Instead I dropped the phone and felt for the leather case of pepper spray I'd never used. Bought so long ago, I wasn't even sure if it worked. Did pepper spray have an expiration date?

I felt spindly fingers climb around my shoulder, then a pinch of pain. "Lost?" the man said.

"What?" My mouth was dry. "Excuse me?"

"You heard what I said." The man spoke too closely, spraying me ever so lightly with foul breath. We were face-to-face, eye-to-eye. My only assessment was that he had to have been beating on a woman. He was too small to be a real threat to another man. I gripped the tubular case, thumbing the safety shield off.

"Get away from me," I finally screamed. "Get the hell away!" I pulled out the pepper spray and pointed it at him like I meant business, and I did.

"Just passing through," he said, darting glances past me, to the sides, and back to me. "Have a nice day." He stuck his hands in his pockets and whistled as he casually walked into the overcast dawn.

I ran in the direction of the moans. A pair of legs and feet squirmed from behind a car. I approached with caution.

"Jasper! Oh my God, Jasper."

He rolled over, still scrunched in a ball, holding his ribs. His face was swollen. Blood smeared across his mouth and nose. His glasses were twisted, hanging on his badly bruised ear.

"I'll get help."

"No. Please. No, I'm okay." Jasper's thick fingers weakly grasped my sleeve. I knew someone this badly beaten up with possibly broken bones shouldn't be moved by an amateur like myself. More important, all I could think of were the bloodstains he was about to leave on my cream-colored three-quarter-length jacket. I even had on the cream leather boots to match. Okay. This was serious.

"Jasper, I have to go get help. Don't move. Please, I'll be right back."

I trotted inside the emergency entrance and straight through to the triage. I grabbed a young resident who looked like he should still be in high school. I'd seen him, Dr. Warner, a few times in the cafeteria and around the hospital. He in turn brought one of the nurses, and they hurried behind me back to the parking garage.

"He's over here. Wait. No. Maybe he was over . . ." The parking garage was empty enough to see in every direction.

The car was gone, and so was Jasper.

"We better tell someone." Dr. Warner said, "At least the police can go to his house and check on him."

I stood dumbfounded. "Why would he leave? You should have seen him—he was a mess. He needed stitches. His ribs were cracked, the way he was holding himself." I shook my head. "Doesn't make any sense."

"You sure the guy didn't come back and take the car? Usually carjackers just want the car. They only beat the person down when they're in the way. Maybe Dr. J hobbled inside." The nurse folded his thick arms over his chest. Each forearm was covered in a bevy of tattoos. He was built and athletic and looked like he'd seen his share of trouble in his former life.

"No. No. It wasn't about a carjacking. It wasn't about the car. The guy walked off without it anyway. He was long gone by the time I went in for help. The guy acted like Jasper owed *him* money." I pointed to the darkened spot on the concrete. "Look. See. There's blood."

"Doctor, heal thyself," the nurse said under his breath. He kneeled down to get a closer look. "Maybe the old doc rather get medical attention somewhere else. Don't trust Jack the Ripper."

"I assume you don't go around using that euphemism?" Dr. Warner let out an agitated sigh. "I'm sorry. I have to get back," His professionalism superceded his youthfulness. "If you need me, you know where I'll be."

I turned my attention back to the nurse. "You knew Jasper when he was practicing here?"

"Oh yeah, wasn't that long ago."

"Well, no one else seems to know. What happened? Why isn't he practicing medicine anymore?"

"They know. Everybody knows. Just uptight like the young Dr. Warner there. Another blemish they'd prefer to keep off the record. Got a image to maintain, but the image is pretty much shot right between the eyes."

"Okay." I goaded, "Jasper Calloway?"

"The good doctor was caught playing house with little boys."

"Patients?" I said, horrified, as if the crime could be made any worse.

"Well, one patient they're sure of. A boy, fourteen. He was hospitalized in pediatrics where Dr. J was in charge."

"Please don't call him that," I said, squinting from the association.

"Okay, Dr. Jasper. People sure are sensitive to the name game around here."

"I'm sorry to interrupt. Go on. The boy was a patient."

"Yep. Family had some serious dough. They had planned to donate a wing and everything, feeling like the care and facilities of this great establishment brought their son back to life. The kid had sickle-cell," he said, putting a rough knuckle to his chin. "Sickle-cell. Yeah, I'm sure. Anyway, the kid ends up killing himself."

By this time the parking lot had begun to fill up with staff. "What? How? Why?"

"Hey, Big C, whad up, dog?"

"Nothing but you, man." The nurse, Big C, gave a little nod.

The morning staff was starting to arrive.

"You mind if we go to the cafeteria and finish?"

"Not much else to tell. The kid killed himself. The parents found some Internet diary on his computer about his undying love for the good doctor. The parents were furious, ready to shut the whole place down. Lawsuit. Prison for Dr. J—oh, my bad. Anyway, the hospital made a deal with the family that he'd never practice medicine again and would never be near children. Only way they could guarantee that is if they kept him right here where they could keep an eye on him. He can't leave and go work somewhere else, ever, or everybody will suffer, ya know what I mean. It's like he's chained here like some kind of yard dog. Can't get off the playground."

"Why didn't the family just crush him? Send him to prison? I would've, if it was my son."

"Pride. People like that don't want the world knowing something like that about their boy. You know how we do. Pride," he said again, extending one of his thick arms. The tattoos were more visible. A cross. Words,

JESUS SAVED MY LIFE. "By the way, I'm Calvin—or C, if you will."

"Venus. Or V, if you will. Thanks for talking to me."

"No problem. I've seen you on TV trying to look all hard and about business. But you a little cutie."

"Thank you, Calvin, C, Big C," I corrected. "Thanks a lot."

"Anytime. Don't be a stranger."

"I won't." I waved. He fell in step with a few nurses arriving for morning duty. He threw a satisfying arm around one woman as they walked. I thought about Jasper and what a despicable thing he did. A patient. A boy. Wrong. Disgusting. He deserved to get his ass beat. Maybe? All I knew for sure is that it made sense now. Jasper had to be the one sabotaging the hospital. He was angry enough to do it. Hell, I'd be angry, too, a prisoner with no hopes of ever getting out.

Implicated

Clint peeked inside. "You're here. I heard about what happened this morning." He kept his hands in his pockets and seemed to look over his shoulder before coming inside. "Must've really shaken you up."

"I'm fine. I don't know whether to wish Jasper well or hope he's laying dead somewhere. Knowing what he did, having a relationship with a child. Gives me the creeps that I had to share an office with him. I just hope he doesn't come back. You know, this proves what I've been telling you all along. He's been sabotaging this hospital."

Clint's mind seemed to be drifting. "Yeah," he said, peeking over his shoulder a couple of times.

I got up and did what he didn't have the nerve to do. I closed the door. "Afraid the missus will see you?"

"You have no idea."

"I think I do." I sympathized but only briefly.

Clint responded quickly, "This hospital is the most important thing in my . . ." He paused and thought about what he was trying to say. "Some things are worth fighting for." His skin, usually the color of ripe darkened berries, seemed a little dull except for the beads of moisture that suddenly appeared on the bridge of his nose. His shaven head glistened with perspiration as well. "We have the staff meeting. I'll see you there."

"Yeah, see you there."

He left my office, peeking first then stepping out the doorway with caution.

I closed the door behind him. Goodness, was all I could say. Kandi had the man scared for his life.

"You've been working overtime, I see?" Speak of the She-whore. Kandi pulled her fullness into my office. She pushed the door a small ways closed.

"Oh, you just missed your hubby," I said, as if she didn't know. "He just wanted to brief me on a couple of things before the staff meeting." I took a deep breath. "Kandi, I don't know why I'm making up excuses. I'm just going to be honest with you. There is absolutely no interest between Clint and me, none whatsoever. I don't want you to be concerned, or stressed about it, especially with you being pregnant."

"Do you think I'm stupid? You think I'm falling for this act. Of course you want Clint."

"Excuse me?"

"Excuse you is all I've done." She pushed my office door all the way closed.

"Kandi, honestly. I don't think this conversation is a good idea." I attempted to go around her and she wouldn't budge.

She was a solid head taller than me. "If you were thinking at all, you would've never come here. Why are you even here?" she asked mildly.

"Okay, this really isn't supposed to be happening."

"No, it isn't. You're not supposed to be here." Kandi tried to smile, but her lip quivered. "You may get this job, but I'm still in the position you really want to be in. Don't even try to fake it. Let it go, Venus, for once and for all." She shook her head and coughed out a sarcastic laugh. "I don't even know why I'm worried. Look at you. Nothing much has changed. I never could see what Clint saw in you. The rapper's girlfriend, now that's a stretch." She scrunched up her nose in disgust.

"The rapper's *wife*. If you're going to try to be insulting, get it right."

"I don't have to try, it's actually quite easy. I mean really, look at you and look at me. There was no contest then, and there's no contest now."

"Then *why* are you so worried? If you've got it all together, why is my being here such a threat?"

To my shock, she reached out and put her finger in my face. "You don't want this job. When are you going to let him go, Venus? You and Clint are history. They say it takes as many years to end a relationship as the time you spent in the relationship. Time's up. You're done. Four for four. I'm standing here with a baby in my stomach. Clint and I are happy together. There is no need for you to continue popping up every time you're not happy in your own state of affairs."

I kept my arm and hands entwined against my chest. My heart beat wildly against my ribs. "You better get that finger out of my face 'cause I'm about three seconds from kicking your ass."

"I wish you'd try," she said.

I shook my head and threw up my hands. "I feel sorry for you. I truly do."

Her big eyes crystallized. She tried to blink the moistness away. In our fiery conversation, I hadn't realized how close we'd gotten: nose to nose, nearly toe to toe.

I backed up and went around her. "If you want to talk about something besides Clint, you're more than welcome to come back."

She cut her eyes. "I'm not going anywhere. And I mean that in every possible way."

If looks could kill, we both would've been laid out on the floor. But the staring contest was wearing me down. I grabbed my purse and left her standing in my tiny office as I snatched the door closed behind me.

The conference room filled until it was standing room only. I was among the lucky ones to get there fast enough to have a seat. Kandi circled twice, cradling her belly before someone finally gave up a seat out of compassion. She graciously accepted. Clint and the heads of their departments were already seated around the large table.

Morgan stood in the front of the room. "Now this is the kind of enthusiasm that's going to save this hospital. Thank you for coming." She rested her hands together in prayer. "We have been invited to the health commission's overview hearings this week in Washington, D.C. We're going to propose the privatization of Jackson Memorial."

A few claps and a whole lot of "thank gods" carried across the room.

"I'm not saying this will solve our problems, but it will be a start in the right direction. I first want to acknowledge Venus Johnston, who came up with the brilliant idea. She did a full proposal on the good, the bad, and the ugly, and I must say the good outweighs them all. So I'm asking her to go to Washington, D.C., to represent us. Does anyone have a problem with that?"

Morgan took a moment to look around. "Secondly, I'd like one of you to go with her, offer the credibility of actually being in the trenches, the effort and integrity component." Once again she looked around. A tall lean man with graying sideburns raised his hand.

"If we're voting, I'd like to nominate Dr. Fairchild. He's the newest among us, but I have to say his dedication and enthusiasm give him the upper hand. Besides, he's not burnt out like the rest of us." A few chuckles came from behind. Everyone nodded and moaned in agreement.

My eyes never left Kandi's. She looked like she was drowning but no one could save her. What she didn't know is that I was drowning, too. I couldn't go out of town with Clint. Of all the craziness I'd pulled in the last few weeks, that would definitely seal my doom.

"Is there anyone else who would like to be considered?" Morgan eyed the group. "Then we all agree. Dr. Fairchild, would you do us the honor of representing us in Washington, D.C.?"

Under the gun was an understatement. Clint looked around as if he were faced with twenty shining rifles all pointed and ready to fire. He stood up, apologetic. I already knew the answer, especially having just dealt with Kandi's wrath. Clint stretched himself to get through the crowd and finally visible. "I'd be honored to go and speak on Jackson Memorial's behalf. It's just that . . ." He paused. Kandi softened with relief, anticipating what he would say next.

"While I'm gone I'm going to need a promise from everybody here to step it up and guard my babies with their lives."

Devastated, Kandi looked like she was about to faint. The rest of the group let out relieved sighs. The mainstay of tension melted away with hopes of sunlight at the end of a long dark tunnel. Dr. Clint could save them.

"Don't worry about it, Dr. Fairchild, we got your back," someone voiced.

"Your babies will be in good hands," another voice said from the rear.

"How much damage can we do in a couple of days?"

The room went silent. "Let's not go there," Morgan chimed in.

I felt Kandi staring at me the entire time. I let my eyes slide over to hers and saw fury. I dropped my eyes and turned my attention back to Clint. I wanted to mouth the words, *Are you crazy,* but knew she was drinking in my every move. So I clapped and nodded, too. But there was no way we could leave town together.

Clint rubbed a hand over his smooth shaven head and turned to his wife. "Baby, it's up to you. You need to watch my babies, 'cause I don't know about these guys." He reached over a few broad bodies and kissed her lovingly. "Can you handle it?"

She forced a smile in the cusp of his forearm. "Sure." I could see she wanted to cry but held it in. The crowd cheered. She feigned embarrassment by the display of affection then immediately raised a threatening eyebrow in my direction.

Now what? I was thinking. How in the world was I going to be able to explain this? After Jake had already accused me of wanting to be next to Dr. Ex-Lova, now we'd be on a plane and in a hotel alone together. It just wasn't going to happen.

I stood up. "Um, excuse me."

The group of doctors slowly quieted to hear what I had to say.

"Well, I certainly appreciate Dr. Fairchild taking out time to go in front of the commission. But . . . I can assure you, I can handle the job."

Morgan cleared her throat. "I think it's necessary. We'll put all our personal issues aside and handle business as it should be handled," she said with slightly gritted teeth. "I'm sure Mrs. Fairchild understands what's at stake here."

The rest of the group looked mystified, wondering what underlying drama they'd missed.

I took a deep breath. "The important thing is that the message get across that this hospital is worth saving. I think I can do that."

Morgan stood up. "I know you can, and thank goodness we'll have Dr. Fairchild to also get the message across. I'm going to close this meeting. I know everyone here has important things to do."

I sat down feeling doomed.

No way out.

Several hands slipped encouraging squeezes to my shoulder as they passed. They probably didn't realize I needed every good wish they could offer. Kandi passed in a huff. Couldn't she see I'd given it my best shot? Couldn't she see I wasn't thrilled about the idea either? Hell hath no fury like a woman scorned, and soon I'd know how much.

Two Wives Club

I arrived home ready to throw myself on the mercy of the court. Jake was going to have to understand my predicament. The entire hospital was depending on me. If I didn't go before the health commission and present the case for Jackson Memorial, I feared they wouldn't get the funding to privatize. I would feel responsible, as if I'd failed an entire community.

I practiced my humble pie speech, relishing briefly in the common sense of it all before being hit by a very distinct smell throughout the house. I kicked my shoes off quickly at the door and sniffed lightly at first, and then a second time, identifying the distinct scent of fried food. *In my house!*

I knew the smell well. Buttery and tart, swearing to stick to everything in its path. My father was the king of fried fish. He cooked it outside because my mother pitched a fit about the grease splatters ruining her walls and grouted tile.

I followed the scent straight to Trina in the kitchen. Music was blaring. She bounced to the beat of 50 Cent "In da Club," singing along where she could and humming the rest. Her jeans fit better, revealing a shapely bottom and athletic thighs. Her T-shirt was knotted at the waist.

She spun around and dipped a fleshy piece of fish into a flour mixture. After punching it around, she transported it into the hungry grease. She caught sight of me. "Hey there, how was your day?"

"You're frying fish?" was all I could say before instinctively peeking up at the white ceiling and the many inset lights that would be a bitch to clean. Then to the stainless steel refrigerator, dishwasher, and stove, wondering if she realized this was a job even the Brawny man couldn't handle.

"Don't worry, I'll clean it up. I just couldn't resist," she said, following my concerned eyes. "Found this in the freezer and thought, mmm, I haven't had fish in weeks. If I remember, Jake loves him some fried fish. Catfish, but you know, one sea creature is as good as another."

"But it's Chilean sea bass, Trina. Nine dollars a pound. You grill it, you sear it, you bake it. You don't fry it."

She came toward me with a white meaty chunk flanked by a light fluffy batter. I said no thanks, but the sample piece found its way into the center of my tongue with the tips of her fingers to boot. Before I could spit it out, I tasted heaven.

"Mmmmm."

"Good, I know."

I moaned some more, chewed and swallowed, then waited for the next feeding. Trina grinned. "Ain't talking so tough now, are you?"

"Kaaat." Mya slapped her hands together and gave a glistening smile while she sat in her high chair. She grabbed a handful of something mashed on her plastic saucer and stuck it to her mouth.

"What's that? Is she eating fish?" I panicked and grabbed the small plate. Mya let out a wail.

"It's fish, but there's no bones. Not one," Trina said, continuing on rhythm dropping a healthy piece of battered fish into the cackling oil.

I went to remove the plate and Mya screamed at the top of her lungs. "Shhh, I'm sorry, Mya. Mommy has to look out for you." I turned around and saw a flash of hurt on Trina's face.

She turned her back to me and tended to her fish fry. I took a long deep breath and tried again. "I'm sorry for stepping on your toes. Really. It's just been a long day, and my brain is on lockdown. Really, I'm sorry."

"I understand." Trina used her shoulder to brush away the dry sprig of hair that tickled her ear. A righteous-sized diamond stud sparkled. Real, I quickly surmised from the setting.

"Those are pretty."

"Oh, yeah, thanks," Trina said, as if she'd forgotten she was wearing two karats in each ear.

Of course my second question was, *Where'd you get rocks that size?* though I stopped myself. Nor did she feel the need to volunteer the information. She must have felt me staring and used her shoulder to put the hair back in place.

"What's that smelling so good?" Jake came into the kitchen completely ignoring me and went straight to the steaming plate of freshly fried fish. He picked off the same piece I'd tasted. "Oh-ma-gawd. Umph."

"I'm going to take a quick shower." I headed upstairs still hearing Jake's praises of Trina's cooking. A few lip smacks, some overblown *umphs,* and a *whew* for good measure.

After my bath I came out feeling relaxed and light. I wrapped my robe tight, ready for round two of Trina's fried delight. I heard laughter as I got closer to the kitchen, Jake's honest belt of amusement traveled the halls and rose above the stairs.

"Hi." I arrived, just missing what was so funny. I looked between them. Jake's long lashes blinked slowly while he avoided eye contact. Trina sat across from him while Mya used the milk from her sipper cup to make finger paint on the high chair tray. The three of them looked like a full-fledged family. No missing parts.

"You ready for a plate?" Trina asked, wiping the corners of her mouth. She got up from the table, taking his empty plate and glass. "The macaroni and cheese is going to knock your socks off. Isn't it good, Jay?"

"Exquisite."

I took the seat she left and sat beside him. I waited until he finished chewing then leaned in for a kiss. Trina reached across my face and set the plate full of food down in front of me.

"You want some hot sauce with that?"

I shook my head.

"Try it with the hot sauce. It's good." Jake rubbed his lean stomach, standing up for a stretch. "Delicious, Trina. You outdid yourself." He reached into his pocket and pulled out a wad of cash. "Here you go, an early bonus."

Trina smiled. "Why you keep giving me money like some drug dealer? You don't have a bank account?"

"Do you?" Jake asked, already knowing the answer.

"No. But I plan to get one . . . if I had a check to deposit."

"I'll write you a check," I added.

"There you go—the lady of the house has spoken." Jake washed his hands at the sink, then checked his watch. "I gotta go. Thanks for dinner, Trina."

I was unable to taste the food in my mouth. Something missing this time, maybe Trina's fingers. "Where are you going?"

"I have a mixer. Trina has grease duty." Jake let a sly grin rise on his face.

"Shut up 'fore I make you do some cleaning. I bet you don't even know where the soap is."

"I know where everything is. You're forgetting before I was descended upon by all you women, there was just lil' ol'e me, and I did all right."

I was looking for the punch line, ready to laugh on cue. Trina smiled wide and flung a dish towel at him. Jake blocked it and knocked it to the floor. Any minute I thought they were going to start butt-slapping each other.

"Tell him he better be grateful for what he's got," Trina said to me, but not looking in my direction.

"Yeah, most men only have one wife." I appreciated the opportunity to play along.

Jake shot a look that said I wasn't invited to this game. "See you tomorrow, Kat."

"Later, Jay." Trina started spraying 409 on everything in sight.

There comes a time when you know a mutiny is on the rise. But you ignore it so you can go about your immediate business. I sat alone at the end of the eight-foot table and scooped food into my mouth, pretending I hadn't been snubbed publicly by *my hubby*. I ate everything on my plate, though it was tasteless from my misery. I got up and rinsed the plate.

Trina took the plate from my hand. "I got it. Aren't you going to the party?"

"Oh . . . no. It's just a mixer. I don't need to be there."

"A mixer. Jay said it was a merger party. Not that I know what a merger party is. All this business lingo has been going to my head."

What the @#$%? A merger?

Before I knew it, I was upstairs squeezing gobs of gel into my hair and pulling up the zipper to my one and only little black dress.

I came back downstairs ready to roll. "You sure you don't mind staying?"

Trina smiled. "Please. I like staying overnight here."

"If I haven't told you lately, I do appreciate you being here and taking care of Mya."

"My pleasure." She shooed me to the door, and I was on my way.

Uninvited Guest

I pulled up to the downtown building where the windows were lit on every floor. A young valet opened my car door when I pulled to the curb.

"Ma'am." He took my nervous hand, helping me rise. I threw both legs over with perfect toes in my black strappy heels and pretended I was supposed to be there. "Thank you." I pushed my shoulders back, my chin up, and walked in with manufactured confidence. To my shock everyone was wearing white. It looked like a summer party in the Hamptons. I scanned faces, thinking I wouldn't recognize my own husband in the mix. Men dressed in conservative suits but all having a bit of slick wildness in their look. Women. Women everywhere in tight white dresses or belly-baring two pieces.

I muttered hello to anyone who managed eye contact long enough with the outcast in black who obviously hadn't been invited.

Jake was nowhere in sight. Music of a lazy techo nature spun the room. Not Jake's style at all. He liked solid R & B classics, neosoul, and real jazz. I took a glass of champagne off the serving tray before it darted in another direction with the fast-moving server.

I looked for Beverly Shaun, the one familiar face I

could strike up a conversation with. Immediate relief
took over when I saw her. I tapped her on the shoulder.
She turned around. Blue eyes scanned me up and down.

"Oh, I'm sorry, I thought you were someone else."

Her piercing blue eyes focused particularly on my
hair. For a self-conscious moment I fingered the nape
of my neck, taking note that my spiral mane was still
moist from the shower and fresh gel.

"Fenny Maxwell." She extended a hand, "And you
are?"

"Venus Johnston." I extended my own nervous hand.

"Welcome," she said, as if she were the hostess with
the mostest.

"I'm sorry. You look a lot like someone else. Do you
know Beverly Shaun?"

"Beverly?" She crowded her face into a frown. "Yes,
of course. I guess it's the hair. I usually wear mine
similar to yours, but I had it straightened for this special occasion."

"Special occasion?" What Trina said earlier about a
merger came back to me.

"JP Wear and the Rocknell department store chain.
We're fifty-fifty partners now. I'm sorry, who are you
with? I'm so busy chatting, I didn't get what company
you were from."

"I'm Jake's wife."

She suddenly found me of no interest. "Well, good
to meet you." She turned her back, diving into her original conversation with her small diverse group, two
white men and an Asian woman.

I tapped Fenny Maxwell's bare shoulder. "Sorry to
interrupt. But what about Jake? Have you seen him?"

This peppered her interest. "Jay, haven't seen him.
Strange when the party boy doesn't show up to his own
bash, don't you think?"

But he'd left an hour before me. I looked around. By this time, I was breathing underwater. My heart was working overtime to keep up with the adrenaline pumping through my veins. For some reason, I couldn't control my hand when it reached up, tapping her a little harder. "I'm sorry to keep interrupting you."

She faced me as if I was taking up way too much of her time.

I licked my lips and tried to remember they were artist perfect and not to ruin my pale gloss. "So you're part of the merger?" I asked, my voice nearly failing me.

"You could say that. I put the deal together. Funny, Jay hadn't mentioned he was married."

That did it. I was ready to kick off my shoes, snatch the dangles out of my ears, and put Miss Blue-Eyed Soul in her place. "He never mentioned you either, I mean the partnership." I took short fuming breaths. My feet started to hurt. "So you haven't seen Jay all night?"

"Not once. Beverly Shaun either," she added with a smirk. "If I see either one, I'll point them in your direction."

"Thank you." I turned up the glass of champagne and swallowed until it was gone. I moved up the stairs holding my empty glass and tried to look like I was having a good time. Light came from underneath Jake's office doorway. I brushed against the long stalks of a palm like a secret agent. I waited for a few moments, thinking someone would eventually come out and I'd catch them red-handed. I squeezed my arms down to catch the small trickles of nervous perspiration. My heart beat off track.

I knocked. "Jake," I said weakly, hoping he didn't answer. No one answered. I touched the knob and turned. The door was locked. "Jake, it's Venus." I knocked harder. Listening with my ear pressed, waiting for the sound of bodies in panic, pulling up pants and zippers. Imaginary hushed voices telling each other to stay calm.

Movement. Footsteps. I stood back. The door swung open.

"Well, well, it's the missus, and wearing black. What happened, sweetheart, didn't get the memo?" The affable Legend Hill stood with his freshly twisted locks hung over the shoulders of his crisp silk-and-wool-blend suit. His bold menacing smile crept to deep lines on his chocolate rugged skin.

"What are you doing here?"

"Is that my welcome? I didn't even get a wedding invite, haven't seen you in all this time, and that's the greeting I get."

I moved past him, looking inside Jake's office. A long-legged beauty sat on the couch, waiting to resume whatever position I'd interrupted. She rolled her eyes and looked at her nails.

I turned back to face Legend. "Why are you in Jake's office? Don't you have your own?"

His deep baritone voice belted a laugh. "You lost something already?"

"Get out."

The sexy woman stood up and moved quickly to the door. Legend grabbed her by the arm. "Hold on, sweet thing. Not so fast."

"Legend, I swear, you don't want to play with me right now." Legend and I had a history that included eye-gouging and backbiting. I was just shy of kicking and swinging.

"You're probably right. You're looking out of sorts, to say the least." He took his accessory and led her out by the hand. "If I see your man anywhere, I'll be sure to send him up."

I shoved the door closed, pulled out my phone, and

dialed Jake's cell. There was no ring. Straight to voice-mail it went, meaning his phone was off. I left a message as though I were the picture of sanity. "Sweetie, I came to JP Wear studio hoping to support you and you're not here. I'm waiting in your office." I slapped the phone closed. I took a seat at Jake's desk and did what any wife would do.

I rustled through his desk drawers. I didn't know what I was looking for, it just seemed the natural thing to do. The last drawer I opened revealed something I never thought I'd see. There right on top of everything, next to the paper clips was a shiny red package, a Trojan condom. I picked it up and flipped it over in my hand.

EXPIRES 6/07, printed boldly on the edge. It was definitely a postmarriage purchase. I shoved it back in his drawer then on second thought placed it in my purse.

I turned out the lights and closed the door. The party was still in full swing. The music was charged up a notch. Bass pulsated through the floor and reverberated in my eardrum. I headed to the door. I couldn't stand another minute.

"Venus . . . wait a minute." Jake was coming toward me.

I pushed through the double doors out into the cool night air.

"I didn't know you were here." He reached out and grabbed my hand. "Legend just told me you were upstairs."

I dug in my purse and threw the condom at him. "Why was that in your desk? And don't try to tell me it's from before we were married because I swear . . ." I turned away from him.

"It's not mine."

"Oh, that's even better. And while you're searching for a better explanation, could you also go over where you've been for the last two hours, 'cause you sure as hell weren't here."

He took my hand. "Come back inside. We'll talk upstairs in my office."

"Then explain how you could sell off half of JP Wear and not even talk to me about it." I wasn't going to cry, I'd already told myself. "Which one you want to tackle first?"

"You are some piece of work, you know that? You want to talk about secrets? Not being honest, I don't think you want to go there," he said.

"I've been completely honest with you. You're the one adding in motivations, trying to make me seem conniving. I haven't lied to you about a single thing. I told you where I wanted to work. I told you why, period, end of story. No secrets. Now all of a sudden, I'm enemy number one. I'm not crazy. Don't try to pretend all of this is my imagination, Jake."

"Come inside," he said calmly.

"No, hell no. I'm going home."

"Then I'll call a cab. You're not driving drunk."

"I had one glass of champagne while I was looking for you."

"Fine." Jake started to walk away.

"Don't you dare leave me out here. Not until you tell me where you were."

"Sounds like you got it all figured out." He turned and talked to the valet before going back inside. I stayed outside, blubbering like an idiot.

I felt a quick tap on my shoulder. "Ma'am, your car." The valet had shown up with my car just as Jake told him. I looked up at the well-lit building to see if Jake was standing there, and he wasn't.

Walk of Shame

Jake and I treaded lightly around one another. So many times I thought to say, *By the way, I'm going to Washington, D.C., with Dr. Ex-Lova,* but I knew it was too late for that. He'd think I was taking revenge, acting out of spite when none of it was true. I was hurt, yes, but nothing could trump finding a condom in his desk, him being missing in action and refusing to explain his whereabouts, then worst of all selling JP Wear and not bothering to discuss it with me.

"So are you ready to talk?" I asked while we lay in bed, both pretending to be asleep.

He stayed silent.

"Then I'll talk. I admit I probably overreacted about finding the condom. You're right—it could've been Legend's. He's the one I found in your office with an unidentified female. But can you at least try to explain where you were while I was looking for you? Two hours, Jake."

"I told you I was there. How many times do I have to tell you?"

"Okay. All right. You were there, but where? I looked, I asked everybody and not one single person had seen you."

He took a long deep breath. "Do you think I'd mess

around on you? Is that what you believe? 'Cause if you do, there's nothing I can say to change it."

I wiped my eyes and tried not to sniff. I knew if I played the crybaby card, he would simply turn over and throw his arms around me and make everything all better. "And what about selling your company, and not even talking to me about it."

"That one's easy. I didn't think you cared."

"Of course I care. How could you say that?"

"I think you can figure that one out."

I couldn't fix my lips to say another word. Yes, I could figure it out. I was being punished. Fine. I only wish the punishment were tangible, like when you were a child, you're sent to your room. No television. No phone for a week. Maybe even no dessert after dinner, but good grief the silence was cruel and unusual punishment.

"I have to go to Washington, D.C., tomorrow to present a proposal to the health commission."

Silence.

"I'm coming back the following day, so it's a quick trip."

Silence.

"Okay, then . . . Jake, I've already decided to quit when I get back. I want to do the presentation because this could actually save the hospital, this one trip. But when I come back, I've decided. I'm through. I can't stand you being mad at me like this. It's not worth it." I said into the darkness. It's just not worth it. I closed my eyes and let the tear slide down into my ear.

Silence.

Up, Up, and Away

The next day I sat on the airplane, checking over the heads of seated passengers for Clint to arrive. Southwest Airlines had banished the idea of assigned seating, giving customers permission to choose their flying mates on a first-come–first-served basis. A large man with an eye for petite passengers who took up less than their share of seat space spotted me. I picked up my satchel and threw it into the seat next to me just as he arrived by my side.

"Is this seat taken?"

"Yes, sorry. My friend is in the restroom."

The man labored on. I decorated myself with various deterrents from further offers. I sat in the aisle seat and gave my coat the middle and my laptop the window. I gathered a few tissues and pretended a runny nose was giving me havoc. Saving seats had to be the worst offense, an unfair practice, leaving those who'd taken the energy and time to arrive early with fewer choices.

"Is this seat taken?" An older lady with slumped shoulders and kind wrinkled hands stopped right next to me. She looked as if one more step would do her in.

I peeked past her ratty coat, still no sign of Clint. I saw only a family of raucous children with oblivious parents who appeared anxious to get past. Behind them a steady stream of people, none of which were black guys with bald heads.

The older woman stood blocking the aisle, patient and unfazed by the irritated passengers. I gave it some thought. Clint probably wasn't coming anyway. And even if he did, he could still take the middle seat. I raised my coat with me as I stood to let her in.

"I need the aisle, dear. A woman my age can't pray about going to the restroom. It's either right then, or it's too late."

"Yes, of course." I grabbed my satchel. I piled everything into the middle seat and sat against the window. The rose scent of Jergens lotion moved into the seat with her. I stared out, watching piles of luggage rolling onto the carriage of the plane. I wondered if Clint's bag was among them.

After the plane looked like it was closing up, I accepted the fact he wasn't coming.

"Is this seat taken?" a voice asked.

Not again.

"Why yes, I think it is." The older woman said, happily taking over the dirty duty of saving seats.

I looked up to see the sparkling whites of Clint's eyes. He hadn't lost any sleep. The picture of health. I was relieved Kandi hadn't tried to poison his soup or anything.

"He's with me." I moved my bag and coat out of the way.

"Hold on, I'll get up in a moment, dear, then you can slide on in." The older woman gripped the headrest in front of her with a feeble hand while she tried to stand up. After a few attempts, Clint put out his hand and she took a hold. "Thank you, you're a dear." Clint climbed in and shoved his bag under the seat.

"You two make a stunning couple."

"We work together," I said, leaning past him.

"Do you now? What kind of work is that?" She asked.

"Hospital public affairs, and he's one of the doctors on the board. Director of Pediatrics and Neonatology," I said, feeling slightly proud.

"How interesting. My husband was a doctor. He passed away in 1991. I didn't think I would live another day after he left this earth, but here I am. Life does go on."

He whispered in my ear. "You did it now."

The sweet older lady continued. "I have three sons, not one of them wanted to practice medicine and follow in their father's footsteps. It hurt him so. My Allen dedicated forty-one years to medicine."

As I was about to ask her sons' chosen careers, the roar of the engine silenced me.

Her voice rose with the engine. "There's something about being a physician," she continued without a prompting. "The dedication and the honor that comes with helping people. People look up to doctors." Her voice kept rising with the engine. "Doctors are the angels of our world."

Clint leaned into my ear again. "I should tell her what you really think, that we're all the anti-Christ." He smirked, showing a deep dimple line down his cheek.

"Not all doctors, just you, remember."

"I thought you changed your mind about all that." His voice was a warm whisper in my ear. "I thought I was granted immunity."

"Never," I said.

"Never?"

"Never ever." I turned my attention to the flight attendant doing her safety thing. I always felt obligated to give flight stewards their due. Our courageous attendants dealt with hostile customers, irate drunks, not to mention the fear of terrorists every single day on the job. The least I could do was pay attention for two and a half minutes while they talked about safety.

"If I'd known you still felt that way about me, I would have stayed home," he said, pretending to be offended. "I'm married. And don't try anything while we're on this trip."

I reeled back as far as the tight quarters allowed and socked him in his arm. His eyes squinted and his mouth opened in a fake yelp, but no sound came out. He massaged the sore spot while suffering silently. The plane ascended straight up as if we were heading to the moon. My ears plugged; my eyes went heavy. I was near sleep before I felt a tap on my thigh.

"Did you tell your husband you were coming to Washington, D.C., with me?"

I took a deep breath and said what I wished were true. "Absolutely. He's completely secure with our relationship."

"Yeah?"

"Yes," I said, adjusting my cream wool coat like a blanket over my body.

"That's truly a secure man. Either that, or he thinks I'm chopped liver."

"Rancid chopped liver," I confirmed. I stared blankly out the window at the clouds. The truth was Jake knew nothing of Clint sitting beside me for a five-hour flight. Nothing of our conversation, how we'd talked about the hospital, Clint's desire to turn the hospital around, or my being afraid of Jasper Callaway, the incident in the parking garage and how he'd creeped me out. Then unavoidably, the conversation turned to the past.

"How's Sandy doing these days?" Clint always started our back-down-memory-lane conversations with Sandy, my little cocker spaniel. Sandy was the only true proof we'd ever been a couple. Sandy arrived in a box with a beautiful fluffy satin bow for my birthday present instead of the engagement ring I was totally expecting from Clint. The beginning of the end, I liked to call it.

"Big, healthy, and lovable. She's still in D.C. with Wendy. Her kids got used to having her. I didn't think it was a good idea to move her to California."

"Why?"

Because I'd have to live with the constant memory of you, I almost said. "Our house really isn't a dog house. I mean, the floors are all hardwood, you can practically see yourself in the shine. She'd slip and slide all over the place. She couldn't run around, the house is kind of . . . it just wasn't meant for animals," I said, wondering if it sounded as ridiculous an excuse to him as it did to me.

"You sure you didn't want her around to remind you of me?"

"All dogs remind me of you."

"That's cold."

"I thought about giving her back to you, but I didn't want you to think I didn't appreciate your gift and all."

Clint couldn't get out his reply for laughing, holding his belly. "You, you . . . tried to throw the poor puppy out the window."

"I threw the box. Last I looked, she wasn't in it."

"Okay, yeah, anyway," he said, recovering slightly. "When you opened that box and saw her cute puppy face, you looked at me like it was a snake and a rat all balled into one."

"Not because I didn't think she was cute. She was supposed to be my ring. I showed you the ring like five times at the jewelry store. You sat there beside me and watched me try it on. You even asked the guy if they had payment plans—then you show up with a puppy."

"So I guess you made up for it, huh?" He picked up my hand and tilted my ring finger to catch the light of the two-carat diamond, "Going around collecting them like pets? So what is this, like your third engagement ring?"

I pulled my hand out of his. "Wonder how many Kandi's had."

"One. The only one I gave her."

"Is that what she tells you? I guess she was a virgin as well?" *Temper, temper.*

He quieted for a moment. "V, do you think we would have made it together?"

I looked around the huge plane for the exit signs, wondering what the damage would be if I shoved the door open and gave Clint a push. "It's just such a ridiculous question. Really, it's moot. It's buried. It's such a nonissue. Really," I said one more time for emphasis. "Relationships work if you want them to work. That simple."

"You believe that?"

"Absolutely."

"You think any two people can come together, and if they have enough fortitude, they can stay together forever?"

"Yes, I do."

"So let's say this guy here with the red comb-over and—" He leaned forward to see the people across the aisle. "—and say, that lady with the serious sideburns over there, they could make it, just by telling themselves they should?"

"Millions of people do it every day. They stay in dead-end marriages or relationships because they're either too lazy to get out, or have no self-esteem to believe they can do better. So they put into motion the 'cheaper to keep her' or 'love the one you're with' scenario. So to answer your question, yes, guy with bad comb-over and woman with pointed sideburns could make an illustrious couple.

"But honestly, Clint, I don't want to be part of the masses. I wanted someone who wanted me as much as I wanted him. No reasons behind the relationship whatsoever. Not to stay together for the children, stay together because neither can afford to live alone, or stay together because people think they're a great couple and everyone likes to have Christmas holiday at their house, none of that. With Jake and I, we have no reasons, no logic, no strategy, we just love each other. Everything else is secondary." *He completes me*, I thought but didn't say out loud.

Clint had nothing to say for an awkward few seconds, digesting the information and tone. He stared straight ahead, no doubt wondering about his current relationship with Kandi. Were they together for all the secondary reasons, or did they truly love one another, hell or high water? It was definitely a question he would have to answer and very soon.

"So we could have made it," Clint said out of nowhere, answering his own question. "We could have."

I pretended not to hear him. I pulled my coat up around my shoulders, feeling frightfully chilled. My body shivered from head to toe. I watched the clouds through the side window change shape and then disappear to a blank canvas. Open sky, without rules or boundaries. We didn't talk to each other for the next hour or so, both wondering if we really *could* have made it.

House Calls

The evening hours shut down Washington, D.C., like a bank at five o'clock. The streets cleared, the taxis stopped lining up, and tourists gave up waiting outside the White House to get a glimpse of the president. The sun was setting behind the large cherry trees that lined the streets of downtown. The taxi pulled up to the Watergate Hotel, where a bellman dressed in a traditional overcoat and hat opened the car door.

"Greetings, welcome to the Watergate." The bellman extended a hand to help me out of the cab. Clint let himself out on the other side and paid the driver. Not many words were exchanged inside the hotel. We both stood at the reception desk to check in like we hadn't flown the entire way talking and bumping shoulders, like we hadn't lived together for four years not long before.

The pretty brown desk clerk took notice of the doctor prefix on Clint's name and then commenced to flirt with him openly. She smiled too much and asked if he needed any extra services during the evening. Clint took the bait. "What kind of services are you offering?"

"Room service has a full menu with twenty-four hours' service. If you need fresh towels, sheets, or any toiletries of any type, I'll personally deliver them." She added, "with one push of a button." She fluttered her sparse long lashes.

"I'll keep that in mind," he said, looking over his shoulder to make sure I was still in earshot. I rolled my eyes. He came to where I was standing and finally offered to carry my bag.

"No thanks, I got it."

"What's all the hostility for?" Amusement funneled through his mask of seriousness.

"Why were you flirting with that chicken head?"

He laughed while he pressed the button in the lobby. "You're calling someone a chicken head. Ms. Hair Aware. Ms. Hair Doesn't Matter."

"She's a chicken head because she obviously saw me come in here with you but it didn't stop her from making a fool of herself."

"So chicken head doesn't have anything to do with the cockatoo thing she had working on the top?" He made three fingers spring and wiggle over his forehead. "Besides, we got separate rooms. She's a bright girl— she can add."

"Clint." I shook my head and left it at that. The elevator arrived. He pushed the number eleven, then looked to ask which one he should push for me.

"Same floor," I said stoically. "Why don't you wear your wedding band? That's misleading to people."

"It gets in the way of work." He splayed his smooth palms. "I work with my hands."

"Oh please."

We rode up, staring straight ahead. When I couldn't stand it any longer, I turned to him. "I don't care about you flirting with that girl at the checkout desk. That's not my problem. I just can't figure out why you're trying to get a rise out of me. I don't have the patience or the time to second-guess your motivations like I used to. Just spit it out."

"I wasn't trying to get a rise out of you."

"Yes, you were."

"Guess it worked then," he quipped, thoroughly amused with himself. Clint hadn't joked much over the past few weeks. He was tired and humble most of the time at the hospital. It was refreshing to see him with a lighter spirit, even if he was using it to aggravate me.

The elevator stopped and the doors opened to a huge framed mirror. We were Clint and Venus again. Him without a care in the world, me, angry and annoyed, just like old times. We turned the corner of the long slender hallway and walked in the same direction. We both stopped at the same time.

"I'm here," I said, fumbling with the envelope that housed my keycard.

"I'm right across from you." And that's when it happened. Clint whispered my name before he closed his mouth around mine. He slipped his arms ever so gently around my waist as if he were testing the waters. When he was sure it was safe, he unleashed, kissing me with full force. We stood pressed against each other, my hands gripped around the perfect smoothness of his oval head, his palms closed around the small of my back. My eyes remained closed while I drank in the comfort, the softness of his lips. I knew once I opened them, reality would be too hard to swallow.

I wiggled my way out of his grasp and stepped away. I bent over and picked up my room key and then his; both had fallen out of our hands during the melee. I held them up. "I'm not sure which is which." I handed him his. "All I know is that we're going to be in different rooms." Of this I was sure, regardless of the splendid beating of my heart or the warm surge pulsing through my body.

He took the plastic card then picked up his leather bag. He stuck his key in and nothing happened. My hand shook while I stuck my key in, the red light flashed. I turned toward him, afraid to get close enough to exchange keys.

"Let's just trade rooms," I said, moving past him with safe space between us.

"I'm not going to bite, V."

I squeezed through the door, sliding into the darkness where I was safe—from myself. My heart was beating out of my chest. The kiss meant nothing. Absolutely nothing.

I double-locked my door and said a little prayer. Twenty-four hours, it wasn't a lot to ask for. After the morning we'd be back on the plane headed home to our loved ones. Me, safe in Jake's arm before the next sunset. Clint . . . well, he was on his own.

Jus' Dinner

"V, I made reservations downstairs for dinner." Clint's voice came through on the other end of the hotel line as if he were sitting right beside me. I hadn't planned on going anywhere the rest of the evening. The long flight, the bumbling kiss in the hallway, both episodes had sapped my energy. I only wanted to focus on the morning. My suit was already laid out, my laptop was opened so I could work on my speech for the congressional committee hearing.

"I'm going over what I'm going to say tomorrow. And you should do the same," I told him, staying on the straight and narrow path of professionalism.

"We can go over it together. I'll check yours, you check mine. If you want, I can come over and we can order room service."

My silence prompted him to keep selling. "Just dinner, V, I swear."

I'd heard "jus' dinner" from Clint many times in the past, and it never ever entailed just food. "No . . . ," I stammered.

"V, we both have to eat."

"I'm tired. Seriously, this day needs to end."

"Yeah, but tomorrow will be here before you know it.

It's a perfect time to go over our presentation. You're the one who said we have only ten minutes to make miracles happen."

I surveyed the green chaise in the corner, then the chair and desk directly in front of me, old-world furniture with nothing to say. No answers or warnings. "Okay, downstairs at the restaurant. I'll meet you there in half an hour."

"I'm across the hall, remember, we'll go together." He hung up before I could protest. I didn't want to be in the small space of an elevator with him. Nor did I want to be within arm's reach, sitting at a dinner table.

Yet exactly five minutes later, he was knocking on my hotel-room door. Through the small peephole I saw the back of his charming head. He turned abruptly. "Open up, V. I know you're standing there."

I opened the door. "I said, half an hour." I pushed my turtleneck higher around my neck and pulled at the hem to make sure my belted low-rise jeans weren't revealing any skin.

He stepped inside. "Your room is nicer than mine. I should have kept it."

"I'm sure they're exactly the same. This is a corporate hotel—they don't do anything different from one room to the next."

"Yours is definitely bigger." He stayed by the door with his hands behind his back, trying to look harmless.

"Where's your prepared statement?" I noticed he wasn't carrying any papers.

He pulled out one sheet folded in a square. "Right here."

"Where's yours?"

"I have to find someplace to print it out." I slid on my shoes and grabbed my laptop. "That's why I needed the thirty minutes." We left the room. I took my key but left my purse.

"I must be paying," Clint said the minute he noticed I didn't have my purse.

"Damn right, you are."

Drop a Dime

Jake drove home determined to stop being angry and quit taking it out on his wife. His company being railroaded wasn't her fault. Someone he trusted had betrayed him. His wife and Mya were all that he could really depend on, and here he was letting her believe it was all her fault. The bitterness he felt was a general mistrust, something he'd fought over years to keep contained. Why did people always think he could be faked out and messed over? It was exhausting always having to put people in their place.

He'd planned to apologize for his selfishness. Start fresh with the idea that his wife deserved her own life. She'd had a full one before they'd met. What made him think she'd stopped needing her own identity once she became Mrs. J. Parson?

Eventually he would have to tell her everything. He didn't see how he could keep what happened with Byron Steeple a secret. His wife wasn't stupid. She'd make the connection.

"Trina, you here?" Jake came through the door with as much gusto as he'd had all day. He threw his keys and cell phone on the table near the door and peeled off his cashmere jacket. "Trina!" He called again.

"Right here, where's the fire?" She wobbled out on high heels and a fitted minidress.

"Girl, where'd you get all that?" Jake was surprised at the new Trina standing before him and couldn't believe the transformation. When had it happened? Why hadn't he seen it before?

"The dress or what's underneath?" She smiled and did an unsteady turn, revealing an apple-shaped bottom and slim waist. "I'm hittin' the club. Remember the reason I asked you to come home early so I could leave? My friend's picking me up."

"Oh, right, right. You look good." Wondering how he'd missed the transition. Her makeup needed a bit of work—too much eye shadow and way too much lip gloss reminding him of Jamie Foxx's character, Wanda, on *In Living Color*. But the weave was nice. Long and straight. A new hairstyle gave confidence and character to any woman.

"Nice dress," he added. "Where'd you get it? Looks familiar."

"I bought it. You don't like it?" she said, concerned.

"Oh, no, it's just that it looks—"

"Like it cost a lot. And it did. You're the one paying me."

"Right, but the money is so you could get on your feet. You shouldn't be wasting it on clothes and stuff."

"Jay, I can splurge once in a while." She leaned in closer. "I wish you'd stop being so sad all the time."

Jake couldn't help but let his eyes fall to the long line of cleavage centered in his face.

She noticed the attention. She blushed and pushed back her freshly applied strands of hair around her ear.

"Where's Mya?" he asked, gaining his composure.

"She's down for the count. I tried to keep her up so she'd sleep through the night, but she was exhausted. Y'all have a late night last night?"

"Yeah, kind of."

"Ooh, I gotta go. He's here." She leaned in the window and then steadied herself. "Are you going to be all right?"

"The question is, are *you* going to be all right?" Jake was concerned about her high heels.

"Fine. I'm going to shake my booty." She moved toward him with definite caution. She grabbed his face and kissed him on the cheek. He'd known her for what seemed like all his life, and he'd never seen her this happy. He hoped it worked out. She was Cinderella, and he felt like the Fairy Godfather—without the wand, but with a hell of a bankroll. The door closed.

The house felt empty and quiet. He looked at his watch and assumed his wife would be calling soon to let him know she was settled in Washington, D.C. It always made him nervous when she treaded old territory. An assemblage of memories and emotions he was no match for. He'd been in her life only a short time. He didn't have the armor of relationship history to rival with her past. They hadn't spent more than one Christmas together, a birthday each between them, and maybe one or two trips out of town including their honeymoon. All he had was now and each moment after. He depended on each day adding more value than the last. Lately, it had gone astray, but he was determined to put everything back the way it was meant to be. Her loving him. Him loving her. He felt bad for giving her such a hard time.

I sing this song for you . . . make me feel brand new.

He kicked off his clothes and shoes and planned to take a long shower and then be ready and relaxed when Mya woke up, as he knew she would. It was only seven. Maybe they'd take the stroller down to the Third Street Promenade, where she could ride the carousel. They'd buy ice cream and cotton candy—well, maybe just ice cream, he thought, picturing her with cotton candy in her hair and pretty much everywhere else her small hands could reach.

He was a step away from getting into the shower when the phone rang. He almost didn't answer because of the unknown caller ID and remembered it could be his wife calling from Washington, D.C.

"Is this Jake Parson?" the voice asked on the other end of the phone when he finally picked up.

"Yes, it is. Who's calling?" He was prepared to hang up, angry with himself that he'd fallen for a telemarketer's call.

"Hi. Um, my name is Kandi Fairchild. I'm married to Dr. Clint Fairchild. Does that name ring a bell for you?"

"Yes, it does." Jake pushed the knob and stopped the water from beating on the shower walls. Though it sounded like he'd stopped nothing. The sound that pulsated through his ears was his own heart crashing, then pumping as fast and hard as it could to catch up.

"I'm sorry to have to call you, but it's kind of an emergency," she said slowly. Emergencies required some type of urgency. She was taking her time, enjoying each and every word spoken.

"Speak your mind," Jake said, walking back to the bedroom, bracing himself on the edge of the bed.

"Well, my husband and your wife are in D.C. together." The woman paused. She continued on after he said nothing for too long. "I didn't know if you were aware or not. They're alone on a business trip. I found it strange that only the two of them were going alone." She emphasized the word *alone* one too many times. "I've already tried to reach him, Clint, my husband, several times and haven't had any luck. I was hoping . . ."

She paused. "I was wondering if you'd heard from Venus, your wife."

Jake was too busy spinning to be able to answer coherently. Maddening. The room had already shifted so many times, he didn't know exactly where he was. Then it stopped, the rotating coming to an extreme halt. His eyes landed on the framed pictured of him and Venus on the dresser. The mirror hanging over it held a reflection of himself, though he had trouble focusing. It was he, Jacob Marcus Parson, JP, right? The man everybody thought they could walk over and get away with it. At every turn, he had to step it up. No chance to rest for the weary.

It was him, all right. He recognized the boy when he was being teased for being a "pretty muthafucka." Too soft and pretty, so he had to act hard. Always a heartbeat away from getting into a fight because someone thought he was beatable. The person who tried always lost—he made sure of that.

"Why are you calling me?" he said, unsympathetic, finally getting a hold of himself.

"Because . . . I thought you'd heard from Venus. If you had, I could stop worrying about them. I mean, you know with everything that happened not so long ago with the terrorist attacks on the East Coast, I was worried about them traveling to Washington, D.C., alone. Anything could have happened and Clint isn't answering his cell phone. I have no idea what's going on out there with them *alone*. I just wanted to know if you'd heard anything."

He grabbed his chest and then moved slowly to the drawer that held his inhaler. *Bitch*. He didn't know if he was referring to the caller or his wife. Or possibly even Clint Fairchild himself, Dr. Ex-Lova, the kind of man who'd pull a stunt like this and expect no repercussions. He took another puff and held his breath, hoping the next exhale-inhale would be easier. Within seconds, the smothering cloak lifted off his chest and face.

"That's what your local news station is for," he said with his first good breath. "If that doesn't work out, try CNN. And a tip—the next time you think about calling here to ask where your husband is, you better be willing to live without him." He hung up the phone. The oxygen so many took for granted was all his again.

"Bitch." This time he was able to say it out loud. He was definitely referring to the caller.

He dialed and waited patiently for the voice mail to answer as he knew it would. He started talking. "Babe, give me a call. Just wanted to make sure you arrived and everything is cool. I miss you." His voice shook in a tremble of fear he hoped could pass for exhaustion.

Two hours went by before the phone rang. "Yeah, hey, how you doing? You made it in all right? Good." He paced while he held the phone in a death grip against his ear, listening hard for any signal, any notice of alert.

"So where're you staying?" A nonchalant question that held his life in the balance. "Oh yeah. Is it nice?" He had to sit for a minute. His knees weak. "No. I've never heard of it. You're going to dinner alone? I thought maybe you'd call Wendy." He tried to sound lighthearted and steady.

"I always hate to eat alone." He paused, waiting for the statement to take effect, but no admission of a traveling companion. "I do. I miss you. Mya misses you, too— because I just know. Yeah. Ah-huh. I love you, too."

He slapped the phone closed and threw it as hard as he could, the second one he'd have to replace in the better part of a month. He hoped the other one would never be found. In fact, he did better than hope, he prayed.

He yanked the towel from around his naked body and went to the closet. He dressed hurriedly. He went downstairs and grabbed another phone. He dialed Henry and Pauletta's number. The machine picked up. He paced some more then decided he couldn't waste time with phone tag. He dialed the other number that he knew by heart. She picked up after only the second ring.

"Trina, I'm sorry to interrupt. Listen, I have an emergency. I need you to come back and watch Mya . . . all night. I have to leave town. I wouldn't be asking if it wasn't an emergency, you know that." He had to strain to hear her whisper, something about this being her chance. She was having a good time, the first time in forever.

"Please, please, I'm begging, Trina. I swear, I'll make it up to you in a million different ways, but I need for you to get back here."

Let It Ride

Waves of doubt moved under his feet while he stood in the long airport security line. Nervous and even a bit light-headed, he'd given himself ten reasons to go back home. One of which, he was exhausted. Seemed he was on a nonstop uphill battle. His company, his wife.

He'd tried to calm down and let the whole thing ride. He knew in his heart of hearts it was all a big misunderstanding. He wanted to do the right thing, but the shroud of jealousy and anxiety surely would sneak in during the night, suffocating him to death and he would never have known the truth.

Jake moved up to the security line, dropping his cell phone, pen, watch, and keys into a plastic tray. He stepped through the metal detector. The loud piercing alarm made everyone look in his direction. His tender wool sweater suddenly felt itchy and tight, a noose around his neck.

"Sir, please step over here." The bland man in a white shortsleeve shirt and gray pants waved a hand for assistance. Jake was used to it, but found it no less annoying. He wore diamond studs the size of quartz rocks in his ears, but no heavy gold bling around his neck. Nothing excessive—simply well-hung denims and an expensive camel suede jacket that was being scrutinized very closely on the X-ray screen on the security belt. He was a young black man of obvious means. He had money, which for everyone else equated to drug dealer, entertainer, or athlete. Drug dealer being the top of the list.

He stood patiently while the wand surfed his body. "Sir, do you have any items on you that you'd like to volunteer?" The younger expressionless security guard held out a plastic basket, probably expecting Jake to toss in a Luger or a blade.

"Nah," Jake said in disgust. He spun around so the magic wand could surf his back and the rest of his body.

"You're going to have to take off your shoes."

This was a new one. "My shoes?"

"Yes, sir."

Jake looked to his watch, where it was no longer fastened around his wrist, then around the airport for the nearest clock. "What time is it?"

"Sir, we're trying to move everyone along as quickly as possible. Being in a hurry isn't going to change the fact that we still need your shoes."

The flight he'd booked was the last one for the night. Both airport security guards waited with their colorless knuckles resting on their thick sides as if they had all the time in the world and wouldn't mind a bit of excitement to make the night go faster. Jake sat down and took off his shoes. One took the shoes while the other used the wand around his sock-covered feet. He ground his teeth and felt his heart rate quicken. There wasn't much left in the way of degradation. He looked to his wrist again out of habit. He felt naked without his watch and noticed his wedding band. The span of diamonds placed evenly around in the platinum setting gave him a moment of peace. He felt silly. Ridiculous, even. Rushing out to D.C., for what? What did he expect to find? His wife and her ex-lover, that's what. Jake tried to appear calm, but his eyes darted to the large scale clock on the wall.

"What time's your flight?" the younger one asked quietly while he tickled the bottom of Jake's feet with the wand.

"Ten twenty."

"We'll get you out as soon as possible—long as there's no problem with the shoes."

The older guard came back holding the thick soles out like they were armed nuclear missles. He paused seemingly to give alarm but then he said, "All clear."

Jake snatched them out of his hand. "Where's my watch, my phone, the rest of my sh—?" Jake caught himself. All in a day's work. He actually felt sorry for the little men who had to do this work. It was embarrassing. "It's been a pleasure," he said in a mock salute with his middle finger extended.

Pushing past the throng of tired travelers, he moved swiftly to the gate. He panicked from the obvious emptiness of the waiting area, a bad first sign. The gate door being closed, the second.

"Excuse me, this is my flight. I need to get on this plane."

A bushy-eyebrowed man at the counter looked at his computer screen. "Last boarding announcement for that plane was fifteen minutes ago."

"But it's right there. The plane is right there. I'm looking at it."

"I know, yes, but once the doors are closed, that's it." The bushy-eyebrowed man put up a hand.

Jake wished he were dealing with a woman. He'd have no problem getting those doors to open. "Look, this is the last flight to D.C. I have to be on this plane.

It's an emergency. My life depends on it," he said believing his own words.

"Sir, I'm sorry."

"No, you're not." The more obstacles that slowed him down, the more resolute he became. He had to get to D.C. He stuck his hand in his pocket and pulled out his wallet and did the only good and right thing. The thick wad of one hundreds accidentally fell from his billfold and onto the man's shoes. Jake shoved them forward a bit more, kicking them. "Please, I have to get on that plane."

Cold Calls

Kandi's calls were persistent and could no longer be ignored. Clint pretended it was the hospital, but I could tell by the grimace on his face it was his wife.

My feet were propped up on the edge of the seat next to me. I pulled out my flight schedule and counted the hours when I could get home and start everything over. I wanted the tension between Jake and me to subside, to go away completely, and I would do whatever it took to make it right.

Clint came back to the table, unable to mask his strain. "Sorry about that, had to take the call." He picked up the menu, flipping through it. "Is this all they have?"

"Not a steak tartare man?" I asked, grossed out as well. Raw meat was just uncivilized. "What about the seared salmon?"

"I don't like raw fish either. We could go to the room and do room service. Order a nice steak, cooked, some wine."

The funnel of sound became loopy, mired in confusion. I squinted as if I didn't understand correctly. "You just got grilled by your wife and you're trying to be alone with me . . . in a hotel room?" I picked up the menu and studied it. "Not a smart man."

Clint clasped both hands and put them on top of his head. "Is everything a secret op with you, nothing anyone says is what they actually mean? Dinner, V, when will you understand, just plain food, not trying to get anything but a full stomach." He looked around and flagged the waitress. She was already heading our way.

Clint told the waitress we were leaving. Next thing I knew, we were at a bar up the street sucking on buffalo wings. We were both too hungry at that point to be picky. We ate silently until nothing was left but bones.

The Lakers versus Miami basketball game was playing on a television stationed above the glass shelving filled with liquor bottles. I busied my hands in my lap, wiping the grease on my napkin. My fingers tingled with heated nerves. It was something I'd been dying to ask. Not until the last sip of beer did I have the gumption to let it pass my lips. "Do you know what you're having . . . a boy or a girl?"

"A boy," Clint said.

I had a quick flash of what the baby would look like—one part Clint, one part She-whore, and still totally adorable. "When's he due?"

"May."

Now it was his turn. "So are you and Jake having any more?" he said, picking up a carrot stick and dipping it into the ranch dressing.

"We've talked about it. Maybe in a couple of years."

"So does Jake know Mya isn't his?" Clint wouldn't look up during his inquisition, busying himself with carrot sticks and doing last checks on the chicken bones for any undiscovered meat.

I was speechless. No one had ever asked me such a thing. Not even Wendy had broached the subject, and keeping it real was her specialty.

"I just assumed," he said. "She looks like him, Airic. Remember, you brought him to my wedding."

"How could I forget? Lovely wedding, by the way. Now you've got me curious. Do you think the baby Kandi is carrying isn't yours?"

He found my eyes. "No, that's not what I think."

"Well, it's a funny subject to be talking about."

He took offense. "I know I'm the father."

"Good for you." I'd hoped I shut the subject down for good. There was a sufficient pause, long enough for him to give it some justified thought. Fatherhood was a choice, biology not withstanding. He'd have to make his.

"So what came between you and your ex, Airic?"

"You're just full of questions, Clint."

"I'm just curious."

I shook my head. "Differences, I don't know." Shaq had just dunked over everyone's head. The bar crowd booed. "Do you want to go over our presentation for tomorrow? If not, I think I'll head back to the hotel." I began to get up.

"No. Stay. Please." There it was again, the new word he liked so much. "No more stupid questions. I'm sorry. I just figured we were friends, we could talk about anything."

"I don't talk about just anything even with friends. So anything that has to do with my relationship with my husband is off-limits."

"Done." He lifted up his hand to ask for another beer from the waitress.

"Let's talk about the plans for funding. I know the commission is going to ask what kind of programs their money will be paying for." I tried to get comfortable again on the hard barstool.

"First thing I want to do is put some funding into an

education program. Get these women into a program
to teach them about safe condom use. It starts with the
mothers. Slow down the AIDS epidemic, less babies
born to a death sentence."

"I think it starts with the men," I said, grateful to talk
about anything that wasn't centered on my life.

"It's not the men who are having babies. The women've
got to start standing up for themselves."

"Yeah, but it's the men spreading the virus. Women
are being infected seven-to-one faster than men.
Which coincidentally is about the ratio of men to
women. So you have this one man out there sleeping
with about seven different women every year. That
one man is the problem."

"What about the seven women who didn't just say
no? The bottom line rests with them. They're the ones
responsible to what happens to their bodies."

"For."

"What?"

"They're responsible *for* what happens to their
bodies."

"Oh, yeah, here we go. Correcting me. You haven't
changed."

"No, I haven't." I gave him as much disdain as he'd
just given me. "I'm not disagreeing about the responsibility," I continued on the more important subject. "I
just think the education should be centered on both
parties. If a woman believes she's in a monogamous
relationship and believes she's in love, the guard comes
down. And we both know how believable men can be."
I took a sip of his beer.

"That's your way of saying men lie, that men are the
ones always doing the lying."

"I didn't say that."

"Good, that's good, 'cause we don't want to go there," he said, definitively.

"We sure don't," I said, tipping the bottle to my lips.

"'Cause if we went there, I'd have to point out the fact that women mess around about as much as men do. Equally disloyal." He brought a carrot to his mouth and made a loud crunch.

"And I'd have to mention that you're right. And I can guarantee you'll have your firsthand proof soon enough."

"Get off it, V!"

"Get off what?"

"When are you going to let it go?"

"Let go of what?" I said, daring him to say it.

"Let go of the fact that I chose her over you. When are you going to stop trying to make me pay for that? If I admit I was wrong right now, can we be friends? Okay, I was wrong. I chose the wrong woman. Is that what you want to hear? Like that's going to change your whole life. Like every wrong will be made right again. What's done is done. Stop hating me," he added to my shock.

"I guess that would be about as easy as to stop loving you."

"You never loved me. I was just the prize you wanted to win."

Well, that about did it, you see. I waited for the sky to split open and the thunderous applause of clouds but nothing came. It was exactly what I'd wanted to hear. I was finally exonerated. Here I'd lived a good portion of my life believing our breakup had been my fault. The truth was right there laid out on the table. He married Kandi only so I wouldn't win. He hadn't wanted me to be right about one more thing. He wanted to show me he was boss. And what a fine job he'd done. But there was no magical moment of relief. I didn't feel happier or lighter knowing this.

I reached out and touched his hand. "I did love you way back then. But you know what, I get it now. The whole relationship was just a figment of my imagination. You're right, I wanted the prize. Having someone love you back with as much intensity as you love him or her . . . that's the prize. And I did win after all. Trust me on that." I stood up. "See you in the morning, Dr. Fairchild."

Pixie Dust

Being with Clint had worn me out. Back in the hotel, I wanted nothing more than to go to sleep. I heard a soft knock on my room door and thought it was Clint, ready to apologize. I looked through the peephole. The one-sided smile and slick side bangs framing a pixie face was the desk clerk who'd been flirting with Clint. I reared back in shock, realizing she thought she was knocking on his door. I put my hand over my mouth and thought for a moment what to do.

I swung my door open. "Can I help you?"

"Oh, I thought this was someone else's room." She'd ditched the little burgundy hotel jacket, wearing only a sleeveless white shirt and black trousers.

"We switched rooms." Indicating I knew exactly who she was looking for. I never liked people that talked with one hand on their hip as if the world depended on everything they had to say. Well, there I was, hand on hip. "He's across the hall. Maybe you can catch him before he falls asleep." I closed my door, locked it, and then stuck my face back to the peephole.

The desk clerk took a step back and did an about-face, knocking on Clint's door. I held my breath, waiting for him to answer. Clint was about to be busted. The young desk clerk knocked again and waited patiently. I, on the other hand, had run out of patience, waiting for something exciting to take place. I took my face off the door to take a break from the cold metal polishing on my forehead. The second it took to put my eye back to the peephole she was gone. *Damn it.* I continued to stare out the hole, thinking I'd missed the moment Clint opened the door and let her inside. If memory served me right, Clint lasted no more than ten, eight minutes. Being a bit older, I'd give him another two, three minutes tops. I waited.

The cold draft coming underneath the door froze my toes. I gave up and climbed back into bed. I rubbed my feet together under the heavy down and tried to focus on my own business at hand, my speech, but quickly fell asleep.

The knocking on doors and the voices out in the hallway awakened me. My eyes flew open. My first thought was the little desk clerk wasn't giving up without a fight. I hadn't noticed the glimmer of dawn peeking through the heavy velvet curtains. I staggered to the door looking forward to the moment when I'd feel vindicated. This is what Kandi deserved, an unfaithful man who slept with desk clerks. I pushed my face against the metal peephole. By the time my eye came into focus, I was sure I was dreaming.

Clint stood at the open door with his boxers on, stifling a yawn. He stroked his broad dark chest and asked what was going on. What was so urgent at six in the morning? He hadn't recognized Jake. So when the first strike reeled back and landed hard against his face, he hadn't seen it coming. Clint fell backwards with Jake fully on top of him.

I struggled with my door, scrambling with the safety

bolt, then the chain hook, breaking free to find them wrestling inside.

"*Jake!* Stop! Ohmagod!" I jumped on his back wearing nothing more than my underwear and white tank. He threw me backwards then turned to face me with rage. I'd never seen him this way. "Stop it, you're making a mistake, Jake. Listen to me." I touched his arm.

He shook my touch off. "You made the *mistake* when you came here with *him*." He pointed.

"Calm down. This is crazy. Let me explain." I put my hands out to protect myself, pretty sure that I was next.

In those short moments, Clint took the opportunity to swing, hitting Jake solid in the jaw. Now it was Clint who felt my wrath. "Don't you dare hit him! This is crazy. Listen to me, both of you."

For a brief moment, it seemed to work. The calm loving Jake I knew so well had reinhabited his body. He stood up holding his jaw, but within seconds, he was lunging in Clint's direction, tackling him down. The two men struggled, knocking over lamps and shoving back furniture. I jumped on Jake's back, pulling on his shoulders and arms, anything I could get a grip on. "Baby, please. Nothing happened." He let go of Clint and we both tumbled backward. My head hit the corner of the bedpost and knocked the fight right out of me.

The way Jake called out my name, I knew things didn't look good. A thick swell of numbness quilted my thoughts. The room spun. Jake was kneeling next to me. There were two Clints on the opposite side like a pinwheel. I lay flat, wondering how this nightmare could continue even though I was wide awake. I stared up at the ceiling and saw the Sleep Gypsy who used to visit me as a child, laughing, pointing her slender finger, go to sleep now . . . go to sleep.

The blackout was short-lived, though it felt like an eternity. I opened my eyes to Jake kneeling over me.

"Don't move her." Clint came back with the desk lamp, the shade conveniently knocked off. He held the light over my face while he pried one eye open at a time. I tried to blink and shove his hand away. "Stay still," he ordered.

I lay as still as possible, knowing the tank and panties I was wearing were showing too much skin. The sizable lump in the back of my head was getting bigger by the second. "Let me up. Move." I pushed Clint's hand away, feeling the bile rising up through my chest. I coughed and gagged, leaving a mess on the carpet. Jake stayed right by my side. I peeked up, wanting to tell him I was sorry, so so sorry, but nothing came to my lips but more saliva. If I were sick enough, maybe he would feel sorry for me, enough to forgive me. I lay back down and closed my eyes.

"A concussion. It's definitely a concussion." Clint hurried to the bathroom. He came back with a wet towel. He wrapped it around my head. "She might need stitches."

I already had stitches, I was thinking, right here. My hand rose to feel the healed skin above my eyebrow. No, that was months ago, after the car accident.

Jake reached out and wiped the stream of tears moving over the bridge of my nose. *Thank you, honey.* Next, I felt Clint digging around the back of my head, past the mass of hair. *Yeah, right there.* Two men had been my longtime secret fantasy, but not like this.

"A big lump but no cut," Clint said, taking a hold of my hand. "V, wiggle your fingers, now your toes . . . good. Let's move her up to the bed."

"I got her," Jake said, scooping me up by himself then

laying me gently on the bed. He was still fighting mad, anger still in his tone. He sat down next to me.

"She'll be fine." Clint said from nearby. "I'm sorry for the misunderstanding, man. We switched rooms. Our keys got mixed . . . that room was nicer . . . so we switched."

Aah, good work, Clint. Don't forget to tell him how we stood in the hallway and dropped everything from our hands just to embrace each other in a passionate kiss.

"You know, your wife called my house?" Jake's voice cracked. "I wouldn't be here but for that phone call."

"Kandi? My wife?"

She-whore, that's her real name.

"Your wife," Jake said matter-of-factly. "How many wives do you have? She claimed to be worried about you and Venus traveling to D.C. *alone*. All she wanted me to know is that you guys were here, alone in a hotel."

"I'm sorry, man. I swear, Kandi, she's . . ." Clint's words trailed off, as if everything he knew about his wife could only be summed up to her name. "All of this is my fault. We switched rooms. It's all my fault."

No. Don't start a confessional now. No. I screamed for my brain to wake up and get it together. Lives were about to be ruined. Jake had an uncanny ability to see through bullshit. If Clint admitted to one more thing, Jake would see the entire picture in his head. The passionate kiss in the hallway. Dropping the keys and not knowing whose belonged to whom.

I pushed myself up on my elbow and used the other arm to stroke Jake's shoulder. He nudged my hand away.

"I'm leaving, are you coming with me?"

"I don't think that's a good idea right now," Clint chimed. "She shouldn't be moving around."

"Shut the hell up!"

"Look, man, I already explained to you. This was a misunderstanding. You're going to have to calm the hell down. She just had a head injury—moving her around isn't advised."

"Good thing we have a doctor in the house." Jake looked me in the eye. "Are you coming? I'm not asking again."

For a minute, it was an easy answer, a no-brainer, and then I remembered why I was there in the first place. The hospital. The closure. The health commission. Morgan Taylor. An entire staff. The babies.

Jake stood up, found his jacket, snatched it up and walked out the door before I could say a word. It happened that quickly. Jake was gone like a magic act. I swung my legs around and tried to rise up.

"Stay still, V."

"I can't. I have to go." I stood up then sat back down, feeling the weight of a brick putting pressure on my head. I shut my eyes and wished the room would stop spinning.

"Seriously, I don't think you need to rush out in the icy cold, this time of morning looking for him. Let him calm down."

I shook my arm out of his grasp. "You don't know a thing about loving someone enough to go after them. You never have!"

Clint stood up and took a step back, then started gathering his things. "You stay in here. I'll move to the other room." He handed me his cell phone. "Call your husband."

A slow guttural moan leaked out of my throat. I dialed slowly, wiping my eyes and my nose, remembering only one number at a time, and still a man who spoke only Spanish answered. I hung up and tried again. Jake's voice mail picked up. The chime signaled, and I hadn't yet thought of what to say.

"Jake, please don't leave. Please. I want to go home with you. I'm so sorry, for everything." I closed the phone and laid it down like it had spiritual powers, and if I prayed over it long and hard, my prayers would be answered.

It rang. I quickly picked it up. "Thank heaven," I whispered. "I'm so sorry, babe."

"Venus?" Kandi's shock was followed by a shrill scream. I couldn't make out a thing she'd said after "You bitch." I hung it up. When Clint came back carrying my bags, I didn't say a word about the phone call. I tossed him his phone. He scooped it up before sitting on the edge of the bed.

"I thought you said he knew we were here together."

I didn't answer him. I let my head fall into my hands.

"It still doesn't excuse what Kandi did. I'm sorry," Clint said. "So now what?"

"I have to go. I can't stay." The room was still spinning. I dug in the bag Clint had sat beside me and pulled out my jeans.

"You're going?"

"I can't stay."

"What're you trying to do?"

I stuck one leg in my jeans and fumbled with the other. Clint realized how pitiful I looked and started to help. He handed me my sweater and then my shoes. "I still don't think it's a good idea. Look at me." He held my head and looked into one eye at a time. "You're going to be fine." Clint reached out and took my hand. "V, he was wrong about you. Whatever he thought you were capable of, he was wrong. And so was I."

I couldn't hear the rest of what Clint had said. The words came out of his mouth mixed with apology and good wishes to start over.

I left, hailing a cab with the sun barely peaking over the city. I was hoping Jake was at the main Reagan Airport, though there were at least three others to choose from. Regardless, I was getting on a flight and heading home. I couldn't let him down again. I'd already done enough damage.

Home Alone

I arrived to an empty house. No Mya. No Trina, and no Jake.

My cell phone rang before I could start doing the calling. It was my mother. If this were a movie, the suspense horror music would start in a low piano cord, *du du da dahhhh*.

"Hi, Mom." I held my breath.

"I have Mya. Jake dropped her off. I didn't ask any questions," she said, waiting for a voluntary explanation.

Only problem, I was as confused as she was. "I guess Trina couldn't make it to work today."

"He didn't look good. He wasn't himself at all. What's going on?"

"I . . . well . . . he may be a little mad at me."

"Lord," she said, calling to the highest power. "What'd you do?"

"Mom. Okay, it's kind of a long story, and I'm so tired. Can I just hop in the shower then call you back when I can think straight?"

"No."

I sat down and started recalling the last disastrous few months, starting all the way back to feeling bored and needing an outlet. The hospital probably wasn't the best choice, I admitted. My mother laughed. She laughed when things weren't all that funny—in fact, when they were just plain ridiculous.

"I told you. Didn't I tell you?"

"But the point was," I explained, "the trip had nothing to do with Clint, and everything to do with Jackson Memorial. If I announced Clint was going, he would've accused me of every possible scenario anyway. A lose—lose situation."

"And you still believe this?" my mother said, not quite through with the laughter.

"Mom. I believe I was wrong. But Jake was wrong, too. We both did a lot of hurtful things to each other over the last few weeks. I just want to fix it."

"Men will always trump your simple mistakes times two. They're not as understanding as women. Things are black-and-white for them. You mishandled him, so he's going to mishandle you, only he's got bigger hands, you know what I mean?" Her voice turned away. "Mya stop, get away from that basket. What is this girl's fascination with laundry?"

"She likes the smell," I said. "Mom, put her on the phone."

I heard the coaxing my mother had to do to get her away from the probably freshly folded sheets and towels.

"My-My, hi, baby. How are you, sweetie?"

"Hiiii," she breathed out. "Mama."

"Yep, mommy, sweetie," I said softly. "I miss you."

She made a small giggle noise. At least someone was happy.

My mom picked up the phone where Mya had dropped it. "You get some rest. I've got Mya. I think Henry's planning on taking her out to the park, get some sunshine."

"Thanks, Mom. I'll call you later."

"Don't worry about us, you find your husband."

"I will." I hung up the phone and started my phone campaign. Jake wasn't at JP Wear, but I left a message on his business line. "Baby, I'm home now. I left right behind you. I'm so sorry. Just give me a chance to explain." Next, his cell phone. The voice mail picked up instantly, telling me his cell phone was off. "I promise to fix everything, baby, to make it right. I promise. I love you." He refused to call me back.

Plan B

It was like old times: he, Legend, and Beverly hunched around a table sipping on martinis. The restaurant was brightly lit but still maintained an erotic calmness. Words were spoken in hushed whispers. Never-ending music like one continuous chord played just below the surface. For a second or maybe longer, Jake was relaxed, though he couldn't stop the last twenty-four hours from playing in his head.

Legend lifted his arm for the waitress. "Another round?"

"Unh-unh, count me out. I'm right where I want to be." Jake made a cut-off gesture to the waitress.

"You never could hold an ounce of liquor." Beverly looked between the two men. "I want to make a toast."

He wondered if his wife was on her way back home yet. He didn't know how he was going to make it through the night thinking about Venus alone with Dr. Ex-Lova. He thought he was bigger than this. But the insecurity crowded his thoughts. He checked his watch.

"You got another date, bigger name on the other line?" Legend asked with a wiry look of I-know-something-you-think-I-don't.

Beverly didn't chime in. She suspected why Jake kept looking at his watch but kept it to herself. "So, before Jake is completely out of libations, let's make a toast, to our newly named CEO of JP Wear."

"I'll drink to that."

"So kind of them to give you a title at your own damn company," Legend added.

Jake hunched his shoulders. "I don't even care, man. I put way too much energy into that place and got nothing back. It's time to focus on what's real. To my friends." Jake raised his glass. "To my only real friends."

"I'll drink to that." Legend gave an appreciative smile.

Jake took a long swallow of his drink. "You guys have been great. Thanks for hanging in there with me. A man needs loyalty. A man needs friends who will stick by him."

"I see it's time for an intervention." Legend reached across the table and pushed Jake's glass away. "Now you can go ahead and tell us what happened to your face. Seeing how we're your loyal band of thieves and all."

"I fell."

"Venus do that to you?" Legend asked with a menacing smile.

The mention of her name tore through Jake. For a minute he thought he was going to push up his drinks plus the failed bites of sushi.

Beverly jumped in. "I'm just afraid of what the other person looked like."

"I think I know." Legend shook his head. "But if you don't want to tell me the truth, that's cool. I can't be a good character witness if I don't know the real deal."

"Character witness for what?"

Beverly put her head down and stirred her martini with the sprig of orange peel.

"Byron Steeple was found beat to death sitting in his pretty new Bentley, and you know nothing about that?" Legend asked with a smirk.

Jake put his hands up. "I don't know what you're talking about, man. But I'm sure he got exactly what he deserved. He must've robbed somebody else blind besides me."

"Good to hear." Legend gave a wink to Beverly.

She ignored him and tried to change the subject. "We need to get back on track, guys. Just because we were infiltrated doesn't mean we should give up."

"Right," Legend said. "Let's discuss Plan A, 'cause lord knows Plan B was a bit messy."

Jake got up, stumbling slightly backward with his seat. "I'm not in the mood for jokes. I'll check you guys later." He slipped a hand to Legend to shake, then squeezed Beverly's shoulder. He could feel both pairs of eyes on him.

Beverly stood up and grabbed her fake fur stole. "I'm going after him, take care of the check." Her tight jeans swished away while Legend looked at the table full of empty glasses.

"Great."

Outside, Beverly didn't have to move too quickly to catch up with Jake. He still hadn't decided which direction to head, so he stood off-kilter in the middle of the downtown crowd that moved fast and steady around him.

"You going back to the studio?" Beverly asked, putting her hands around his eyes from behind.

He peeled them off and turned around. "Nah, I'm tired. I'm going home."

"You want to talk about it?" She laid a hand on his shoulder, and then touched his cheek. "I don't think it's a good idea if you drive."

"Shaun, you're in no better shape than me." He leaned in too close to her face. She reached out and pulled him into her grasp. Jake had gotten too close to the lioness cage. Their mouths locked hungrily around each other. He squeezed her as tight as he could, letting his hand fall to the full roundness of her bottom and lifting her slightly to her toes. He felt the grip of desire taking hold. Her lips were soft, her tongue sweet, the warm scent of alcohol adding to his already thick buzz. He felt his body giving way while his head continued to spin. He heard a bus pull up and felt the warm exhaust from its engine.

The doors opened. The driver called out. "You two waiting for the bus, or what?"

Jake spun Beverly slightly so his back was completely to the driver. He continued to taste her tongue, reaching deeper, looking for something he'd lost.

Beverly broke away for a moment. "We better move. Legend's going to be out any minute." She took his hand, pulling gently. They got only as far as where the brick building ended before they scooted themselves into the small alleyway. He lifted Beverly with surprising ease and pushed her back against the hard edge of the wall.

His breath was heavy, his heart beating steadily quicker with each taste of her tongue. He shoved her low-cut top out of the way while he reached past her bra, pushing her full golden breast to meet his lips.

"Wait, Jake. Let's go somewhere."

"Right here, right here," he whispered between licks and sucks of her nipples.

She closed her eyes and gave it a shot, but the hard scratching bricks against her back were trampling the magic. She wiggled her breast free of his mouth, slipping it back in its cup. She lifted Jake's face to hers.

"Not here." She kissed him to pad his disappointment. "The W is right across the street," she tilted his head. "Right there." She kissed him again, longer and stronger to seal the deal.

She took his hand and led him to the corner, where they waited for the light to change. He stood behind her, his breath in her ear. She reached up from behind and stroked his head and neck as they lingered. "What's gotten into you, boy?"

The light changed, and the little green man appeared as well as the *beep-beep* signal for the blind. In this case it was appropriate. Jake had become stupefied, deaf and dumb, all at the same time. He reached up and grabbed Beverly's breasts from behind. She knocked his hands away. "Patience."

They made it across the street and through the brass-framed turnstile. The lobby was brimming with guests. The sophisticated gentlemen at the front desk gave them a welcoming smile.

"Checking in today, sir?"

"We'd like a room, one night," Jake said, playing in Beverly's hair.

"Yes, sir, your reservation?"

"We don't have a reservation. Just need a room," Jake said, refusing to take his eyes off Beverly.

"Sir, we have a full house. We're overbooked as it is. We're hosting a large conference for the weekend."

Beverly chimed in, "Please, please check again. We were staying over at the Sheraton, horrible." She grimaced. "We thought we'd switch over here to a nicer place. Do you have anything, just for tonight? I'd so appreciate a good night's sleep." Beverly knew a good ego stroke was always necessary. No one was capable of simply doing a good job out of duty.

"I'm sorry, we have nothing."

Beverly took a hold of Jake's hand. "We can go to my place." She pressed herself against him but felt him pulling away. She reached out and grabbed him by his shirt before he fell backward. "Whoa, you all right?"

"I'm fine." He started toward the exit.

"Wait a minute, Jay? What's going on?"

"I'm sorry, Shaun. I can't do this."

She touched his face. "I know you're hurting. I just want to be there for you, like I always have. We'll just go somewhere and talk."

A discerning look fell on his face, as if to wonder how he got there in the first place. "I'll see you later." He walked off feeling he had no particular place to go. Home was the last place he wanted to be. The JP Wear studio maybe. Neither felt right. The misplacement of something gnawed at him. Something he'd lost but couldn't put a finger on where he'd left it. He stopped at the corner to let the city bus hang a right. The huge advertisement turned the corner with it, *JACKSON MEMORIAL, REAL CARE FOR REAL PEOPLE.*

What he'd lost wasn't all that far away. All he had to do was figure out how to get it back.

Fire Starter

The phone woke me up in the middle of the night. Morgan Taylor's frantic voice piped in full speed. "There's an emergency, Venus. You need to get down here. There's been an accident at the hospital. We've got to put together a statement—it's just awful. You've got to get here," she cried out.

"But . . ." I had been in a fitful sleep. I questioned whether the phone call was part of a continuous bad dream.

"The police are here. The news coverage is going to be brutal—we've got to act quickly."

"I don't understand. . . ."

"Get here ASAP, Venus. Please hurry."

I hung up and looked over to the empty side of the bed where Jake still had not come home. The last twenty-four hours hadn't been a dream. Jake was somewhere out there still hating me while I was home alone, doing an even better job of hating myself.

I arrived at the hospital to see the police car lights swirling in unison. Fire trucks were parked on the grass blocking the entrance. I moved swiftly through the crowd and saw the fire in its final stages being put out.

Black smoke billowed from a broken window. Water sprayed up in the air and landed on the fourth floor. I pushed past the crowd to the inside of the hospital. People ran around scared and frantic.

I touched one of the nurses by her shoulder. "Did anybody get hurt?"

She looked dazed and opened her mouth, but nothing came, as if the tragedy were unspeakable.

I took a deep breath and tried to stop fear from overtaking me. "Please, tell me, what happened?"

"There was an explosion." The nurse broke out in a sob.

I tried to move to the next person but found myself being carried the opposite direction by the crowd.

"Everybody, please keep moving." The firefighter used the megaphone: "We need to keep this space clear for the injured."

Injured.

"Venus . . . over here." Morgan Taylor was waving from a short distance, her head popping up and down over the crowd. I made my way to her. Her eyes were smudged with black mascara. She swiped at her eyes, coughing. "There was an explosion, Venus, a fire on the fifth floor." She broke down into the tissue she was carrying to protect her nose from smoke.

"The infants, the children, who was injured?" A wave of fear engulfed me. I knew Clint was back from the hearing in D.C. and would've beelined straight to the neonatal ward on the fifth floor. I couldn't wait for her answer. I spun around and moved to the area the officer was trying to clear. I could hear Morgan calling my name, but it sounded distant, as though miles of distance lay between us. I pushed through the herd of staff, nurses, and patients with IV bags still attached.

I heard the distinct sound of a camera clicking as I

was turning around, the flash went off in my eyes. There on a gurney was a body partially covered with a sheet. The photographer was taking pictures.

"No! Out of here." I started swinging with all my might, pushing and shoving the photographer who'd made it inside. "Keep them out of here!" I screamed. A few of the male staff took immediate action blocking the doorway and making sure people could get out but not in.

I moved slowly, afraid to see who was underneath the sheet. It was Dr. Langley, one of the pediatricians. I cupped a hand over my mouth. *The fifth floor.* The smell of smoke bit into my throat and eyes. I braced myself and gathered the strength once again. I reached out for the wall to keep from sliding to the ground. I gathered a second wind and squeezed past the firefighter manning the elevators.

"Hey! Wait a minute, you can't go up there." The large man put his body in front of me.

"I have to. I have to see what's going on."

"Ma'am, we're keeping the elevators clear." He put up his hands to indicate I wasn't getting past him.

I turned my eye to the stairwell then made a mad dash.

"Wait!" he yelled. I was already through the steel door. I took the stairs two at a time, covering my face with the collar of my jacket. The smoke was in thick pockets. I stopped every few steps, out of breath, and coughed so hard, a lung may have shaken loose.

"Who's down there?" The voice rang inside the stairwell. I looked up and down, not sure where it was coming from. They called out again, "Anybody down there?"

I answered weakly, "Here. I'm here in the stairwell."

"What floor are you on?"

"Third," I said after checking the number on the exit door.

"Are you all right?"

"I'm fine." My voice cracked.

"Okay, you should be safe the rest of the way down."

"No . . . I was on my way up. I need to come up."

"Absolutely not possible," the heavy voice boomed overhead as if the Ten Commandments would be quoted next. "We're evacuating . . . wrong way," he said.

"I need to see the damage. The fifth floor is pediatrics. There are children and infants on that floor," I tried to explain to the firefighter.

"Not anymore. Everyone is headed in one direction, and that's out of here, ma'am. You're going to have to do the same," the booming voice echoed before the door slammed shut.

It wasn't like me to give up so easily. My lungs made the decision for me. The higher in elevation, the thicker the smoke, the more difficult to breathe. I made my way back down, one dizzying step at a time. I nearly fell through the last door when I landed against the metal bar latch.

The continued streak of panic and chaos I was expecting was nowhere to be seen. For a brief and scary moment I thought I'd been left abandoned while the fire department had cleared everyone else out. But relief followed. I'd simply traveled too far down, ending up on the basement floor. The air, though stale, allowed me to breathe without inhaling smoke. The quiet was unsettling. Knowing there was a catastrophe taking place right overhead, I felt a world away from the sorrow but still sadness crept inside me. The realization that I had control of *nothing,* absolutely nothing, was a hard pill to swallow.

Standing there, I realized my life, the lives around me, were all a finger push away from being extinguished or changed forever, and none of it could be controlled by the decisions we so valiantly made every day. Career choice, friends, lovers, husbands, where to live, who to live with—I wanted to laugh, but only liquid pushed through my nostrils, tears rolled down my cheeks. It all boiled down to one second in time, when it could all end for no good reason. All I could think of were those babies, innocent and helpless on the fifth floor after they'd fought so hard to live.

After a few more hiccupped cries that I knew no one could hear but me, a calm took over. As if an angel came down with fluttering wings to show me the way. I figured it all out. If I had no control, I should have no fear. No matter which path I'd chosen for myself, some puppet master was at work pulling the strings. Whether I thought I was safe or in peril, doing the right or wrong thing, the end was already decided, decisions made for me.

But did it have to be now, I thought as the humming sound turned into a roar. The rumbling towered over me and through the walls. Another explosion? I scrunched into a corner, covering my head with my arms and expecting the walls to cave in as the thunderous sound got closer then stopped. It was only the elevator. The doors sprang open.

I was prepared to plead my innocence to the firefighter. Instead it was Jasper. He quickly shoved a stick against the door panel to jam it.

Realizing he wasn't alone, he took a few quick steps toward me. "What're you doing down here?" He extended a hand to help me up. I stood up on my own, ignoring his hand. "That's some mess up there, huh?" he said nervously, looking around. The beating inside the parking garage had left him with a cut under his eye that healed badly, making him look like an ex-boxer.

I pushed myself deeper into the corner.

"If you'll excuse me." He headed directly into the room with the sign on the door, KEEP LOCKED. Jasper moved frantically, knocking over boxes before hitting the light switch. He swept past me as quickly as he'd come carrying a stack of boxes almost taller than himself. The stickers on the side were marked through with a handwritten EXPIRED across the pharmaceutical label. On closer inspection I saw the name, PSEUDO-EPHEDRINE, the everyday cold medicine used to make crystal meth.

The huge supply of drugs had probably been stored down here one box at a time by Jasper himself. Jackson Memorial nurses had been accused of stealing and peddling the medicine and here it had been stored the whole time.

He pushed the boxes onto the elevator and went back for more. He wiped his brow on his sleeve where he'd begun to sweat and ooze the smell I couldn't identify until now. The smell of an addict.

"What happened, you started out selling it, then couldn't resist testing the product yourself?" I said, angry beyond control.

I stood trembling, not knowing what he was capable of, but too furious to keep my mouth shut. "That's why the guy was trying to beat the crap out of you in the garage. He's paying you to bring him supplies but then you had a better idea to go independent? You started the fire to distract everybody, just for these boxes?"

"What!" he snapped. "I had nothing to do with this fire." He sucked his teeth, dismissing me. "Typical."

I stayed calm, telling myself if I didn't move, he wouldn't attack.

"I'm here to save the only thing worth saving before this hospital goes up in flames. You think I can live off the little pittance of money they pay me? I was a good doctor. This hospital, this spineless group fed me to the wolves, never once asked my side of the story. They simply made deals with the devils of this world. Forget about all my years of dedication. I did nothing to that boy. When I told him he and I would never have a relationship, he killed himself. But did anyone believe me? No," he said too calmly. "My only joy will come when this place dies a slow death the same way I have."

He snatched the stick from between the elevator doors. "Coming?" he said with a knowing grin. "Suit yourself." The doors closed and he'd made his escape.

The reporters were back like old lovers clamoring for attention.

The captain of the fire department stood in the midst of microphones and cameras stuck in his face still covered with grit, answering questions the best he could.

"All I can say right now is that the fire started on the pediatrics floor, most likely caused by an oxygen tank. I've given the hospital clearance to put the patients back in their rooms." The questions were hurled all at once.

He waved a hand. "I think I'll pass the rest of your questions on to the director of the hospital." He stepped away leaving all eyes on Morgan Taylor. If the disheveled look in her eyes was any indication of what was about to come out of her mouth, Jackson Memorial would never live down the night.

I signaled to Morgan that I was coming to her rescue.

"Please, I have to get through, please. Excuse me," I pushed back and forth before finding an opening. I got to Morgan's side before the first word was spoken.

"The fire was an unfortunate accident," I said quickly. "At this time we don't have the exact information on how the fire started, but we will investigate fully. As for the patients, all are accounted for. A report will be filed and distributed for release tomorrow morning. One of our doctors was lost in this fire. We're grieving his loss at this time and hope you can respect the fact that no information will be released until his family members are notified. Thank you." I put an arm around Morgan and pushed her along. The night air held the stench of smoke and bewilderment. Her body tensed as we entered the hospital doors.

"I can't," she said, "I can't do this. Not now." She backed away.

"I'll get someone to drive you home." I left Morgan noticeably shaking in the lobby. When I came back, she was still standing in the same spot, in shock. "Morgan," I gave her a gentle shake. "Morgan, Leslie's going to drive you home, okay?"

She nodded. The frailty of Morgan's usual stern exterior was heartbreaking. At the moment, Jackson Memorial had no captain at the helm, no one in charge. Jasper Calloway was still running around free to cause more tragedy and chaos. Patients were sprawled about like there'd been a train wreck. The lobby resembled news footage during a war. People with oxygen tubes, saline bags attached to their bodies, and bandages wrapped around their head and chests lined the walls, waiting for someone to tell them what to do, where to go.

The fire captain came in holding a clipboard. He had a *Magnum, P.I.* mustache almost wider than his face. I could tell he was looking for who was in charge. My first instinct was to go hide. He caught sight of me and headed in my direction. His hero uniform, heavy jacket, and firefighter helmet were all intact.

"I'm giving the hospital clearance. But if I were you, I'd have every oxygen tank in this hospital professionally serviced. Those tanks are fueled by nitrogen. A lot of pressure. One tank in the wrong hands could blow up a full square block."

I signed the clipboard and handed it back. He tore off the top sheet, giving me a copy. "I know the kind of trouble the hospital is in. This isn't the kind of night you need. Good luck."

When was the nightmare going to end? There were probably hundreds of tanks spread from floor to floor, each potentially tampered with. K-I-T, keep it together. *Don't panic. But breathe, yes, breathing is necessary.*

"Venus."

"Huh!" I jumped when I felt a hand on my shoulder. I turned around to see Clint with a huge gauze bandage covering his right eye. His face was riddled with tiny cuts and abrasions. "You're all right."

"Yeah, I'm fine," he said solemnly.

"Clint, I know who did this. I know what happened. This entire hospital isn't safe."

"C'mon." He led me off a few steps.

"We've got to tell the police. Jasper is getting away. I saw him—he practically admitted to trying to destroy this hospital. This is murder."

Clint looked like someone had socked him in the gut. "It was an accident, V. That's all. It had nothing to do with Jasper."

"An accident? No. It was Jasper. He was downstairs in the basement after the drugs he'd hidden. He's selling them, he's addicted to them, that's why the guy beat him in the parking lot, they were in business together." I was short of breath by the time I finished.

Clint simply looked annoyed. "V, you're wrong." He shook his head. "It's my fault. That's all I can say right now, okay. It wasn't Jasper. I accidentally left one of the oxygen tanks loose when I was changing them."

The shock rose on my face. "Are you sure?"

"Let it go, V," he said with finality before walking away.

"Venus." I heard my name being called.

I turned to see Jake. I didn't ponder whether or not he'd just witnessed Clint grasping my arm. I didn't care what he saw: I only knew the truth. Through all the sadness and tragedy, he was all that mattered. I rushed toward him, threw my arms around his neck, and held on for dear life. "Baby . . ."

"Shhh, I got you. I'm here," he whispered. "I'm right here." He rocked my body back and forth in his arms. "It's going to be okay, everything's all right. I got you."

Front Page

The fire at the hospital was on every channel. I watched the television on mute while I lay in bed with Jake still sleep beside me. The small clip with the subtitle underneath, JACKSON MEMORIAL IN REAL FIRE. As if all the other incidents were just a trial run. This was the real one that may shut the hospital down for sure. A doctor died. A smiling picture of Dr. Langley appeared on the screen with dates underneath, 1959–2005. I clicked the TV off and pushed myself back under the covers. I didn't want to face the day.

Jake lay peacefully beside me like he hadn't known sleep for a couple of days. I watched his eyes flutter and took the opportunity, stroking the side of his face and kissing him gently on the lips.

I snuggled so close, I'd pinned myself underneath his weight. He wrapped his arms around me, then fell back to dreamland. For a brief moment everything seemed perfect and right. I got up and decided to make breakfast. It'd been a long time since it was just Jake and me alone in the house. I planned to fix my husband coffee, toast, and sliced fruit and serve him in bed. The term "scared straight" kept entering my mind. Close call. Dodging a bullet. Lucky. Blessed. I could go on and on—all I knew is that everyone deserved a second chance, sometimes a third or fourth in my case.

As I was headed back upstairs with the breakfast tray, I heard the newspaper land on the porch. The paperboy had perfected throwing it over the seven-foot-high gate. I set the tray down and wrapped my robe tight to get ready for the morning cold. I scooted fast and grabbed the Sunday *Times*. Having the paper delivered first thing in the morning started out as part of the job; now it was a relaxing ritual. I slipped the thick newsprint under my arm and headed up the stairs.

Jake was sitting up but relaxed against a stack of pillows.

"Hey, sleeping beauty, got some coffee and cinnamon raisin toast."

He sat up as I came toward him with the tray. "I've got something for you, too."

I gently scooted the tray on his lap and kissed him lightly on the lips. "Honey, no. Your coffee's going to get cold."

"I'm not talking about that," he said, biting into his toast.

"Oh, right." I stood up straight, pulled my robe tighter. He reached into the side drawer and handed me an envelope.

"Open it."

"What is this?" I pulled out a check made out to Jackson Memorial Hospital. I kept squinting to see if the row of zeros would shorten or keep getting longer.

"A donation," Jake said sweetly.

"I can see that. This is a half a million dollars. You didn't have to do this."

"I did." He shook his head. "I didn't know how else to say I was sorry."

"Jake, no. I was the . . . I'm the one. You don't have

anything to apologize for. I knew taking that job would make you nervous. I was selfish—I could've done something else, like you said, if I wanted to work so bad, it could have been anywhere else but there."

"No. All that was my fault. The minute I challenged you, tried to put down your decision, I knew what I was setting myself up for. I know the woman I married. Your stubbornness, your passion, those are half the reasons I fell in love with you. Throw in a hospital with a threat of going down and I had a serious cause on my hands. And you know what, I'm proud of you for trying."

"You are?"

He nodded his head. "I was born at Jackson Memorial," he said softly. "I never wanted to see it close. I wasn't angry about you working there. I was angry about a lot of things, a lot was happening, stuff I was too embarrassed to tell you about."

I sat down on the edge of the bed. He moved the tray and pulled me against his body. "I caught Byron Steeple stealing from my company. Millions, and I couldn't figure out how he was doing it until it was too late. Byron is the one who gave ammunition to Fenny Maxwell, the one you met at the party, the blue eyes," he added, knowing that was description enough. "Byron was feeding her information. She knew JP Wear was in a serious hole, dependent on the Rocknell stores. She gave me an ultimatum. Either I merge with them to be a private label or she'd pull JP Wear off their floors, leaving me even deeper in red. JP Wear wouldn't have survived if I didn't fall in line. That's why I had to sell."

"Jake, no." I held on to him. "I don't care how many times I've already said it, I'm sorry I wasn't there for you."

"You were there—I just pushed you away." He kissed me on the forehead. The soft touch of his lips sent a storm of emotion through me. Our mouths pressed against each other. I wanted to climb inside his arms and stay there, loved and safe.

He peeled my arms away and looked me in the eye. "Promise me we'll never let anything come between us again."

"I promise," I said. I meant it. I'd spend the rest of my days giving all that I had to give, loving him without reservation.

Jake hopped into the shower. I rolled over and grabbed the newspaper off the tray I'd brought up. I knew there would be plenty on the Jackson Memorial fire. A large color picture of the firefighters shooting water up to the fifth floor while frantic hospital staff stood in the background.

Dr. Clint Fairchild, Head of Pediatrics and Neonatology at Jackson Memorial is currently under investigation for negligence after the accidental death of Dr. Burt Langley due to nitrogen explosion. The California Board of Health plans a full investigation to explain why the doctor would be performing unauthorized maintenance on potentially dangerous nitrous oxygen tanks.

Just as Clint had said.

I read the one paragraph in the newspaper and refused to read the rest. I flipped the *Times* closed then folded the paper over. The obituary section faced me. A photo of Dr. Langley caught my eye. Remembering his face on the gurney. Seeing the hurt and scared faces all over again. A wave of sadness hit. Dark wet spots appeared on the newsprint. It took me a moment to realize the spots came from my tears.

I read the small write-up for Dr. Langley, survived

by his wife and two children, memorial services will be held Monday at 2 P.M. at Greenville Morturary.

Down below another picture caught my eye. Under the grainy sepia-toned headshot was a small caption. IN MEMORY OF BYRON STEEPLE.

The sound of the shower stopped.

Jake was still in the bathroom drying off. I folded the paper, prepared to show him when he came out, *Look, this man who robbed you is now dead. Karma, huh?*

My mouth suddenly went dry, and my head hot. The buzzing in my ear grew louder. The sense of awareness, the ability to hear, see, feel, all too much at one time. I wanted the sound to stop, the small voice in my ear that said, Jake knows, of course he knows. I jumped out of bed and grabbed my laptop. I tapped a few keys and started a search on the Internet for how the man died. Within seconds the story, not more than a few lines popped up. Beaten to death. Found in his car. Nothing stolen. I read the same thing over and over again. No leads. Found dead.

"Already back to work?" Jake came out with a loose-fitting T-shirt and jeans. His hair was moist when he leaned over and kissed me. I closed my laptop. My eyes darted to the newspaper still facing Byron Steeple.

"Jake," I said, then nothing else. I blinked the tear away and it streamed down my face before I could catch it.

"Babe, it's going to take a while but the hospital will get back on its feet." He slid the tear away with the back side of his soft hand. "You want to do something today? Go to a movie, something to get your mind off everything?"

I shook my head, because I was still unable to speak.

"We should at least pick up Mya from your mom and

dad's house. I miss my baby," he said, slipping his feet into his socks one at a time. I watched his hands, his wrists, his arms, tight with muscle, and had no doubt of his strength. I'd seen him with my own eyes take down Clint, a solid few inches taller, with one blow. I covered my mouth but the sound still came, a hoarse cry followed by me trying to shut myself up.

Jake rushed by my side and threw his arms around me. "I got you, sweetness. Shh, it's okay. Right?"

I nodded my head. Eventually, yes, everything had to be all right. I wasn't in the kind of world where people died by another's hand. My world was safe. I held on to Jake as tight as I could, burying my face in his chest and arms, hoping I could read his heart. I knew the rhythm, his beat, the pace, but I couldn't find the answer to the question. It just wouldn't go away.

Smoke Signal

I was grateful for Monday morning, which signified hope and new promise for the week. I woke up early and called Trina, letting her know Mya would be with my mother so she didn't need to come in.

"How about tomorrow?" she asked cautiously.

"Why don't you take the entire week off," I said, knowing that a week would probably mean forever. My mother was right. There only needed to be one Eve. If things were going to change, I had to start in the obvious areas. Jake and I didn't need any more distractions from third parties. I wanted to be his wife and take care of our child and be the mother I knew I could be. I wrote out a check for Trina along with a letter of recommendation.

The smell of dampness and smoke hit me the minute I entered through the hospital lobby. The receptionist station in the entrance sat unattended; phone lines blinked and went unanswered. The sky had a solid cloud hovering low and menacing. No rain was in the forecast. The weatherman predicted a bright and sunny beautiful day. I kept looking at the large ominous cloud and knew the weatherman was wrong.

"You're here." Morgan stood at my door, markedly a

changed woman from the devastation. Her usually coiffed hair was pulled back in a rubber band. Her blouse was loosely tucked into a pair of elastic waistband pants. She was unraveling before my eyes.

"How're you holding up?"

She came inside with slumped shoulders and sat down. She began to tear up. "Burt . . . Dr. Langley and I were very close, more than friends," she added. I understood what she implied, though Dr. Langley had a wife and two small children. Her face began to tremble. She stared off before a single tear trailed down her face. Morgan dabbed her eyes with a balled piece of tissue. "He said he was sorry and it was his fault."

"Clint?" I said, "You're talking about Dr. Fairchild?"

"Yes." She wiped again. "He's responsible."

I came around and sat next to her. "Morgan, I'm so sorry for your loss, but if there's a breakdown, any semblance of this hospital going against a doctor, especially, Clint . . . Dr. Fairchild, Jackson Memorial won't stand a chance of getting through this."

"What . . . I'm going to protect him? I've lost someone I loved. I'm not going to protect him on any level."

I thought about what Jasper said, how no one wanted to stick by him. Every man for himself. "Please think about it, Morgan. If this hospital is ever going to survive, everyone has to stick together."

"If he's responsible, then he needs to pay the consequences."

I rubbed my tired eyes. "Let's just get a positive statement out there, put on a good face, and deal with what really happened as it was, an accident."

"That's just the issue, isn't it," she said defiantly. "We don't know what really happened. But we do know who was responsible."

We both looked up at the same time to see Kandi

blinking slowly, standing halfway behind the opened door. "I have the rest of my things."

Morgan stood up. "I wish you the best," she said with restraint.

Kandi cut her eyes toward me then back to Morgan. "I wish you the best, too."

I took a deep relieving inhale, then exhaled. Maybe real work could get done. Kandi and I in the same building, let alone the same room, was a dangerous mix. I was about to tell Morgan about the donation from JP Wear before I heard the commotion coming from the hallway. Morgan and I both trotted out, landing behind the small crowd that had already gathered.

"I'm not going to jail for what you did!"

"Someone call the police, this man is insane," Kandi's voice rose. "Get out of my way."

"They're already coming. I knew you'd point the finger at me eventually to save your husband. It'd only be a matter of days before you tried to pin this whole mess on me."

After finally pushing my way through the crowd, I saw Jasper pointing a shaking finger at Kandi.

"No one's blaming you for anything," Kandi said coolly.

"I already know what's going on. You think I didn't know what you were up to. She did it, she's the one unplugged the incubators." Jasper spun around to see if anyone believed him. "She started the fire, too."

Kandi adjusted the box in her arms. "Has someone called the police on this lunatic yet? Doesn't matter to me. I'm out of here." She attempted to pass, but Jasper stayed in her way.

"Okay, that's enough," I said. "Haven't we all had enough?" I faced Jasper. "Get out and don't ever come back. Just stay away and don't ever come back."

Jasper looked past me to Morgan as if he needed her permission. Was he really free? Morgan dabbed her eyes with tissue then turned away.

Jasper's face was covered with perspiration. He blinked the moisture from falling from his eyes. "I didn't do any of it," he said before turning and stumbling quickly away.

"He's a lunatic and you people just stand there." Kandi headed out.

I reached out to slow her down. "You'd better wait a few minutes until he's gone."

"Did you just put your hands on me?" She recoiled as if she'd been hurt. "I'm not Clint. I'm not going to fall for your goodwill bullshit."

"Look, we've all had more than we can handle. I just don't think it's a good idea if you go out there. He could be lurking in the parking lot or anything."

"He's the one better be afraid of me," she said before turning on her heels—and in that moment, I believed her.

I caught up with her before she got on the elevator. "Kandi, how did the fire start?"

"Are you insane?" she asked, stepping toward me. "You're going to believe a drug addict? You know, I've put up with all I can from your little meddling ass. If I wasn't pregnant, you and me would be down and dirty right about now. Stay the hell away from me."

"Clint could lose his medical license," I blurted, knowing that was the only thing she truly cared about. "If you know something, you have to tell what really happened."

"He's not going to lose. If anything he's gained his life back. This wretched place was sucking the life out of him. Anybody that walks into this hospital is destined to lose his soul. I'm glad. I'm so glad he can walk away, finally."

"You seriously need help."

"You're the one that's going to need help." A half smile rose on her face as the elevator doors closed.

No truer words had been spoken. It was time to roll up the sleeves and get to work. I'd nearly sacrificed my marriage for Jackson Memorial. I wasn't going to sit and watch it go down without a fight.

By the day's end I had a list of events that would give Jackson Memorial a head start to the finish line. The best part about throwing myself in headfirst was that the mystery of Byron Steeple's death, right along with all the other unanswered questions, quickly moved to the bottom of my slush pile. I had calls to make and sponsors to beg for donations.

I left the hospital well past dark, feeling positive and hopeful. I strolled through the parking garage carrying my bag and leather attaché, relieved I didn't have to worry about Jasper creeping up behind me anymore. What I hadn't expected to see was the word *BITCH* scratched on the hood of my car. So right about here is when I was through with the happy-go-lucky we-shall-overcome crap. I walked around the car looking for the rest, maybe a sentence or two, a long scratch down the side for good measure. There was nothing else but the childish scribble on the front hood.

Of course Kandi was the first person who came to mind. But since I had no witnesses, I'd never know. I threw my things in the car and locked myself in tight. I was about to start the engine when someone rapped on my window. I grabbed my chest before looking up to see Clint tapping, indicating for me to roll down the window. I pushed the button, giving him an inch and not much more. "You scared me."

He breathed heavily, looking up past my car every few seconds. "Did you talk to Kandi?"

"You know, don't you?"

"What'd she tell you?" His fingers gripped the side of my door.

I shook my head in disgust and started the engine. "Back up, move," I said, putting the SUV in gear.

"V."

"No. No . . . I get it. You're protecting her. I mean, was she that unhappy and jealous of your precious hospital that she was willing to destroy it? You were right, it wasn't Jasper, was it? It was Kandi, and you knew the whole time."

"V, tell me what she said?"

"She said enough. I know what she did. But you know what, I don't care. I really couldn't care less. Now move, Clint, unless you want your feet run over."

"V, give me a minute. Just shut up a minute, please." He rushed around to the other side of my car and pulled on the passenger door. I wouldn't unlock it, but he kept trying. "Just open the door, V."

I knew I would regret it. He climbed inside. "Can we go somewhere else to talk?"

"I'm not going anywhere with you. You see what someone wrote on my car. Who do you think did that? Take a wild guess."

"Just drive, V. Please," he said sadly.

I put the SUV in gear then pressed it back into park. I turned the engine off. If Kandi was willing to take down an entire hospital to see her husband in a better light, I was toast. We weren't leaving that parking lot together. I turned to face him. "It doesn't matter. Okay. I'm done. I'm out. I don't care what happened. I should've never come here and got involved with you and her. I knew it was trouble, but something bordering on insanity kept me from walking away. But it's not about you or her. It's about that hospital and all those people who

might lose their jobs and this community that has nowhere else to go. And you and her can just go—"

"If I told the truth, somebody would go to jail," he
interrupted quietly. "Maybe even both of us," he said,
shaking his head with regret. "Kandi showed up at the
hospital with a letter I wrote. She found it. She wasn't
supposed to find it. It was like a practice run. I was telling her in the letter, that I wanted to leave . . . a divorce." He paused long enough for my shock to subside.
"She brought the letter to the hospital after she found it.
She cornered me outside the neonatal ward in the hallway. I told her to go inside where we could talk. She
went off, completely off, talking about killing herself
and the baby. She said she rather be dead right along
with my unborn son then let me run off with . . . you."

I gasped. "Me?" I shook my head with disbelief.

"I told her that you had nothing to do with my decision." He paused as if he wanted me to say something.
I couldn't. "She held up the letter with a lighter," he
continued. "I tried to snatch it out of her hand. Then I
heard the sound, the air pressure coming out the tanks.
Earlier in the day I'd reset them. That part was true, I
didn't get the connector on tight. It was leaking, as well
as the nitrous that backs it up. When Kandi struck the
lighter, I heard the searing sound, the pressure building
up. I grabbed her just before it ignited. I covered her
and the explosion happened. I got her out then went
back for all the babies. Everything was out of control.
The fire, the smoke.

"Dr. Langley came and started trying to put out the
fire. I didn't realize he'd collapsed until the whole room
was engulfed. I couldn't get him out. It was my fault,
any way you look at it. I don't need to involve Kandi.
It's not going change the end result."

I stared out the window and chewed on the inside

of my jaw, contemplating. "Clint," I said, frustrated. "I have to go."

"V."

"No, really, I have to go."

After a few moments he pulled himself together, stepped out of the car, and closed the door. I didn't hesitate, driving off as fast as I could.

I swung between lanes on the freeway, passing drivers who weren't trying to get home to their husbands. I wanted to get home to Jake. I wanted to hear him say, *It's going to be all right, babe.*

Other Fish to Fry

It wasn't so easy when I was playing in my own back-yard. Pointing the finger at Clint, judging his decision to protect his wife was the same crossroad I'd come to. The question of how Byron Steeple died hung in the air every time Jake walked into the room. The weight of the answer would've destroyed us, whether he told me what I wanted to hear or not. I swore I'd never ask. I just couldn't.

I was on automatic pilot. I woke up every morning putting my head and body to the grindstone. I packed Mya up and took her miles out of my way to my mother's house before going to the hospital. Trina was sent off with a healthy Jake the Fairy Godfather severance package. I could run my own household. I could handle the care of my own child and husband. I relished waking up to the sound of Mya screaming my name. *Maama!* I'd been granted queendom and all that the title required I willingly gave. I think the word I'd used was *fulfilled*. Which meant a full day of working at the hospital until I was exhausted and couldn't see straight. Then coming home to the challenge of trying to keep our feet from sticking to the floor. Never mind the un-folded laundry and piles of dirty dishes in the sink. Fulfilled, I said to myself daily. Sometimes I even spelled it out. *F-U,* well we know the rest.

I was admittedly wiser and more mature, perks of the job of being a working wife and mommy. The afternoon Wendy called to announce the finality of her divorce, I was full of advice and flowing with a positive outlook.

"He says he wants to get back together," she said over the phone. "He waits until the final papers come and now he's all apologetic and sick over losing me. I asked him, What about the little whore . . . what about her? He says there was nothing ever serious. He says the baby was born just as white as pancake flour. Not his. Ha! That's what his ass gets."

"Exactly," I said. "No one was ever satisfied with what they had until they'd experienced the threat of losing it all."

"He can forget it. I's a free woman. I won't go back, I can't," Wendy proclaimed in a fake southern drawl. She sounded strong and light, dignified and vulnerable all at the same time. "I plan on making some serious upgrades. I'm already registered for school. Moving back in with moms gave me the freedom to go back to school. . . . Can you believe it? I'll be forty-two when I graduate, and still in my prime. Do you realize people are living past ninety? That's too damn long to be alive and not have fulfilled your dreams, your goals." Wendy was preaching to the choir.

I said my *um-hums,* and *amens* on cue.

"I should be thanking that tattooed wench for sleeping with Sidney so I could find myself."

"Everything happens for a reason," I added to the stack of metaphors and clichés we'd already piled up. Knowing that once we hung up the phone we'd both wallow in self-pity and wonder why if change is so good, why we felt so afraid. I fell silent watching Mya unfold all the towels I'd folded. She laid them out in perfect rectangles on the floor, taking pride in her straight corners. When her round feet waddled over to straighten one side, she'd ruin the other, causing a lot of back and forth.

"So before I buckle down and start hitting the books, I need to do some serious rump shaking. I still got it, why let it go to waste?"

"Rump shaking?"

"Clubbing. Girl, how long has it been? We need to go out to celebrate my freedom."

"Eeeew, can't we just go to a day spa and get our eyebrows threaded or something? It's a lot less painful." I checked my wild brows in the mirror. Hadn't been tamed in quite a while. Between the hospital and trying to take care of home, I hadn't much time for anything. "No one goes clubbing anymore. It's like a bad scene from *Waiting to Exhale* the movie. Grown-ass women at a nightclub. It's just not right."

"Grown or not, I want to get my swerve on," she purred like a kitten. "This weekend. It'll be fun. We can go to dinner, go out for drinks, then find a hot spot and get down and dirty on the dance floor."

I crawled onto the floor next to Mya and helped her straighten out a towel before needing to lay down myself. I spread out on the plushness. Lucky me, I'd discovered Trina's secret for soft fresh-smelling laundry. One cap of softener on a second rinse cycle. Now all I had to do was learn how to fry some fish, but I'd get there.

Spreading out my limbs and flexing my toes, I tossed in a belly crunch. "It's not like I know where the hot spots are," I exhaled, letting my feet drop.

"Well, you've got forty-eight hours to find one."

"And then can we go to the spa?" I asked, hoping for a reward for submitting to dangerously loud music that could bust my eardrums.

"In case you don't know, there aren't any men at the spa, unless they're named Hugo and like to paint their toes a soft peach when no one is looking." She smacked her lips. "I can see already, I'm going to have to find me a new best friend. You're way too happily married with child." This Wendy assumed because I never mentioned a single thing about the hospital and Clint drama. I hadn't let it slip that Jake came home later and later in the evenings and sometimes into the dark morning when the sky was violet blue. Nor had I mentioned the constant ache just below my rib cage, better known as a terrible gut feeling that arrived each night right before bedtime, the anxiety of not knowing what was really happening in his world.

Mya got up and grabbed another towel. This one she spread over my face and body. I kept the phone at my ear while she covered me from head to toe. Mya's coal black eyes peeked at me, pulling the towel just low enough to match our eyes and nose. Both of us grinning insanely, I lay back down letting her cover me up with another layer or two of towels until the light of the room closed out completely.

"Wendy, you couldn't be more right, very happily married with child." When would the lies stop? "Hey, when you come, bring Sandy?"

"Sandy? I'm not carrying that dog with me on the plane. What am I supposed to do, put him in my Gucci dog case? That won't work, 'cause I don't have one. And secondly, Tia has grown much attached. I wish I would try to take that mutt away from her."

"Not to keep, just for a visit."

"Girl, please. You want to visit, you're going to have

to make the flight out here." She got quiet. "Is there something you're not telling me? Seems like you start yearning for your little cocker spaniel when you're having sad attacks."

"What the heck is a sad attack?"

"You thinking about what you coulda-shoulda had different."

"Wendy, tssch," I sucked my teeth in exaggeration. "I was just thinking Mya would love to be around a cute little doggy. Wouldn't you, Mya?" I poked the phone up through an opening of the towels. "Say hi to Aunt Wendy."

"Hiii," Mya said in her soft wispy voice.

I pulled the phone back in time to hear Wendy's excitement and baby talk ensued. "It's me," I cut Wendy off in the middle of a long syllable.

"She is growing up so fast. I can't wait to see my little princess."

"Yeah, she's running the place . . . and me." I flinched from Mya's foot stepping on me like I was part of the floor.

"What happened to your au pair via Compton?"

"Funny, ha ha. Trina left. I mean we let her go," I said, conveniently leaving out the full connecting story whereby she made me feel completely insecure in my own home. "See you this weekend."

"Who was that?" Jake came in or had already been in the room. I was lying flat on my back buried under towels. I rose up to see him go straight to Mya, picking her up into his arms. "How's my baby girl, huh?" Jake and Mya did the nose nuzzle. He put her back down and did a quick survey of the room.

"I know. Mya did it." I scooped the towels into the basket then followed him into the kitchen. Dishes from earlier covered the counter and filled the sink. Pasted cereal on the bowls. Milk film on the sippy cups. "Wendy's singing the praises of young, single, and free."

He pulled the microwave open and closed it just as quickly. The oven was next, the hinge squeaked from lack of use. Stellar clean since Trina left. I liked the spotless shine of the black ceramic top and chrome trim, and hadn't so much as boiled water or baked a frozen pizza to keep it that way.

"I didn't cook anything. . . . I got busy. My conversation with Wendy was over two hours, playing catch up."

He smirked and pulled a brown banana off the bunch. "So how's Wendy doing?"

"She wants to come out and celebrate her divorce being final. Go out dancing, eegh."

"Take her to Gotham Hall in Santa Monica. It's a nice place," he offered.

"No club is a nice place, and what do you know about Gotham City?"

"Hall," he corrected. "Gotham Hall is a restaurant but they have a dance floor. I've taken a few buyers there to entertain. It's cool. The club crowd is more your age."

My mouth dropped a little—not much, I could still carry my tongue. "Well, thanks. I hope they have a cane station so no one trips over us old fogies and all."

He grinned. "Mommy thinks she's old," he said to Mya, who was leaning on his leg getting her share of mushy banana, too.

"No, you think I'm old." I walked by and opened my mouth for a bite as well. Instead of breaking off a piece as he did for Mya, he stuck the whole banana to my mouth. I closed my lips around the curved fruit and sucked gently before taking a piece. I leaned against him. "I bet I know something where being older is an advantage. Especially when I lose my teeth and gum ya into ecstasy." My tongue skimmed the edge of my teeth for emphasis.

"Babe . . . not a good visual." Jake dropped the floppy peel into the garbage, leaving me standing alone near the sink. Mya was already trailing behind him, dragging a towel around her shoulders like superbaby.

This wasn't the first time in the past few weeks where I'd felt small, strangely incomplete. Like standing outside myself and watching from a distance. But I got used to it. I understood some things had to be compromised. We weren't the same people as two years before, eager and passionate, hanging on each other's every word. We were married now.

Open House

Wendy insisted on renting a car and taking the drive from the airport all by herself. Newfound independence and a nice plump divorce settlement gave her the freedom to do a laundry list of small things that boosted her self-esteem. The newly found woman was standing on my doorstep looking like a magazine spread for spring fashion. Only thing missing from her ensemble was a straw bonnet with silk flowers on the top.

"You look marvelous!" I pulled her inside for a long warm hug.

We danced around, then hugged each other some more. "So this is the Ponderosa. Whoa, girl. Just whoa. I love what you've done with the place."

"Well, I can't take any credit for it. It was like this when I got here," I confessed.

"So I'll give you credit for finding a man with good taste, 'cause the place is laid."

She screamed, "Mya! Oh my goodness, look how you've grown. Look at her."

I spun around to see Jake holding Mya's hand. Mya did a running step then slowed down not sure if all the excitement was over her.

"How you doing, Jake?" Wendy hugged him, and then kneeled down to Mya's eye level.

"Oh sweetie, you're beautiful. You remember your aunt Wendy?"

Mya stuck her tummy out as an offering. Wendy quickly scooped her up, kissing every part of her face. "Oh my goodness, I'd want to stay home and eat you up all day."

Jake caught my eye to say see-told-ya-so.

I gave him a yeah-we've-already-covered-this look.

Soon enough Mya started to squirm, requesting to be put back down. She made her way against Jake's leg, leaving Wendy to deal with the slighted feeling I was so used to.

"Here . . . come on. I'll show you to your room." I grabbed her suitcase, noticing the weight and wondered how long she'd really planned to stay.

"Nice. This must be where the au pair stayed," her voice dragged in a fake English accent.

I scrunched my face. Anything regarding the past few months made me uncomfortable. "Yeah. Sometimes."

Wendy slid her arms across the satin duvet then plopped onto the fluffiness. "If this is the guest room, I don't even want to know what your room is like. You know what . . . your life *is* perfect."

That was my chance to tell her how wrong she was . . . or technically, how right she'd been all along. The many times she'd corrected me . . . nobody is perfect, Venus, nothing is as good as it seems. The many times I'd refused to come down off my mighty cloud of joy, now I was willing to admit nothing is as it seems.

I stayed quiet, thinking if I opened the can of worms . . . they would turn out to be snakes. Dangerous. Poisonous no-turning-back snakes. I'd end up saying something stupid, like . . . I was living in this perpetual state of emotional separation, keeping myself blind and busy so I couldn't see the big snakes. The kind that lived under your bed each and every night but moved around invisibly. I was so afraid that the knock would come and there would be a detective so and so at my door, from the so and so division, to politely ask questions about so and so, murder.

"So where we going?" Wendy asked.

"Jake told me about a club. He said it was a nice place."

"Not too nice, I hope." She unzipped her suitcase and pulled out the Marilyn Monroe–style dress with a deep cut halter and billowy chiffon on the skirt. "Is this bad, or is this bad? You ought to see it on. Sexy." She held up the highest pair of stiletto heels I'd ever seen, the kind in the Frederick's of Hollywood catalog. "I'm on a mission."

"Indeed."

The emotional stress of worrying about Jake and the untold secrets in our life had taken a toll and I was looking forward to getting out of the house and spending the weekend with my best friend, even if it included a loud nightclub. So there we were, sitting at a small round table, the two of us, sipping on the second free round of drinks courtesy of the man with braids coming out of his head like Pippi Longstocking and little barrettes on the end. Thumping music vibrated up our feet and out the holes of our ears.

"Want to dance?" The free-drink guy stood over me, glaring with precision down my halter top.

Wendy darted her eyes. "Go. Dance."

"No more drinks," I said to Wendy, "the price is way too high."

The crowd seemed impossible. Too many people on one dance floor. I stood at the edge, afraid to move near the frantic bodies. "I gotta go to the bathroom," I yelled near the free-drink guy's ear.

"What?"

I pointed in the direction of the ladies' room. He gave me a disappointed nod. I steadied my walk so as not to look like an easy target. Still I'd warded off the obvious interest by looking no one in the eye. "Where you goin', pretty lady?" I let out an exhausted sigh. A couple more hours, I was thinking, that's all I'd need to endure. I entered the bathroom, and my entire life changed. The woman in red made it clear Jake had divulged secrets. He'd shared his pain. He'd made it clear. He was unhappy. Unfulfilled. I'd wondered if pretty red toes knew about the biggest secret of all, Byron Steeple. It was only a matter of time before the charade would end.

Woman in Red

So who do you think it is?" Wendy asked while I drove erratically in the darkness.

"I think . . . maybe, I'm not sure, but . . ." I wished I could tell Wendy everything. Some secrets should remain only between husband and wife. I'd seen the mistake made so many times, just friendly release, unburdening oneself of information hoping to feel better. Never worked out that way. The release into the universe gave it more power, where suddenly you were required to take action, to think and move and make decisions that would change your life forever.

"Spit it out. You know, in your heart you always know," Wendy said, more devastated that I hadn't told her about the hospital position with Clint and the whole scene with Jake showing up to find us at the hotel together. She couldn't care less about overhearing the woman in red stilettos. It seemed a minor symptom to a much bigger problem. I had to admit she was right.

"I think it's Beverly Shaun. You met her a while back. She's a designer for Jake's company. She went with us to lunch that day you came out."

"Beverly, yeah, the sista with all the hair."

I nodded.

"She was cool. I thought she was cool. She wouldn't do that, would she?"

I gave Wendy a sideways glance. "Didn't you just say you know when you know?"

"So, doesn't make it gospel. I didn't know Sidney was banging the babysitter." Wendy sucked her teeth. "Yes, I did," she confessed.

"She and Jake have been friends for a long time, but they were also lovers."

"Lovers, as in a long-term relationship, or it happened once and there was no chemistry kind of lover?"

I shook my head and gave her a look I couldn't put into words. "There's no one else it can be."

"I must say you are mighty calm to be a sista who just found out her man was screwing on the side."

Yes, I was calm. I was picturing myself high above in a cloud drifting off to a place called yesterday. I didn't want to deal with what was happening, what I knew was going to happen.

Jake was asleep when Wendy and I arrived. I let him sleep. I listened to him breathe and fall into a light snore. The next morning, I woke to an empty bed. I listened for sounds of running water in the bathroom, a tap of the shaver against the sink or maybe the stir of an electric toothbrush. I got up and put my ear to the door. Gone. What had he done, set his alarm?

The red stiletto voice in the bathroom replayed in my mind in echoes and double-toned words. I'd drunk too much. One free drink less and the room may have stopped spinning long enough for me to make a clear identification.

In his home office I sat in his big leather chair where my feet barely touched the ground and spun myself around slowly until I was too dizzy to focus. But still after a few moments the chant came back, *It could only be Beverly.*

I dialed Jake's cell phone. "Hi, you left early this morning," I said, holding the phone tight against my face. "Ah-huh, well, I was going to take Wendy out for a nice brunch. I was hoping you could come. I mean, she's only here for the weekend. Okay, yeah, I'll make reservations for a nice dinner. What about the Moustache Café? Is anyone else meeting you at the studio . . . just you?"

I spun myself just enough so that I couldn't quite hear him, another bout of dizziness. "What time do you think you'll be back? Okay. Um, I'll see you later, then. Love you, babe." He hung up first. I held the phone a few seconds longer. It wasn't like the old days when you could hold the line and listen while the person on the other end thought the line was clear and started dialing—then you could bust in and say, *Ah-ah, caught ya.*

"There you are." Wendy stood at the office doorway. Her long slender legs extended way past her T-shirt.

"Umm, do you need a robe?"

"Oh, yeah, forgot, there's male species here."

"No. He's gone. Had to get to the studio early this morning." I rolled my eyes with disbelief.

"Oh, now, there you go," Wendy said. "Let me tell you something, if you seek—"

"You shall find," I interrupted with a flip of my hand.

"Trust me, it's the oldest law on the books, and it's true."

"I didn't seek that woman in the bathroom, okay . . . she found me. I've seen everything . . . in this case heard everything I need to hear. I've accepted it. It's probably what I deserve."

Wendy stuck her lips out for a patronizing pout. "Don't cave in so early, mocha love. I put up with lies and alibis for almost twenty years. You're only in year two. Have some endurance for goddess' sake."

"I'm not doing the Whitney and Bobby thing. If Jake is messing around, we're through."

"I've heard absolutely everything. You will never cease to amaze me. There should be a display of you at the circus. Meet the amazing Venus Johnston. See her deny the fact that she was the one messing around in the first place, then want to burn the man at the stake for giving it back to her in double dose."

"This has nothing to do with me. I was never messing around. I explained that to you. Clint and I went to D.C. together on business. That's it. Besides, you have no idea what I've accepted, what I've put up with. He has no right or reason to want to give me anything back in a double dose except unconditional love and respect, like I've given him."

"Oh baby girl. Look at you." Wendy came by my side and put a warm hand on my shoulder. "Why don't you just ask? Get it over with. I'll take care of Mya. This isn't how I planned to spend my newfound freedom weekend, but for you, I'll sacrifice."

I took the offer. Within an hour I was on my way downtown to the JP Wear studio, hoping I would find the answer to every question and quiet every fear.

Pinning Ain't Easy

Jake switched the engine off and sat in the car wondering what he was doing in front of the JP Wear studio. He wished he could stop caring. It wasn't his company anymore, at least not like before. But there he was putting in work and dedication.

He locked himself inside the studio. The huge loft-like building covered a full square block. The building was part of the JP Wear assets, he was proud of that. Not like most companies, leasing everything from the sewing machines and chairs to the air they breathed and the water they drank.

"What're you doing here?"

He jumped when he heard the voice. Beverly stood at the top of the stairs. Her face was free of makeup. Her hair pulled back into a ponytail. Her weekend look wasn't lost on Jake, fitting in with his own overwashed denims and T-shirt.

"The question is, what're you doing coming in on a Saturday?"

"I work many weekends without gratitude or a simple thank-you. Didn't you know?"

"Yeah, I think I knew. Thank you," he added as an afterthought.

"So what's your excuse?" Beverly leaned on the steel banister, letting her elbows rest gently. "I thought you bowed out except in name only."

"This is me. Everything this company is, I built."

"And what a fine job you did, Mr. Parson. I appreciate the fact that you're still in the pursuit of excellence. Speaking of which, I'm up here busting my ass on these macho-man pants the new dragon-slayer wants to see by Monday morning and poor you has nothing to do. As a matter of fact, I know exactly what you can do." She directed him with a sly finger curl. "Get up here."

Jake took the stairs two at a time, glad to oblige.

"Take off your clothes," she ordered once he followed her inside the sample room.

"Shaun, I thought we already went through this."

She grabbed a pair of the sample pants off the table and threw them at him. "Put those on. If I was talking about the other way to get your pants off, I'd need a jackhammer."

"Turn around."

"Are you kidding? I've seen everything you've got."

"Not lately," he said.

She turned her back to him while he slipped off his jeans and changed. "Done?" she asked, facing the wall.

"Okay. Yeah, these are cool."

She snapped a tomato-shaped pincushion on her wrist. She kneeled down and grabbed a handful of fabric and turned him around by the seat of his pants.

"Ay, watch those pins."

Beverly blew out a sigh and flipped her ponytail over her shoulder. "You're talking to a professional. Just stay still."

"Now, see, that's too tight."

"That's not too tight." She released a bit.

"A man doesn't need fabric wrapped up his ass. You wonder why men got their pants sagging. It's because the crotch is too close."

"I assure you, my research indicates you are truly in a class all by yourself." She grabbed a handful of his manhood.

He gasped; still he didn't knock her hand away. A sign she could continue with her work. She accidentally stuck him with the first pin.

Jake flinched. "You trying to draw blood?"

"Stop being a baby. It barely touched you. Let me see. Want mama to kiss it for you, huh?" She lowered her voice to a soft connecting whisper. She pulled the fabric open, exposing his Calvin Klein underwear. "Humm, must not have hurt too bad." She stroked the fullness.

With the stroke of her hand, he thought he'd drop to his knees. He fought to stay standing. Every ounce of energy in his body diverted to the mass of hardness.

"Shaun, don't," he said, barely able to hear his own voice. He gripped her hand. "You keep messing around, you might get hurt."

"I like the sound of that," she said. The heat of her touch penetrated the fabric as if it wasn't there. She stroked harder.

"Shaun, don't. Stop."

"Okay, I won't stop," Beverly toyed, knowing exactly what he'd really meant.

She dug her finger around the loop of her ponytail, freeing her hair to fall over her face. Long sensuous strands brushed against his skin, seducing him to relax.

He grabbed her wrists, yanking her up to her feet. "Beverly."

She found his strength more of a turn-on. She leaned forward, ready to start fresh, a kiss, a flick of her tongue

across the line of his bottom lip and he would be all
hers.

He held on to Beverly's wrist. "Stop playing."

She refused to give up, leaning her body into him.
Pants fallen around his knees and the involuntary thick
erection exposed. He'd lost his balance, and squeezed
tight waiting for the fall.

"Jake!"

He let go to soften his own fall. She landed on top
of him. The fog of light-headedness cleared slightly.
The voice sliced through the haze.

"Ohmigod!"

Beverly stood up, her hand cupped to her mouth,
and was fast to the door. Jake shook his head, trying to
get the imagery of how it'd all started in the first place,
wondering how his guilty conscience could conjure up
his wife's voice so real. He looked around at that precise moment and knew it was going to happen. Knew
inevitably it was going to happen.

The slap across his neck, then his head, he felt the
pelts grow stronger with sting and precision. "You son
of a bitch!"

It took that long for him to realize it was really happening. Real-life blows. He was still on the ground.
His wife's tiny powerful hands socking and scratching
at his head. The tear of his skin under her nails. The
reality sank in. Pants down around his ankles. The fog
completely cleared.

"It's not what it looks like."

"You . . . son . . . of . . . a . . ."

He put his arms up to defend himself. And then she
was gone. His only proof that she'd been in the room
and not some poltergeist was the sting of air hitting the
open scratches on his neck.

He tore out of the room holding up the pants with no

zipper. He leaped over the last set of stairs, pushed out the double doors and onto the downtown street. Gone. Disappeared as effortlessly as she'd appeared. The street was desolate, as it should be on a Saturday downtown. Then what was she doing there? He let his hands fall into his knees while he hunched over to capture his air. The pound of his heart vibrated through his eardrums. What had he done? He tried to stand up, take a step forward, and knew he wasn't going to make it back inside. The grip around his chest clenched tight, twisting the air out of his lungs. His hands scratched and banged at his chest again and again. *Breathe.* He felt himself losing consciousness as he fell to the ground.

Jake sat down on the stool against her design desk. "Sit down, Beverly," *he said dryly.*

"Uh oh, the minute you start calling me Be-ver-ly," *she pronounced her name hard and studious, mocking him, "I know there's trouble. What now, Jay?" She stroked the fine hairs of his goatee.*

"You have to stop doing that. We work together. If you want to continue working together, you gotta stop the accidental touching, the hand slipping, warm shoulder squeezes, brushing against me."

"I didn't think you noticed."

"I'm married now. I want to stay that way."

Beverly reached across and stroked his brow. "Then I probably shouldn't have done that." Jake took a hold of the offending hand. He kissed her palm then placed it back in her lap. "Please, no more."

"You already said that. And like always, it won't happen again. And like always, I say, that's cool. Then I go back to doing what I do. You go back to doing what you do. I don't have a problem with that." She stood up. "Now, where were we before we were so rudely interrupted." She kissed him on the forehead,

"Oh yeah, let me get my pins." She winked at him then tugged at his shirt. *"Take off your clothes."*

"Take off his shirt," the doctor's voice boomed overhead. Jake could hear them doing their best to seem calm and in control. But he knew the urgency, no denying the panic in the room. "Start the IV, two cc's of prednisone."

The scissors sliced up the front of his shirt, each sleeve shed away easily.

"Blood gas is seventy-two. Let's move. Speed it up, please," the voice said.

Hands moved on all sides of him. Jake didn't ask anything of himself, or them. He knew what little energy he had should be centered on talking to his lungs, asking them to cooperate. People were trying to save him, so he didn't want to let anybody down. Others depended on him as well. His mother hadn't worked since his hit song went platinum nine years earlier. He tried to explain this to his mother, that the music business was smoke and mirrors. He had very little money once the record company, the manager, agent, publicity, and radio hands were greased. With the small amount he had left, he started JP Wear. He paid off his mother's house, so at least he didn't have to worry about that. But all the other things, putting his brother through college, keeping everyone satisfied, he still had work to do. Mya needed a father. He was her father, regardless of how many times the tiny little voice in his head reminded him otherwise.

The needle pricked his skin, entering at a bad angle. His body flinched as the injection settled underneath the flat surface of his hand. The first time he had an IV in his veins he was thirteen having an allergic reaction to the grass turf someone had dug his face into playing touch football. Fifteen years later, he was a grown man; this wasn't supposed to happen. He'd gotten control of everything that mattered. His health. His wealth. His lifestyle. He wasn't supposed to be lying on his back fearing for his last breath.

An eye for an eye, he thought. Maybe this was what he deserved.

The bone-chilling cold ran up his arm, splaying into his blood stream. Didn't they have the good sense to at least warm the bags at room temperature? Refrigerated fluids ran the course of his veins. The commotion in the room reduced to an instant calm.

"Blood gas at eighty," the woman's voice announced. Nice voice, young, East Indian, probably married with two children. Jake had the knack, an ability to hear as keen as a blind man. The rhythm of voices and sounds told him everything he needed to know.

"Bouncing between eighty-five and eighty-six. He's stabilizing."

He's stabilizing? No. Unstable. Bound to be a statistic. That's what he'd heard all his life. The scary myth that a young black man would either end up in jail or dead. He was going to die. If the inability to breathe didn't kill him, his wife would.

"We're at ninety." The voices all sighed relief in unison.

The solid pair of hands lifted from thumping on his congested chest, an odd process, but the vibration loosened the fluids that clogged his lungs. "Make sure the prednisone is on a steady drip," the physician ordered. Black. Definitely a black man from the bass in his voice, the slight song at the end of his words. One more who'd slipped past the burgeoning numbers. "And call his wife," the familiar voice said.

Jake's eyes flew open. The white light above his head blinded him.

He tried to speak, but nothing came. Clint. Dr. Clint Fairchild had just saved his life.

"Don't worry, I'm calling your wife. You're going to be fine," the nurse whispered soothingly. "Try to relax."

Shame Game

That's what he gets," Wendy said as she drove me to the USC Medical Center where Jake was taken in an ambulance. The hospital called and said he was in stable condition.

She tapped my hand. "It's going to be okay. He's going to be fine . . . but still, that's what he gets."

Chill and shivers quaked through my body. I wanted to curl up in a ball and get back under the covers where I'd run and hidden after managing to drive myself home. I was worse off, in no condition to drive, unable to handle large machinery just as the small label on the prescription bottle read. Three little white pills left over from my accident I'd swallowed without water to make me numb. I'd swallowed the pills the same as I'd swallowed the painful unbridled truth of what I'd seen. I may not have believed Jake was capable of beating someone to death, but this crime I saw with my very own eyes.

Wendy stroked my arm. "I've got some tissue in my purse."

I used my sleeve. "I'm fine, please keep both hands on the steering wheel."

"You must be okay, giving orders," she said, taking

her hand of comfort back and putting more diligence
into getting us to the hospital in one piece. I don't know
why I was worried. She'd managed to drive all the way
to my mom and dad's house to drop off Mya with very
little instruction from me. She'd hit the freeway running,
going ninety miles an hour, and hadn't once fretted
about how crazy everyone else drove.

"This is just all too weird, I mean, the way this is
playing out is kind of kismet, don't you think?" She
didn't wait for an answer. "That's what he gets."

Wendy pulled the car to the emergency entrance.
The double doors opened to a serene picture of orderli-
ness and calm. There were so many directions, so
many different ways to go. Where did they house husbands who'd been struck down after being caught with
another woman? I sidled up to the friendliest-looking
triage nurse. "My name is Venus Parson. My husband's
name is Jake Parson. He was admitted a couple of
hours ago."

The woman peeked over her glasses and calmly said,
"Have a seat." Wendy took my arm and guided me back,
away from the glass partition. She knew I had no plans
on sitting anywhere, let alone waiting around for when
the receptionist decided to do a patient check.

The receptionist punched a few keys on her key-
board then twirled her chair to another computer to
type again. I watched her every move, deciding if she
hadn't called my name in the proceeding few minutes,
I'd planned to go through the double doors and find
Jake myself.

"Mrs. Parson?"

Relief washed over Wendy, who was more afraid of
what the situation might entail. "Over here." She waved,
rushing me back to the window.

"Mr. Parson is in Triage A. Go through these doors,

make a right, and follow the red line all the way back to room eleven." She pushed up her glasses and went back to her computer.

"Thank you," I whispered.

The hallway corridor seemed endless. The red line became wavy and blurred. I stopped. "I can't do this. Why am I even here?" I wiped the endless stream of tears from my eyes and nose.

Wendy turned to face me, giving me a long warm hug. "You love him, that's why you're here. You just love you some him, sweetie. And it's okay. That's good. You know how I know? There wouldn't be all these tears if you didn't. So, let it out, it's okay."

I couldn't begin to count how many times I'd cried on Wendy's shoulder. She was there when it counted, always on time regardless of the distance in our life. I wiped my face. My sleeve had become soggy for all the work it was doing.

"He's going to be fine. You guys are going to get through this."

I took a deep breath and believed what she'd said. We strolled the rest of the red line, stopping in front of the room. "I'll wait out here." She stayed outside the door while I went inside. Jake lay with his eyes closed, though I knew he wasn't sleeping just by the tenseness of his facial muscles, the placement of his hands across his middle. He was thinking, not sleeping.

His eyes opened slightly when I took the first step. I couldn't go any closer. The tubing clipped into his nostrils prevented him from lifting or turning for a better glimpse. "I'm sorry, babe. I'm so sorry," he said into the air.

"I'm sorry, too." I swallowed and fought hard to keep it together. "Are you going to be all right?"

He didn't answer. I moved one more step closer. I

could see the stream of tears rolling down the side of his face. I moved even closer, arriving at the side of his bed. I used the fabric from the pillowcase and patted the next fluid stream before it could tickle past his ear. A box of tissue was on the other side on the white countertop, but seemed too far away. I kissed the cool skin of his forehead, then the bridge of his nose.

"You're going to be all right." I squeezed his hand.

"It never happened," he said. "I swear, it never happened."

I shook my head, letting him know I didn't want to talk about it. I peeked at the various monitors and knew enough to understand I was affecting the extra bleeps on the screen and the numbers jumping up and down. I backed away. "I better go."

"No, baby, please don't leave me."

"It's okay, I'm not leaving, just right out there." I pointed past the door. But Jake knew what I meant, and I knew what he meant when he'd asked, please don't leave *me*.

Outside the door, Wendy stuck her hands in her jean pockets and walked slowly toward me. "What's the diagnosis?" Her question asked more than for a simple answer.

"I don't know."

"So I guess you're waiting to hear from the doctor." Her eyebrow went up. "And here he comes." She looked past me. We both faced Clint as he strolled toward us. I was taken aback. He looked tired, thin, like he'd lost a lot of weight. As he got closer, he tried to pull up a smile.

He hugged Wendy first. "How you doing, Wen-Dixie? Long time no see." He cupped both hands over her tiny curls and ruffled them a bit with approval. "Cut it all off, huh? I know what that means."

"That's right, don't start none, won't be none." Wendy handed him off to me.

I reached around his shoulders and forced myself not to inhale his familiarity. His friendship. His shoulders seemed frail, breakable, but he squeezed tight with undeniable strength.

"You okay?" He asked near my ear.

"Fine." I backed away, depending on the stability of my sneakers to keep me grounded. "You're like the Fairy God-Doctor. You magically appear every time I'm in a hospital."

Wendy shook her head. "He wasn't there when you delivered Mya. That reminds me, I thought you were a pediatrician. What're you doing around gunshot wounds and stabbings?"

I cut my eyes at Wendy.

"I left Jackson Memorial," he said in stride." "I took this position until something else comes through. I'm looking to move back to the East Coast." He omitted the whole ordeal of the state board of health investigating him and charging him with negligence. Lucky to have any position in medicine, let alone emergency medicine.

My eyes grudgingly turned to the door where Jake lay quietly waiting for judgment. "So it was you. I wondered how anyone would know to call me."

"Soon as I saw him, I recognized him and took extra care because I knew who I'd be dealing with if anything went wrong." He sort of grinned but it smoothed out quickly to seriousness. "He went into a state of hypoxia." Noticing the haze, he cut it down to layman's terms. "Loss of oxygen to the brain. Not a good thing. He's lucky."

I gave Wendy another look; she ignored me.

"What?" Clint noticed the unspoken communication between Wendy and me. "What's that about?"

"No. Nothing. I'm just glad he's fine." I bit the inside of my jaw, grateful God hadn't heard my call. Only for a millisecond had I wished upon Jake a slow suffering death. Then we would never have to talk about what happened, what I witnessed with my own eyes and never have to deal with it. Instead, now it would become a mainstay of our marriage, a stain on the carpet eventually accepted and ignored. But newcomers would see it, notice the wide dark circle, not sure what caused the stain in the first place. They'd notice how we hardly touched, hardly smiled or truly looked each other in the eye. Maybe they'd assume it was from time, simple wear and tear.

Clint looked closer, nudged my arm. "You sure?"

"Ahum. Wendy, I'm hungry, you think you could check for something edible in the cafeteria?" I squinted my tired eyes.

"Sure. Yeah. Okay. Be right back. Not right back. I'll be back a little later. Take your time," Wendy said, turning and walking away with no sure direction.

Clint and I faced each other. "I just wanted to know how you're doing. Everything, you know."

"As long as Jake is fine, I'm fine," I said, wishing my face hadn't given me away.

"It's okay," he whispered, coming toward me with comforting arms.

I took a step back. With a solid deep breath I decided to get it together. "What about you? How are you, really?"

"Kandi and I are trying to work everything out. We're seeing a counselor."

I nodded my head. "I hope it does. I hope everything works out. I'm going back inside, see how he's doing."

"V, I've thought about calling," Clint said quietly. "Do you think it'd be okay . . . if I called?"

I shook my head. "Probably not."

He let the answer linger for a moment, understanding its full meaning. "Okay." He nodded his head in acceptance. "Okay."

I blinked my tired eyes, returning the same understanding. I went inside and found my way next to Jake.

Aftermath

The next day I brought my husband home. We said no more than two or three words to each other in the car. He asked where was Mya; I said with my parents. I helped him up the stairs and into a hot shower. I shoved all his clothes into the laundry basket and then came back when I heard the distinct sound of his cell phone ringing. I pulled his pants out and dug into his pocket. The animated envelope spun around to announce a message. I flipped the silver phone open and pushed a few buttons, until I figured it out.

The text message showed up, "I hope u r all right," it read. "Called hospital no info."

It was from her. I closed the phone. On second thought, I opened it back up, *"F-i-n-e,"* I typed in. I pushed SEND and waited. The next response read, "Call OK."

I closed the phone, and then opened it back up. I couldn't resist. I listened as the water continued to run in the shower. I took the phone downstairs. Someplace quiet. Out to my car parked in the garage. I got inside and locked the doors. I didn't want anyone to hear what I was about to say or do. I didn't want it leaking out into the air like poison, lingering on the walls or the furniture, settling into cracks or flowing through vents.

She picked up on the first ring.

"I'm only going to say this one time, and you better know I'm serious. If I see you, if I hear you, if I even think you're lurking around, I am going to find you and give you a beatdown you *will not live to regret*. Do you understand?" The rest that followed was probably only for therapeutic purposes because she'd hung up long before I was through screaming into the phone.

It felt good, if only for a few relieving seconds. Tearing her down, ripping her to shreds, envisioning all kinds of heinous acts against the two-faced bitch sent my adrenaline racing. Thoughts rushed in and out, swirling thoughts of Jake, what I'd seen even before opening the door all the way. The scene would forever be etched into my mind. I wondered how, if ever, we were really going to get through to the other side. Make it back to where we'd started.

I heard a tapping sound on the window. My heart nearly leaped out of my chest. I dropped the phone, letting it slip between the seat and the gearshift.

"What're you doing down here?" Jake was leaning against the door.

I got out of the car, heart still beating wildly. "You should be upstairs." I tried to keep my eyes centered on his chest, his throat, anywhere but on the worry and heartache in his eyes.

He had no idea why I was sitting in the car, but that's where he'd found me. He reached out and pulled me close. His body trembled, still moist from the shower. "Please don't leave me," he breathed into my hair, against my face. "Please," he whispered, assuming I was planning a getaway.

"You shouldn't be moving around like this," I said, somewhat satisfied. I helped him back upstairs and into bed.

Wherever I landed, he was underfoot. It went on like that for days. He didn't go back to the studio for almost a week. He said it was okay—he just wanted to be at home with me. I think he thought the day he came home after being gone, I wouldn't be there. I thought it, too. I thought, the minute he leaves, I'm right behind him, out the door, running screaming, like a madwoman. But I stayed, and I held my breath, and watched my words because I didn't want to shame him the way he'd shamed me. It wasn't any fun and I didn't have the energy required to follow through.

"Do you think it would be okay if I went to the studio?" He looked tired and miserable. I wanted to say, *It doesn't feel too good does it, staying home all day feeling of no use to anyone?*

"I haven't stopped you from going anywhere, from doing anything. Don't ask me if you can leave the house like I'm keeping you here. I'm not. I'm not keeping you anywhere. You want to go, go."

He stepped away, as if I'd given him exactly the reaction he'd expected.

I paced around the house, still glad my mom and dad had kept Mya. "You guys need time to heal," Pauletta said over the phone when I couldn't get all the words out. "Don't worry about it. Take as long as you need."

The minute I heard Jake's car pull out of the garage, I got dressed, pored through the yellow pages, and landed on Josie's House of Style. The ad was the biggest on the page. Relaxers. Weaves. Color. All in seventy-two-point font. No customer leaves Josie's unhappy.

Josie's House

"What I don't understand is if old-school hottie is still hooked on you and you still seem to be catching feelings for him, why didn't you just take the opportunity and make it happen, get it over with and out of your system for good?" For the last hour, Shane had listened compassionately, right along with the rest of the salon populace. They all listened, waiting for the next dramatic part of the story. So many parts I'd left out because husbands and wives are allowed their secrets.

I threw my head back. "I'm in love with my husband. And regardless of what happened, I know he loves me, too."

"He had a fine way of showing it," a woman from a couple of stations away added. A liberal amount of get right cream covered around her temples. Her eyes cut through me. "So I guess you believed him when he said it never happened." She coughed out a mild laugh. "You gon' believe me or your lying eyes. That's a classic."

I ignored her sarcasm. Of course I didn't believe him. I was no fool. And yet, I did believe him, though ashamed to say it out loud. Jake was allowed this one mistake. Just one.

"Now you say this woman whose mouth accidentally swallowed your man's tongue, was one of those gorgeous got-it-all-together types? So this is your way of fighting fire with fire?" Carmena nearly burned her customer's hair pausing too long with the flat iron near her ear. A light billow of smoke rose from the hair.

The customer squealed.

"I'm sorry, I'll get some ice." Carmena rushed off.

Josie leaned over Shane's shoulder. "It's a crying shame to straighten all that virgin hair, but I ain't gone lie, you about to knock your man off his feet," Josie hummed moving back to her own station. "Straighten up and fly right."

"So did this Kandi, the doctor's wife, have the baby?" Shane whispered, still stuck in the epilogue of the real drama, better than *Days of Our Lives* and *The Young and the Restless*. Forget about Nikki and Victor, these were real characters with real heartache and pain.

Just the mention of her name left me squirming uncomfortably in my chair. I wanted to feel sorry for Kandi, to be so insecure, to be so desperate to do what she had. "She hasn't had the baby yet. Hopefully, she'll be better by the time it comes. She's in counseling."

"What about the guy . . . stealing the drugs, where is he?"

"He's gone. No one has seen him. I doubt if he can be hired anywhere. I don't think he'll be working in any more hospitals."

"That's a shame. I was born at Jackson," Tikki piped in. "That guy should've been arrested."

I closed my eyes briefly, still not sure of who was doing what. Kandi or Jasper. Either one or both could have been responsible for the malicious acts. But the fire. I knew who'd caused the fire, and the anger still burned in my soul.

"Oh lordy, she needs a healing. See when people stop going to church, then all hell breaks loose."

"She needs to go to jail. In there you find Jesus real quick," Tikki added.

Another customer spoke up, "And did you beat the little hussy down who was messing with your man?"

"Look, this ain't the ghetto chronicles, y'all," Shane announced. "We're talking about the high and mighty—they do things differently."

Carmena cleared her throat. "Not much. Remember Lionel Richie's wife? She beat Lionel and his little floozy down to the ground. Kicked his butt all the way to divorce court."

The salon crowd whooped and hollered.

Shane tapped me on the shoulder. "Okay," he said, pointing out the four separate trays of relaxer he'd stirred into creamy perfection for each massive section of hair, posing it somewhat as a question. The room fell silent, waiting for the drum roll.

I peered at the woman on the end who'd been the quietest of the bunch. No longer screaming mad about her bad weave job. She had a full crowning glory of soft opulent hair. A glowing reddish tint straight with a soft curl on the end. She stared at herself in the mirror. From her beaming smile, anyone could tell she'd been transformed. All was right with the world. She had plans, big plans. A wedding to tend to. A man who'd won her heart. Her confidence overflowed, sweeping a gust of satisfaction over the salon.

"You look beautiful," I said to her, reminiscing in the feeling when things were safe and predictable.

Shane reached over and handed me a fresh tissue. The other in my hand was balled up and shredded. "You gon' have to stop all that crying if we're ever going to get through this day. Please. This is supposed to be a joyous relieving experience. You will walk out of here every bit as lovely as any diva you've dreamed of being. Now buck up. Get it together."

"Don't rush her, Shane," Josie said, interrupting again. She sprayed the finishing sheen on her calm happy customer.

Shane unleashed the clip on the right corner of my hair. He held up one of the plastic bowls of chemical cream and dived straight in with his little black paint-brush.

"Wait." I held up my hand and stopped him from slathering it on. "I can't." I shook my head. "I'm sorry, I'll pay for everything, but I can't do it." I stood up and pulled the plastic cape off my shoulders. I dived into my purse and pulled out the hundreds. I laid them down on his counter. Then put one more bill down. Knowing the going rate of therapy, Shane had been a bargain.

I reached out and hugged his burly shoulders. "I'm sorry."

"Don't apologize. I salute you," he said with mock courtesy.

I turned to the rest of the ladies in the salon and put up a hand. "Thank you, guys, thanks for helping." I pushed the money into Josie's hands for the unruly weave customer.

Everyone had the same pained look of confusion on their faces. I was walking out of there with my hair sticking up like koala bear ears. Still unkempt or worse than when I walked in a couple of hours before but with something far more valuable. My dignity. My strength. Belief in myself and Jake. So what if things were messy. I didn't need to remake myself. Why start over? Lessons were learned that could only make me stronger, *us* stronger.

When I got into my car, I pulled the clips out and

fluffed myself into some form of normalcy. Back to my Spice Girl persona.

Later, parked in front of the JP Wear studio, I put on lipstick with a shaking hand. Every step I took was like walking underwater. Hard burrowing steps to the front door and inside. The open interior of the vaulted ceilings buzzed with energy. I was afraid I'd see Beverly, or worse, Jake with Beverly.

"Mrs. JP Wear, right?" Fenny Maxwell moved away from the few people she'd been talking with at the lobby entrance and beelined toward me.

"Right." I felt like pushing her in the face. "Excuse me." I went around her.

She turned to follow me, moving too close. I was sure her aqua-satin-covered breasts grazed me on purpose. "Jay's not here. In fact I don't think he's coming back. He doesn't have a reason to," she said with pleasure.

"What do you mean?"

She narrowed her eyes. "You seem surprised. He sold the rest of his interest in JP Wear. He's no longer an owner." Her soft translucent eyes twinkled.

I backed away and sprinted out the door and drove home at lightning speed.

Going Once

I knew exactly where to find him. Jake sat on the shore-line with his pants rolled up, his feet burrowed in the sand. The water was still a safe distance away, but there was no guarantee the current wouldn't sweep up with a wave out of nowhere, leaving a crop of stranded seaweed in its wake.

I sat next to him. "What happened? You just walked away from everything you built."

He took another handful of sand and poured it over both our feet. "I couldn't fire Shaun without a serious sexual harassment suit headed my way. She made it clear she wasn't going anywhere without a fight," he said squinting against the sun.

"No one means anything to me but you. No one, nothing. It wasn't a hard choice. Going once, going twice." He improvised like an auctioneer. "Sold."

"It's still sad. Doesn't seem fair."

He hunched his shoulders. "It's cool. I sold my interest to Legend." A mischievous smile rose on his face. "We have an understanding. Before long he'll drive them all mad."

"Now that's revenge. All this time I thought you just ignored his misogyny."

"I know exactly what and who he is. But at least I know him, what he's capable of and what he's not. And I know you." He reached out and touched my chin. We kissed lightly. "Do you know me?" he asked quietly.

"Yes. I do." I wrapped my arms around him and relished in his strength.

"The past is the past," he said with quiet resolve. "It's just you and me, babe."

I held on to his arm and leaned on his shoulder. "If I could, I'd turn this whole world upside down, shake things up to make them right."

"Sounds like a song," Jake said. "Maybe we can start our new career together as lyricists."

"I'll do anything as long as it's with you."

"Um, a duet. I'm loving this song."

"It's not a song. It's the truth."

He draped his arm around my shoulder. "You want to hear my truth? Nothing happened that day. What you saw wasn't what was happening. I don't want anyone but you," Jake said, taking a handful of my wild do. "But I seriously don't know about the Afro puffs. What's going on back here?"

I reached up and felt two clips I missed left by Shane. "Oh, yeah. I was going to get a perm today. Make myself over, long and straight like—"

"Don't even say it. Don't. I love you, everything about you." We leaned back in the sand holding hands side by side, burying ourselves as one big mountain and waited for the big wave to roll through and wash it all away.

I knew it wouldn't last forever. For now, I was glad to snuggle in his smooth chest, his strong arms.

"What're we going to do today?" I said, biting his chin. We'd just spent all afternoon making love.

"Something we haven't done, something adventurous. Hey—" he exaggerated his novel idea "—maybe we should go to the grocery store and actually get food that you cook instead of microwave."

I popped him on his shoulder. "I cook." Top Ramen noodles and frozen vegetables entered my mind.

"We'll stop at the bookstore and pick up a couple of cookbooks."

I bit him, or attempted to on his firm chest before he shifted out of the way. "You know I can cook."

"I'm just playing with you, babe."

"I know you are. I'm seriously the queen of cuisine." I rested my head against his chest. "I'm open for any suggestions, though," I conceded. He was right; it was time to stop being afraid of my oven and stove. As Trina had pointed out, that's what 409 was for. I used to love to cook. I'm almost sure of it.

We showered, shampooed, and shined, picked up Mya from my parent's house, and were on our merry way to being a family again. I couldn't remember the last time all three of us were in one car. First stop, the bookstore. Jake was completely serious about the cookbooks. Not any cookbooks. We had to drive a solid forty-five minutes on surface streets to the independent bookstore in the solidly black part of town.

"You want me to make bean pies, or something?" I smiled while we piled out of the car.

"Nah, I want some serious soul food, some collard greens, corn bread—"

"Neckbones? Pigfeet?" I whispered, not to interrupt the quiet atmosphere as we pushed through the heavy glass door of the bookstore. A slim man with a thick mustache waved from behind the counter. He was too busy reading an issue of the *Black Revolution Newsletter* to look up.

We found our way to a small section of cookbooks. Mya picked out everything at her eye level and handed them to me. Jake grabbed Patti Labelle's cookbook and winked, and nodded.

"Oh please," I said, "I bet Patti's not throwing down on no pork."

Jake took Mya to the kid's section. I kept browsing. That's when I heard it, the voice. The laugh. "Jaaay, what're you doing out here? Look at my baby, look at you. Give me a kiss."

"Hey, girl, you're looking good." Jake's response was laced with a bit of apprehension. "Nice to see you." Apprehension and phoniness.

"You're looking good for a man who was on his death bed."

The familiar twang against the high-beam ceiling bounced off the walls. I spun around, unsure which direction to follow. The voices were hollow, looming over me like angry spirits. The ground seemed to swell. I couldn't move, at least I thought, until the final step sent me stumbling over a raised piece of carpet.

I landed at the feet of Jake and a pair of shiny red toes in pretty yellow stilettos. My stilettos. I recognized the worn lip of the Jimmy Choos where I'd actually used a glue gun to meld it together for one more summer of wear.

"Venus, hey, long time no see." Trina peered down at me, holding Mya.

"Babe, you all right?" Jake reached and was lifting me from the waist. I slapped at his hands. My heart was beating faster and faster with each breath.

"I see you put good use to all those clothes." I swallowed more air.

For a friend, huh.

"Yeah, worked out. Thanks," she said. For an awkward

moment, she and I stared each other down. "Jay, don't be a stranger," she said, cutting her eyes slowly toward him. "See you later, Mya." She put Mya down and did a slow turn walking away in the too-tight pants and sleeveless turtleneck sweater. The sweater wasn't mine, but the pants, she was too damn big for the pants.

I stood stupefied. My eyes continued to dart in her direction long after she was gone.

"Whoa . . . hey, what's this about?" A look of mystery hovered over Jake's dark brows. He blinked. "What's this about, babe? Tell me."

"That's her . . . that's the voice in the bathroom."

"I haven't the slightest idea what you're talking about."

"She's got on my clothes!" I screamed loud enough for the thin man with the heavy mustache to wrestle with his newspaper and come find out what all the shouting was about.

"Y'all going to have to leave. We can't have this kind of thing going on in here."

I brushed past the thin man, scooping Mya up and out the door just in time to see the little sports car with the canvas top pull away. *Jay is miserable, it's about time he realizes his marriage is the reason why.*

Jake followed. "What? Trina? You think I was messing with Trina?"

I broke free and opened the back door, pushing Mya to climb into her car seat.

"Don't you dare lie to me. Don't you dare. I heard it all, but I didn't know who it was until now, Miss Queen of the Makeovers. Now I see, squeezing her ass into my clothes, my shoes. Fake hair and that stupid car. Did you buy that for her?"

"Babe, please, I don't know what you're talking about!"

"Don't you lie to me!" My screaming made Mya cry out. We both peeked to see her struggling in her car seat, trying to get a view of what all the yelling was about.

"Calm down. I swear none of this is making sense."

"You sure talk a good game, Jake. I trusted you. I went against every instinct in my head and I trusted you. All my common sense out the window to believe in you." I shoved a finger in his chest, hoping it hurt him as much as it did me.

"That night at Gotham Hall, she was bragging about how you were finally going to be hers, how I was too busy running off with my ex-charity-doctor to focus on our marriage. I heard her in the bathroom. I couldn't tell who she was, but now I know. Why do you think I went to the studio that day, huh? I was going there to ask you about what I'd heard. Now I find out it's someone completely different."

"Babe," Jake tried to interrupt, but I couldn't be stopped.

"So what else are you not telling me? Let's just clear the air, shall we. I know about Byron Steeple."

What did I say that for? I felt my feet lift off the ground. Jake's arms tightened as I struggled. He effortlessly opened the car door and pushed me inside with one shove then climbed in beside me.

He held up a warning finger. "Watch what you're saying."

"Or what?" I had already broken down, he could have told me anything and I would have said, okay, whatever, so what, because it didn't matter anymore. I was tired and disgusted, ready to walk away and never look back. "What!" I screamed. "Are you threatening me?" Mya screamed, too. I faced her and had an instant flash of the accident. This one may have been worse.

This accident would leave us in pieces, ruined and broken, unable to put ourselves back together again.

"Listen. I'm never going to lie to you. But if you ask a question, you sure as hell better be able to handle the answer."

I bit my lip and tried to stop the tears from streaming. "Get out. Get out of the car."

"Yeah, I talked to Trina and probably told her some things I shouldn't have, but you weren't there."

"Oh, here we go again. My fault, right?"

His face twitched. "You want some more truth? Is that what we're doing, being honest? You need to stop worrying about Byron Steeple 'cause I was this close . . . this close." He held up his hand and pressed his thumb and index finger to the front of my face. "This close to taking your boy out."

I had no response. Still too stunned. He was talking about Clint.

He opened his palms. "Some things are better left unsaid, right?" Jake got out of the car and slammed the door. I scooted to the driver's side, started the engine, and took off. Mya cried all the way home.

I stood in the bathroom with my scissors plied open, ready for the first cut. The first always being the most difficult. Once that was done, there was no turning back. One hand tightened around as much of my hair as I could get, the other holding the shears.

The bushel of hair fell to the ground. It was time to start anew.

Mya picked up a handful and put it on top of her head. She turned up her nose.

"You can have it, sweetie." I snipped and cut to the song playing in my head, soft, melodious, and refreshing. No specific tune, nothing I could identify, just new, and revived. I never thought this day would come. I hadn't planned for it, really, starting over. I wanted this place of security and hope, real life to stay forever. Jake was my hope. My security. My love.

I washed the soft texture, what was left, and wrapped a towel around my head. Next step was to pack. It was simple as that. I couldn't stay. I had no choice in the matter. As I put things in the bag, Mya took them out as if she refused to let this happen and would do everything in her baby power to stop it.

I braced myself when I heard Jake coming up the stairs. He rushed into the bedroom and stopped mid-step when he saw me come out of the closet holding the last of my clothes. His eyes went straight to my leather bag. I ignored him and continued packing.

"Don't do this," he said, grabbing for the bag. I reached for it and he pulled it farther away.

I hunched my shoulders and went for something else. The Samsonite was a bit large, more overstated but it would do. I rolled it out and began to put the few things I had left inside.

"I'm asking you to listen to me. Everything we've been through and you can't hear me now? Just listen," he whispered. "Please."

The truth of the matter was, I didn't want to hear him. People like me were meant to be alone. I was convinced now. I'd fought against it for long enough, believing in the magic of togetherness. Marriage. But I couldn't hide from the natural order of things.

"I'm sorry, I can't," I said, not sure which part I was sorry about. The fact that he'd sold his company for me. The fact that he'd spent the last couple of years loving me, or that I loved him, still. None of those things mattered now.

"I have to go."

"No, you don't. You don't have to do anything except what you want. Remember? You don't *have* to do anything." He sounded as if I were standing on a ledge and he was sent to talk me down. "Please don't go, babe. Don't leave. You promised we were going to always be there for each other."

I shook my head because I didn't remember making any such promises.

"You did, babe. You promised to love me always. Just like I promised to love you. We can't go back on our promise."

"You did. When you stopped trusting me, you stopped loving me. I don't know you, Jake. I thought I did."

"You do know me." He slapped his fist into his open palm. "I promise . . . all new . . . all over again. Promise, from this day forward to love you with all my heart, do you hear me, babe, all my heart. No negotiation. You love me, don't you? I know you do. And I love you. Don't deny what it's worth. Don't pretend like that's not enough, because I know it is." He took a step forward, one cautious step at a time as if I would jump from the imaginary ledge at any moment.

When I looked down, there was no danger. I could walk or I could run. There was nothing keeping me there.

"Babe, please. Look at me. Just look." Another step closer. I felt his hand entwine into mine. Then the other. The smooth pat of skin met his lips one hand at a time. He took the sign as a chance to rest his case, leaning in and cupping my face for a lingering kiss. I pushed him back. The towel fell away, revealing my new haircut. His mouth fell open slightly. Shock, then sympathy. He tried a smile.

I stepped away, zipped up the bag, and slung it over my shoulder. Mya leaned against the bed watching us both, knowing what she was a witness to wasn't quite right, but beginning to get used to it the way children do. I picked her up, hugging her tight. Jake still hadn't said a word.

I wanted to laugh out loud, but the silence felt safe. I was home free to live my life as nature had planned. The same way I realized the night of the fire in the hospital, regardless of what decisions I'd weighed and prayed over, some things were just meant to be.

"If you walk out that door, I'm going to lose you forever," he said from behind me. "I can't let you walk out of here like that." His breathing became labored. I forced myself not to turn around. Not to respond.

"I'm leaving. I don't think there's much you can do about it." I stood at the door, feeling strong. I had the natural order of things on my side.

"If you walk out of here, I've got no chance of getting you back because . . ." He took a long pause. "Okay. You don't need me. Fine. You don't need me, but I need you. I don't want to be without you."

I started toward the door.

"Can I come? I swear I won't complain about a thing." He was talking fast in between breaths. "I'll eat fast food or Top Ramen. I'll even cook. Clean, too. Okay, I might hire someone to clean . . . but the cooking part . . . Babe, please," he said after the stillness wore him down. "I'm sorry for every misunderstanding, every word that wasn't said, every word that was. I should've trusted you. Simple. But you've got to trust me now. As difficult as that might be, you've got to believe in me."

Mya's soft voice broke the silence, "Daddy." She reached out over my shoulder to Jake. When he came to take her, she wouldn't let go of me, tightening her grip, somehow wrapping us both in her small but powerful little arms, pulling us together head to head.

His arms cradled Mya and me both.

"You really gonna cook?" I asked with my face against his neck.

"I'll do anything you ask. Can I ask for one thing, though, just one?"

"What?"

He took Mya and put her down gently. "One second, Mya. Daddy has to talk to Mommy." Jake put my hand on his chest. "You feel that, babe? No one else in this world has my heart." He looked me in the eye. "Please just know it. I will never shut you out again. You know how much I love you?"

I closed my eyes, pushing out the final tears. "I know it."

"You know it?" he asked again.

"I know it," I repeated until my heart felt the same.

A rainbow of balloons floated overhead. A sign hung through the center of the street and connected from one lightpole to the other. Jackson Memorial Health Fair was in full swing. The line for the free blood-pressure testing extended past the line for free flu shots, which extended far past the line for diabetes screening, which rivaled the line for free condoms. Obviously there was still much work to be done.

For once, the media would have something good to say about Jackson Memorial. I marched up to the podium with a speech all ready. I looked out on the full square block full of festivities and hated to interrupt. The white-and-blue T-shirts with the Jackson Memorial logo worn by staff and volunteers and myself sprinkled about.

"Hello, everyone." I tapped the mike. "Thank you all for coming out. I want to thank the sponsors of this great event. Thanks to all of you, we've reached our one-million-dollar goal. They say it takes a village to—" I stopped midsentence when I realized no one was really listening. I folded the speech I'd planned to read and laid it down.

"This is the most amazing day I've ever witnessed," I said quietly. "You never know how far you can go until you feel like you can't go any farther and then someone comes along and offers you a little push, a bit of encouragement and tells you to keep going, you can do it. This day couldn't have happened without all of you, every single person here. I just wanted to say thank you." As I was about to step away, I heard one person clapping. I followed the lone cheer to Jake in the audience wearing his blue-and-white T-shirt with Mya perched on his shoulders. He clapped until it caught on with two or three people, then a few more until it rolled over into a thunderous applause. I moved through the crowd, where he met me halfway.

He kept right on clapping with me standing in front of him. Mya clapped, too, wearing her oversize Jackson Memorial T-shirt.

"I'll always have at least two people who hear me." I tiptoed and kissed Jake.

"What about little JJ? That makes three." He rubbed the small baby bump under my T-shirt.

"Are we sure about the whole JJ thing? I mean, JJ Walker from *Good Times,* remember him?" I made a grimace.

"Gotta have a Jay Junior, absolutely required. You can pick out some fancy name for the next one, like Heathcliff, or Darius."

"The next one?" I shook my head. "Unh, unh. No. Two is my limit."

"Hey, you're superwoman. I'm a witness. We can have

like five or six, and you'll still be able to bring home the bacon, fry it up, and serve Big Daddy all in one sweep."

"Yeah, with five or six kids, you'll be starving in more ways than one. I think you know what I mean."

"Good thing I have faith in you." Jake leaned in and kissed me.

Faith just happened to be the main ingredient in marriage. I closed my eyes and inhaled the moment. Moments added up to a lifetime. Not one would be taken for granted ever again.

Read on for an excerpt from the next book
by Trisha R. Thomas

UN-NAPPILY IN LOVE

Available in trade paperback from St. Martin's Griffin

"This way, over here, JP." The long lens of the camera was pointed our way. The frenzy of photo hounds jostling for spots to get better angles made me nervous. I squinted from the bright flash and saw a long tanned arm reach toward me. I recognized the garish diamond and ruby bracelet before I saw the rest of Jake's publicist, Ramona Scarsdale. She bore a striking resemblance to the actress Lynda Carter, circa 1970 as the comic heroine, *Wonder Woman*. Her dark hair freeze-framed high and away from her face cascaded down her back. Her cheekbones and red lips were artificially enhanced, making her look like the wax figure instead of the real thing.

She slipped her cold fingers around my wrist and gave me a tug. "Wait over here," she growled, adding in a nudge that made me lose my balance.

"Owww." The wail came from behind me, though the young woman was expressing my sentiments exactly. "You stepped on my toe," she squealed.

My ankle had twisted awkwardly in the five-inch heels I'd yet to master so I was only half concerned with her pain and thinking about my own. Four inches used to be the legal limit until someone had upped the ante, making it even more difficult to walk, talk, and look beautiful at the same time. "I'm sorry. I fell off balance."

"I had the perfect shot and you got in my way." She had an earring in her nose, one in her bottom lip and three in each ear. She held up her phone that was in camera mode. "Okay, so like, move," she ordered with a lisp indicating a piercing on her tongue, too.

"Sure." I scooted a bit to the right while she took the picture.

"He is so fine. Even cuter up close and personal. JPeeee . . ." she sang out.

"Yes, he's gorgeous," I said watching proudly as my husband stood against the gold backdrop, poised and looking like a million bucks. His tux was custom-designed and fit over his toned physique.

My hubby's new world was filled with flashing lights and admiring fans. Exotic locales for filming and promoting his new career as a movie star. One day he was my house husband, basically sitting around waiting for tomorrow and more broken promises from his agent, and the next he was being asked to co-star in a movie with Sirena Lassiter, the *Billboard*-topping "it" girl turned actress. Jake and Sirena Lassiter knew each other back when Jake, or JP as everyone knows him, had been a rap artist.

We met six years ago when he'd hired me as a marketing consultant for his hip-hop clothing line, JP Wear. At the time I was engaged to another man, but Jake didn't see that as a hindrance to getting what he wanted. At the time it was me, Venus Johnston, thirty-something, with as Jake likes to say, hips you can't miss, lips that you want to sink into, and eyes that save the day. He's a songwriter by nature, so he's a bit poetic in his descriptions. But on the inside, I was closed off and a bit lost. He found me.

Till this day I question his good sense. Having just found out my mother had breast cancer and my fiancé was under investigation for securities fraud, I was hardly considered an ideal good time. But that didn't stop Jake. He stepped right up to the plate, determined to hit a home run. He was confident like that. Forget about a base hit, getting to second, and hoping to slide into home. He was an all-or-nothing kind of guy.

Looking at him now, thinking about all we'd been through together, made me puff up with pride. Smooth, elegant, with integrity to boot. I slid the tear aside that escaped, threatening to mess up my airbrushed makeup. In such a short time, our lives had come so far. We had a daughter, a beautiful home in Atlanta, and enough history, love, and intrigue between us to make a Friday night movie on a steamy channel seem pretty tame.

We fought for each other when we had nothing left to fight for ourselves.

The minute the crowd started cheering and screaming I knew why. Sirena Lassiter had arrived at Jake's side. He slipped an arm around her waist. She kissed him on the cheek. The on-screen couple oozed chemistry, the kind that made it easy to believe he'd take a bullet for her the way he had in their box office hit *True Beauty*.

"Sirena, JP, over here. You guys are hot." The cameraman with the best pictures would get the most money from the celebrity-filled magazines. Jake's pictures always came out flawless. He gave a sexy smile, then turned toward Sirena who was already staring up at him.

Perfect shot. I could already see the headline, especially since she was engaged to be married to Earl

Benning, CEO of Rise records and also producer of the
film they'd starred in together. Anywhere Earl Benning
walked, a camera followed. Anywhere Sirena Lassiter
sneezed, a newshound reported and offered a tissue.
Having Jake in the fold gave them something to specu-
late. Was Sirena Lassiter falling for her co-star even
though she was engaged to one of the most powerful
men in the business?

Not a chance. I knew these Hollywood types. It was
all an act. The way she looked at him was planned and
rehearsed simply to keep everyone speculating long
enough to get them to the box office. In a nutshell, I
wasn't worried about Sirena Lassiter or anyone else. Jake
and I were locked and loaded. Nothing could come
between us. We'd proven it time and time again.

"Okay, this way. Let's move." Ramona waved the order and her two assistants closed ranks. Each assistant
took Sirena and Jake by the elbow. We were on the
move until I was suddenly stuck behind a barricade.

"Wait a minute. I'm with them," I told the large man
wearing a suit jacket over a yellow security T-shirt.
Jake stopped abruptly as if he'd forgotten something. I
lifted my arm and waved, glad I'd been waxed under
the armpit instead of my usual cheap shave. "I'm over
here, baby."

I knew he wouldn't leave me behind. Six years of a
rocky marital ride, we'd made it through the storm.
The official report was in, we were no good without
each other. Side by side, ready to get through any crisis.
I was the index finger and he was the thumb, or vice
versa. I tried not to quibble about who was in charge.

Ramona whispered something in his ear. He nodded
and then kept marching as she'd ordered.

"Ramona, I'm over here."

She looked back and barely swept her eyes across

the crowd. How many fans were dressed in a red shiny tight dress? I stood out like a chili pepper. It was my first thought when the dress had been sent over by the stylist, hired by Ramona, *Hand picked especially for you,* the note read. The stiff fold on one side kept poking me in the ear. "Ramona," I screamed, the same way I'd done a few hours ago, squeezing into this damn dress. And now she couldn't see me. Beautiful.

I scooted to the last pole of the velvet rope. I tapped a female security staffer on the shoulder. She was mountain large with a melon-sized hair bun.

"My husband is Jake Parson."

"Who?"

"Can you please let me through? My husband is JP," I confirmed. J-P, just two initials like the diamond-laced bling he wore with a swoop on the end. Sirena had it custom-made for him as an end-of-filming gift. I thought about him wearing the chain around his neck and not until this very moment had it bothered me.

The female security guard kept her eyes straight ahead. "Sorry, not without ID."

"Do I look like one of the gang? I'm freezing out here in this dress with shoes that are killing my feet."

Her eyes rode me up and down, then focusing on my glowing shoulders. I'd been spray-tanned with Honey Gold #6, the darkest color on the chart, yet I had still turned out radioactive red. Typical *Hollyweird*. Enough said. She unclipped the velvet rope and stood aside to let me through.

**Don't miss the other novels in Trisha R. Thomas's
Nappily series!**

NAPPILY MARRIED
ISBN: 978-0-312-36130-3

NAPPILY FAITHFUL
ISBN: 978-0-312-36131-0

NAPPILY IN BLOOM
ISBN: 978-0-312-55764-5

UN-NAPPILY IN LOVE
ISBN: 978-0-312-55763-8